DEADLY SWEET DREAMS

Connie Shelton

DEADLY SWEET DREAMS

Samantha Sweet Mysteries, Book 14

Connie Shelton

Secret Staircase Books

Deadly Sweet Dreams
Published by Secret Staircase Books, an imprint of
Columbine Publishing Group, LLC
PO Box 416, Angel Fire, NM 87710

This book is a work of fiction. Names, characters, places and incidents
are either the product of the author's imagination or are used fictitiously.
Any resemblance to actual events or locales or persons, living or dead, is
entirely coincidental. Although the author and publisher have made every
effort to ensure the accuracy and completeness of information contained in
this book we assume no responsibility for errors, inaccuracies, omissions,
or any inconsistency herein. Any slights of people, places or organizations
are unintentional.

Book layout and design by Secret Staircase Books
Cover images © Unholyvault, Andreas Meyer, Makeitdoubleplz, Andrey
Anishchenko
First trade paperback edition: October 2020
First e-book edition: October 2020
* * *
Publisher's Cataloging-in-Publication Data

Shelton, Connie
Deadly Sweet Dreams / by Connie Shelton.
p. cm.
ISBN 978-1945422911 (paperback)
ISBN 978-1945422928 (e-book)

1. Samantha Sweet (Fictitious character)--Fiction. 2. Taos,
New Mexico—Fiction. 3. Paranormal artifacts—Fiction. 4.
Bakery—Fiction. 5. Women sleuths—Fiction. I. Title

Samantha Sweet Mystery Series : Book 14.
Shelton, Connie, Samantha Sweet mysteries.

BISAC : FICTION / Mystery & Detective.
813/.54

For Dan, Daisy and Missy—my pack.
I have loved being "stuck at home" all year with you three!

Author's Note
Dan, Stephanie, Shirley—each of you contributes and makes my writing life so much easier and so much more complete. Deepest gratitude to all. And to my beta readers who catch the many little things that my eye misses: Marcia, Sandra, and Judi—you are the best!

And especially to you, my readers—I cherish our connection through these stories.
Thank you, thank you, thank you!

Chapter 1

Kelly Sweet-Porter peered at the sticky substance in the mixing bowl. "Mom, this is not at all blue. What's wrong with it?"

Sam adjusted her reading glasses and looked more closely at the leather-bound book on the worktable in front of her. "Oh, rats. It says five petals from a cornflower. I thought it said *cone*flower."

"Yeah, no. Those are yellow."

"I guess the big question is, are they edible?" Sam took off the glasses and stared at the mixture.

"They are, but the order was for cornflower blue, and this won't cut it." Kelly's shoulders slumped. "I have the feeling we're never going to get this."

"So much for all-organic ingredients for our picky

customer—I can always get the right color from my bakery supplier."

"That's what I would do." Kelly was quickly learning that not all plants were friendly. Research it first—her new motto. "Let your all-natural customer experiment with plants in her own kitchen." The book didn't always spell out the differences between foods and poisons. Poisons, potions … whatever.

A loud crash sounded from two floors down.

"I'd better check that out," Kelly said, dashing for the open door. "Scott's supposed to be watching Ana but …"

"Go. I'll do something with the icing." Samantha gave a chuckle as she heard her daughter call out.

From the dormer window at the front of the attic, Eliza, the family calico cat, watched her with unblinking green eyes.

"Forget it—cats don't eat desserts."

"Mrroww." She was a cat of few words. Unless it was something important.

Sam closed the leather-bound book and the print on the cover immediately became unreadable again. Squiggles, runes, symbols … whatever they were, even the linguist who'd tried to figure it out couldn't decipher it. Only after handling one of the carved magical boxes could she and Kelly read it perfectly. Or—not quite so perfectly, considering she'd mistaken cornflower for coneflower.

She stashed the book on a shelf full of other old books, leftover property from the old house's previous owner, where it blended in well enough that no one would give a second look. Not that anyone ever got the chance.

The worktable looked neat enough. She picked up the dirty mixing bowl and called to the cat, securely locking the door behind her. Eliza led the way down the back stairs.

"What was the crash?" Sam asked Kelly when she got to the kitchen.

"Miss Anastasia was hungry, so she thought she would start dinner."

Sam set the dirty bowl in the sink and squirted liquid soap into it. "Ana, Ana, Ana … I'm thinking you'll need to get a bit taller before you tackle the cooking."

"Popsicle!" The four-year-old held up a box of the frozen treats that had apparently fallen out of the freezer. "Daddy wants dinner Popsicle."

"Yeah, and maybe we'll have a little talk with Daddy," Kelly said, scooping her daughter up in one arm while stuffing the box back inside the freezer.

"Well, I'm going to leave you all to sort that out," Sam said. "I need to get home and check things at the ranch. I'll be back tomorrow to help you get ready for the p-a-r-t-y."

"It's my party!" Anastasia shouted with a giggle. "Not a surprise, Grammy."

Sam rolled her eyes. "I keep forgetting how she picks up on things."

"Scott and his accelerated home schooling. She finished all the first-grade readers so I guess he's got her spelling words now."

"Can Uncle Danny come to my party? Otherwise, he might be lonely."

"Um, sure," Sam said. "I'll invite him."

Danny Flores was Beau's new ranch hand, hired a couple of weeks ago, and Ana had only met him once. Somehow, the young girl understood that he would be alone tomorrow night when the family came to their house for the party.

"Go find your daddy. I need to ask him what he *really* wants for dinner," Kelly suggested, sending Ana toward the dining room door. Once the child was out of earshot, she said, "You don't have to invite Danny if you don't want to, Mom."

"He's a very nice guy, and I can ask. If you don't mind?"

"Oh, not at all. It's just that I'm not sure where she gets this stuff. How would she know Danny might be lonely if he stays home?"

"I've been telling you, Kel, you've got a very perceptive little girl there."

Sam grabbed her jacket from the peg near the back door and blew Kelly a kiss.

Outside, the wind had picked up, bringing a flurry of snow from the open field across the road. A week ago it had been almost balmy, now it felt like a blizzard. Early spring could bring any kind of weather to the mountains, Sam had learned long ago. She settled into her hybrid all-wheel-drive SUV and started the engine, leaning back against the headrest while it warmed up.

She picked up her phone and called Beau.

"Hey darlin' what's up?" In the background, she could hear the whoosh of the wind.

"You're outside. I'll keep it quick."

"Yeah, we've got a section of fence down. Danny and I are kind of in the middle of a repair job."

"Okay. Just tell Danny he's welcome to join us for dinner tonight. I'm heading home soon and planning a big pot of chile and some cornbread. There'll be plenty. See you soon."

"But everything's okay?"

"Absolutely fine. See you later." Her heart went out to

the wonderful man she'd married. He had been through so much these past few years and yet he always placed her welfare above all else. There wasn't a doubt in her mind if she'd needed something, he would let the broken fence go and rush immediately to her side.

By the time she pulled off the county road onto the long driveway at the ranch, the snow had abated somewhat. Across the field she could make out the dark shape of Beau's pickup truck, a quarter-mile in the distance, and the faint figures of the two men. She didn't envy their task, wrestling barbed wire and metal posts into submission in the frigid air. But she wasn't going to trade her warm kitchen for the chance to join them.

The house smelled wonderful—of onions and meat, pungent red chile and spices—when Sam walked in. The slow-cooker was doing its work. She set aside her backpack purse and phone, pulled off her heavy coat, and rubbed her hands together as she walked into the kitchen. She lifted the lid on the pot and gave the fragrant mixture a stir, satisfied that the meal was on schedule.

Beau would be at least another thirty minutes, so she used the time to tidy the house a bit and set the dining table for three. The carved wooden box sat, benignly dark and quiet, on the sideboard. Sam ran a hand across its top, watching the color lighten immediately to a soft, warm brown. If she picked it up and held it against her body the wood would brighten to the color of honey, and the colored stones mounted in the carved crevices would begin to glow.

She removed her hand, letting the effect subside. Better to have the artifact out of the way when company came. She picked it up and carried it upstairs.

In the beginning she'd been half afraid of the box and its powerful influence, even trying a couple of times to get rid of it. Then she'd learned to use its power to help with everyday tasks, to gather its energy and perform near-miracles. But there was a dark side to using it, she'd discovered. And after the events of four years ago, she was content to treat it with restraint and respect. Now that she felt safer and more confident about its presence, she and the box had somehow learned to let each other be.

"Thanks, but not right now," she whispered, setting it on her dresser.

She heard a sound downstairs, the stomp of heavy boots on the front porch.

Chapter 2

"All done?" Sam stood on the stairway landing and watched Beau step inside. Ranger and Nellie followed, shaking snowflakes from their fur.

"As done as it's gonna get," Beau said. "Ground's frozen solid and barbed wire's a bitch to work with in this weather. But we got it closed off. The cows are all hanging close to the barn today anyhow."

She helped him out of his jacket and gloves, and he unzipped his heavy coverall and peeled it off his shoulders.

"Let me get the fire going," she said. "I haven't been home very long myself."

He turned and pulled her toward him, planting a solid kiss on her forehead. "Smells good in here."

"Is Danny coming for dinner?"

"Yeah. He went to the casita to clean up, said he'd

come over in half an hour. If dinner's ready sooner, just call him."

"That'll work out perfectly," she said.

Beau finished extricating himself from the coveralls, then gave a sniff at the underarms of his flannel shirt. "I'm hitting the shower. Wouldn't think a guy could sweat out there in the snow, but—"

"Twelve layers of clothes will do that," she said with a laugh.

He was unbuttoning the flannel before he even reached the stairs. "Some kind of toddy would taste real good when I get back."

"You got it." Sam turned toward the fireplace, spreading aside the layer of ashes inside, setting kindling and striking a match to it. Two small logs caught the tender flame, and she added a couple of larger ones.

By the time she'd carried in an armload of split logs from the front porch the fire was blazing well, and she added enough more wood to keep it going. Beau's toddy of choice these days was a nip of 15-year-old scotch. She poured two fingers and set the glass on the end table near his favorite chair.

Out of habit she watched him descend from the second story, noticing whether he seemed sure-footed. Her eyes flicked to the door of the downstairs guest room, the sickroom for months.

That was four years ago, she reminded herself. *He's fine now. Just fine.*

Still, she watched. Habit.

Leave it, Sam. Worrying solves nothing.

He crossed the room and pulled her into his arms. This time the kiss was not on the forehead, not a chaste little peck. *He's fine.* She smiled when he pulled away.

"Your drink's on the table," she said. "And I'd better get the cornbread started."

"You're the best," he said with his first sip.

She ignored his groan as he took his seat. Fifty-three was not old. But what he'd been through would age anyone. She refused to look at the place on the living room floor as she walked toward the kitchen—the sight of him, down, blood pouring from the chest wound was imprinted forever. All she could do was ignore it and live in the present. They'd made it through a lot, including the loss of his career. She shoved aside the visions that came back randomly and with force.

She pushed her way through the swinging kitchen door and started grabbing the ingredients for cornbread. Through the window above the sink she saw Danny walk up the front porch steps. She tapped the glass with a fingernail and motioned him to come in. She met him just inside the living room where he was shedding his coat and smoothing back his dark hair.

Danny Flores had come along at exactly the right moment. Beau's older ranch hand had retired to Albuquerque, saying he couldn't do another winter outdoors in the mountains. They'd put out feelers for help but it was hard to find young men who would, or could, do manual labor these days. When the twenty-one year old showed up, saying his grandmother told him the former sheriff needed a worker, they'd hired him on the spot.

"Let's hang your coat here," she said, taking his sheepskin jacket. "And how about something to drink?"

"Oh, no, I'm fine," he said, with a glance toward Beau.

"I'm having a warmer-upper." Beau held up his glass.

"Well, okay, maybe a beer if you have one," Danny said to Sam.

"Sure—I'll be right back with it. Sit over there by the fire." She delivered the bottle of Corona a couple minutes later. "It'll be about twenty minutes until dinner's ready. How's your grandmother, Danny?"

"Feisty as ever," he said with a grin. "I saw her and Auntie Pauline on Sunday."

"Good. You know, Faustina's been a friend of mine forever. She's the reason we didn't even ask for any references that day you came out here."

"Yeah, she told me. But she says it's 'cause I have an honest face. And because I'll feed cattle or mend a fence."

"Okay, true." Sam laughed.

"He can set T-posts in a straight line and knows his way around a fence puller," Beau said. "Can't ask a lot more than that."

As the conversation went toward the specifics of how much wire they'd strung, Sam ducked back to the kitchen. She tasted the chile and added a bit more salt before checking the cornbread in the oven. The chile recipe came from Danny's grandmother, Faustina Lopez, and Sam had made it dozens of times. Danny's mother had attended school here in Taos and worked two summers at the insurance company where Sam was employed during her early years in this town. She remembered when Sally met Hector Flores and moved to San Antonio to marry him. And now their two very handsome children were young adults, and one was living here in Taos County. Small world.

Sam filled water glasses and ladled chile into bowls, sliced the cornbread and put the neat squares in a basket with a cloth on top, then carried a tray with everything out to the dining table, which faced the south pasture.

"Yum, this smells so familiar," Danny said, pulling Sam's chair out for her.

When she told him where she'd gotten the recipe, he laughed. They'd hardly taken their seats when an unfamiliar ringtone interrupted.

"Oops, sorry," Danny said.

"Go ahead and take it, if you want," Sam told him. "It might be your mother."

He hesitated a moment but then pulled his phone from his back pocket. By then it had quit ringing. He took a glance at the screen, and Sam saw something flicker in his expression. He lay the phone, screen down, on the table with a thump.

"Not your mom, I guess," she joked, hoping to lighten the mood.

"I'll handle it later." He ripped his chunk of cornbread in half and practically skewered the stick of butter with his knife.

Sam and Beau exchanged a look, and Beau gave a tiny shrug. It really was none of their business, so Sam steered the conversation elsewhere.

"Before I forget," she said. "Anastasia wants to be sure you're coming to her birthday party tomorrow. I didn't promise—just said I'd be sure we invited Uncle Danny. There may be a couple of kids her age, but mostly it'll be adults, mainly Kelly's and Scott's friends."

Danny's expression relaxed. "Sure—she's such a cute kid. As long as the boss doesn't need another fence mended …?"

Beau shook his head. "Fence or no fence, we're going. Her birthday only comes along once every four years."

At the ranch hand's puzzled expression, Sam said, "February twenty-ninth."

"Well, then, it's a must-do, right?" Danny swept cornbread crumbs off the tablecloth into his hand. "What kind of gift should I bring?"

"As you can imagine, the child doesn't need a thing," Sam told him. "Don't worry about it."

"I wouldn't be any kind of awesome Uncle Danny if I didn't show up with something ..."

"She's big into art right now, and she already has a set of pastels and colored pencils," Sam said, "but I notice the purple ones are getting worn down. Apparently, that's the color of the month with her. If you can find a set of colored pencils or markers that are all shades of purple, you'd be her hero."

He seemed at a loss. "Any alternate ideas? Just in case."

"You know what? Anything purple will be great—a pair of purple socks would make her day."

He grinned. "I'll see what I can do."

"More chile?" Sam offered. Both men shook their heads.

"I heard there was apple pie for dessert," Beau said. "I wouldn't turn that down."

"And I wouldn't turn down a quick trip to the head," Danny said.

Sam pointed the way and began to gather the dishes. She glanced at Beau, who seemed tired.

"Shall we have our pie and coffee in front of the fire?"

He nodded and offered to help with the dishes.

"Nope, you stretch out in your chair. I'll get these and bring everything over there."

As she picked up bowls and plates she saw Danny's

phone, facedown where he'd left it. Beau's back was turned. Curiosity got the better of her. She quickly picked it up and turned the screen toward her. When it lit up, there were just three words: Missed call — Lila.

She set the phone down a fraction of a second before the bathroom door opened and Danny came out.

Chapter 3

Sam sat on the edge of their king-sized bed, applying lotion to the flaky, dry skin on her legs. "Beau, has Danny ever mentioned a girl in his life? Someone named Lila?"

His face appeared in the bathroom doorway. "This doesn't sound like a casual question," he said with a grin. "You snooped, didn't you?"

"Well … okay, yeah. I couldn't help but wonder what provoked that reaction at dinner tonight. I mean, he just about slammed the phone down." She set the lotion bottle aside. "So, has he mentioned her?"

Beau wiped toothpaste from his mouth and dried his hands. "Not by name."

"Meaning?"

"That's not the first call he's received that he wanted to

avoid." He switched off the bathroom light and circled the bed. "A couple of days ago, we were mucking out the stalls and he got a call. He started to take it but seemed shaken when he saw the name on the screen. I asked if everything was all right and he said yeah ... but I could tell it wasn't. He just said it was his father and he'd call him back later."

"Did you believe him?"

His mouth twisted slightly.

"Come on, Beau, think back to your law enforcement days. You *know* how to read people. *Did* you believe him?"

He shook his head. "No. But, hon, it's not our business."

"But this Lila ... it feels like she's some kind of trouble."

"And *again*, it's none of our business." This time his voice was firm and she knew there was no point in pursuing the question.

He switched out the light, and Sam plumped her pillow. But she didn't fall asleep for a while.

* * *

February twenty-ninth. Sam stood back and surveyed her work, a tendril of purple icing threatening to drop from the decorating tip in her right hand. The cake had to be perfect, and yet how did one make a cake perfect for a four-year-old's taste? It was usually the mothers who must be pleased, but Kelly wouldn't care—it was Ana who had placed the order. She spun the turntable a quarter turn to the left and checked the tint of the deep night sky with its constellations of silver dragées.

Surrounding the cake were pairs of calico cats. Sam knew where that came from—Eliza, the family pet. And between the cats was a silhouette, a fair rendition of the Victorian house where Anastasia lived with her parents.

Her granddaughter had been quite specific about these details. The part Ana had been somewhat vague about was that she wanted a witch on top, but no further details. "A witch" was all she had to go by.

She set aside the pastry bag and reached for the topper she'd created from modeling chocolate. A bright yellow-white full moon formed the backdrop for a cartoon-cute witch on a broomstick. Set in place, the moon and witch floated above the nighttime scene on the cake itself. Sam had debated whether the witch should have a traditional green face and black hair, but in the end she'd created a fun avatar of Ana herself—pale skin, red hair, tiny freckles across the nose. She wore a flowing purple dress. Her concession to traditional black for the witch was a pointy hat with purple band and at the last minute she added Eliza, riding on the broomstick with her.

She anchored the topper with some extra icing and stepped back to view her work.

"Nice," said Becky Gurule, head decorator now at Sweet's Sweets. "I have to admit, the theme seemed kind of Halloween-like for February, but this is so cute."

The back door rattled and a gust of cold air rushed in. Kelly followed Ana inside, turning to close the door.

"Wow, the storm's moving out fast," she said, shaking snowflakes from her cinnamon curls.

Ana raced in and came to an abrupt halt, her eyes wide when she saw the cake. "Grammy, it's perfect!"

Sam held up a hand. "Don't touch. Some of the parts aren't set yet."

Ana stepped closer but kept her hands at her sides, taking in details. "Eliza! She's riding with me!"

"Can't have a birthday without the cat, right?"

"Are you going to put a one on it?" Ana asked, holding up her index finger. "I really want a one."

"We can put a one." Sam showed her a numeral she had formed from bright orange modeling chocolate to contrast with the darker color of the sky.

"Yay!" said Ana, dashing off to the sales room to see Jen.

Unlike most kids, who adamantly claimed bragging rights to every year, every month, of their age, Anastasia was quite proud of the fact that, being a leap-day baby, this was actually her first birthday. While Kelly and Scott wanted their little girl to have a party every year, since last year Ana had insisted they not invite friends or make a big deal of it until it was actually her birthday. And the big day was now upon them.

Becky looked up from the tray of brownies she was frosting. "Scott's home schooling is showing off. I swear, she's brighter than my fifth grader."

Kelly waved aside the compliment, although Sam knew it was true. Ana had begun to show uncanny abilities before her second year. Did she have some kind of gift, or was it simply because she spent a lot more time around adults than other kids? Sam attached the numeral 1 to the front of the cake, checked for any little fixups, and reached for a box to set it in.

Ana emerged from the showroom with a coconut macaroon in hand. "Ready, Mommy? I need to finish my spelling words before the party."

Kelly and Becky exchanged a see-what-I-mean look. Kelly made sure their jackets were zipped and they headed out.

Once the witch cake was safely stashed in the large

walk-in fridge, Sam headed for her best friend Zoë's place.

Yesterday's storm had, indeed, blown through, leaving the sky a brilliant blue today and, aside from flakes flying off the trees and a few spots where snow lay in frozen drifts, there was little sign of the ferocious weather of the previous day. She arrived at the bed and breakfast as the last of the overnight guests were stowing skis and poles into a car-top carrier in the small parking area out front.

"Hey there," Zoë said, meeting Sam at the back door. "I hadn't thought I'd see you until later." She wore a turquoise broomstick skirt and a black long-sleeved top, and her shoulder-length graying hair was pulled back in a clip at the nape of her neck.

"Kelly sent me on a mission. The punch bowl she asked to borrow? She's wondering if I can take it over there early. Apparently, she didn't realize she would need to mix the ingredients a couple of hours ahead."

"Oh, sure, come on in." Zoë turned toward the big storage pantry off her kitchen. "The temp really dropped last night, didn't it?"

She carried out a big object that was more beverage dispenser than bowl, explaining that it was indeed what Kelly had in mind.

"I'll have the sandwiches all ready, and Darryl and I will bring them when we come. Egg salad, watercress, and hummus, right?"

Sam laughed with a little shake of her head. "That's what I hear. Our little Miss Ana seems to have very grownup ideas about the party food. I have no idea if she's ever actually tasted watercress. Probably saw the idea in a magazine somewhere."

"I think to be on the safe side I'll add some chicken

salad and maybe some ham and cheese rollups. I can't imagine most of the men loving watercress or hummus."

Sam loaded the punch dispenser into the back seat of her SUV and headed toward her next stop, Walmart. This morning she realized she had no appropriately sized gift bag for the outfit she'd bought Ana. Everything was either way too big, way too small, or of Christmas design. She hoped the big store wouldn't be too crowded.

She still needed to swing back by Sweet's Sweets to get the cake and then get to Kelly's in time to help with the decorations. If she had to guess, she would bet Ana had been up since dawn, and Scott was probably on a ladder right now, placing streamers and balloons according to his little daughter's precise instructions.

A parking space opened up near the building and Sam grabbed it. Inside, she paused a moment to get her bearings. The floor arrangement of this place was always changing, and it took her a moment to remember where the cards, gift wrap, and decorations had last been seen. She headed to her left, hoping she had guessed correctly.

The row she thought she wanted now held candles and silk flowers and she nearly bypassed it when she caught sight of a familiar figure—Danny Flores. He stood with his back to Sam, but the young woman in a short red dress and black furry jacket, who was talking and shaking her finger in his face, paused a moment and stared pointedly at her. Sam ducked to the next aisle and found the gift bags.

The voices carried and, okay, she did edge her way to the end of the aisle where the hearing was better.

"Lila, I—"

"No, Danny, remember, you promised. Honey, you're always forgetting things."

His response was somewhat muffled, and Sam only caught "No—wait!"

This was getting ugly. Sam debated whether to step around the endcap and reveal herself, to give Danny an escape.

"Not *here!*" His voice was strained, as if the words were being forced out through clenched teeth.

"Tomorrow, then," Lila said. "We'll get together and I can explain everything once again."

Poor Danny needed a reprieve. Sam stepped to the endcap and began browsing through the scented candles, pretending not to notice the couple but hoping to give the poor guy a way out.

He didn't notice her, but Lila shot her a look and turned away.

"Bye, honey," Lila said, over her shoulder. "I love you." Her heels clicked decisively away.

When Sam looked toward him, Danny was walking in the opposite direction.

So, *that* was Lila. And what was the story? Sam's mind wanted to put together all kinds of scenarios, but all she really knew was that the young woman seemed way more into him than he was into her. Those things happened all the time, and Sam supposed the situation would work itself out somehow. She sighed and went back to the gift bags.

Chapter 4

Kelly and Scott had left the driveway under the side portico at their Victorian house clear so Sam would have easy access to the kitchen door. She made the left turn, noticing green shoots coming up in the raised flower beds Kelly had added along the front porch of the old house. They had made some nice improvements to the place. Zoë's car sat near the front door. Sam parked under the portico and got out. Beau, in the passenger seat of her car, handed the cake out to her.

Inside, Kelly was stirring something over a burner on the big commercial range that dated back to the house's days as a chocolate factory. She wore a big apron over black leggings and a purple sweater. The apron said Kiss The Cook across the front.

"Hey, Mom," she called out. "Oh! The cake—Ana has

talked about it nonstop. There's a spot for it on the dining table if you want to carry it straight in there."

Beau offered to take it, so Sam handed off the shallow box holding the cake with its night sky, silvery stars, and the cute witch flying past the full moon.

"I'm making some queso dip," Kelly said. "I know— Ana wants this to be an English tea, but once she added a witch cake and gummy-candy treats, I figured we were going more eclectic. And I figured the guys would like something more substantial than watercress."

Sam laughed and told her about Zoë's plans for the sandwich platter.

"Sounds like we'll be fine."

Almost as if she'd heard her name, Zoë came into the kitchen with a large plastic-covered plate. "Can I help with anything? I set a platter of sandwiches on the table where Scott directed me, and these are extras."

"There's a huge bag of tortilla chips," Kelly said, tilting her head toward the countertop near the sink. "You could find a bowl and dump them in. I should have this dip off the stove in a minute, and it's going into the mini-crockpot right here. I'm thinking we could plug it in and put these and the guacamole from the fridge out on the table in the living room. We'll try to spread the guests around or everyone will end up in here, staring at my sink full of dirty dishes."

Sam shed her backpack and jacket, hanging them on hooks by the back door, then picked up the dip and headed for the living room. Kelly's sweet husband seemed to have everything organized. He kissed her cheek and pointed her toward a large side table that stood ready to hold chips and dips, while he directed Darryl where to take coats and went himself to answer the front door.

A low coffee table was already stacked with gifts, and when she saw Danny Flores come in with a purple gift bag topped with a fluff of purple tissue, she sent him in that direction.

"Where's the birthday girl?" she asked Scott when he paused for a moment.

"Oh, she's going to make an entrance." His eyebrows arched upward and a wry smile tweaked his mouth.

Sam's eyes followed the grand staircase from the foyer to the second floor. "Ah. Well, her Grammy probably shouldn't bother her then."

"She kind of has an entourage already."

"Seriously? She's not turning into a complete diva *already*, is she?"

"Just for today. Apparently that's a thing. Her little friend, Hannah, got the princess treatment on her birthday so now Ana thinks that's how it's done. The two of them are probably tossing clothes all over her room up there."

Sam looked around, spotting most of their circle of friends. Zoë and Darryl, of course, plus her close friend Rupert, dressed as usual in flowing soft pants and tunic, with a purple scarf draped stylishly around his neck. The girls from the bakery—Jen and Becky—were in the dining room, and she saw Becky checking the cake for any dings. Becky's two boys hung near their dad, looking bored. Coming to a younger kid's party—a girl at that—was probably not their idea of how to spend a Saturday afternoon. Sam suspected Becky had bribed them with some incentive for later on if they would agree to put in an appearance.

Footsteps on the wooden front porch called her

attention to the beveled glass door, and she went to admit Riki and Evan Richards, Beau's deputy who had taken over for him after the shooting. Each gave Sam a hearty hug and Riki held out a wrapped box.

"In there," Sam said, pointing toward the living room and the laden coffee table.

"And is Kelly becoming a bit insane at the moment?" Riki asked. "The party looks absolutely brilliant."

"Speaking of our hostess …" Sam said, clearing a path for Kelly with her crockpot full of cheese dip.

Kelly set it on the serving table and plugged the cord out of the way. "There! I think I'm nearly ready for a cup of the adult version of the punch," she said, pulling off her apron.

"Shall we, then?" Riki suggested. The two of them headed toward the beverage cart Scott had set near the dining room windows, chatting away about Puppy Chic, Riki's grooming business, as if they didn't already spend quite a few hours a week there together.

Sam turned to survey the crowd and her eye caught Zoë who, out of habit, was looking to be sure everyone had something to drink and a plate of snacks. It seemed no one was alone. Even Danny, who didn't know most of the group, was standing near Beau and talking animatedly with Scott.

A hiss caught Sam's attention. "Grammy! Grammy!" came a stage whisper. She looked up and saw Ana at the top of the stairs. Scott was right—from her lavender dress to the tiara that tried to control her fiery-red curls, the princess was ready for her entrance.

"Announce me!" Ana whispered.

Sam nodded. With a metal spoon from the drinks

table she began tapping a glass. "Attention, attention! All subjects will now step into the foyer for the arrival of Princess Anastasia Sweet Porter!" She winked at Kelly, who led the way.

Little Ana played her role to perfection, flouncing down the stairs in her billowing tulle skirt, her chin held high. Hannah followed along in her own fluffy purple dress, her eyes on the tiara, which had begun to list to one side. At the bottom of the staircase, Ana curtsied to her guests and managed to catch the tiara as it slid off her forehead and plopped into her hands. For a moment she looked shaken but recovered nicely when her audience began to applaud.

"All hail Princess Ana!" Scott announced, saving the moment and making his daughter's day.

The two little girls bounded toward the dining room, wanting to see the finished cake.

Kelly turned to Sam. "Well, she's got the idea of party planning down pat, if not the art of nailing a particular theme."

"I was wondering about that ... depicting herself as a witch on the cake didn't quite seem in keeping with her princess image."

Kelly shrugged. "She's a girl of very definite ideas. I couldn't explain it if I had to."

Zoë approached, a plate in each hand. "You two will get so busy you won't eat anything. So I made two plates. This one's got the tea sandwiches, and this has the New Mexico specialties. Divvy them up however you like."

"Your sandwiches will be amazing," Kelly said, reaching for that one.

Sam snagged one of the chicken salad sandwich triangles and filled the empty space on Kelly's plate with two of her taquitos. Ana and Hannah ran through the room, each with a sandwich in one hand and a carrot stick in the other. Kelly started to caution them to slow down, but they were out of the foyer and headed toward the back stairs before she found her voice.

"Oh well. What kid isn't super-charged on her birthday, right? I'm surprised she hasn't tried to dive into that table full of gifts in the living room yet."

Sam glanced in that direction and saw several of the women had settled into the comfortable grouping of big chairs near the sunny west windows. Meanwhile, the men were still congregated around the dining table with its spread of food. *Good. I won't have to come up with much for dinner at home tonight.*

She saw that the sandwich platter was getting somewhat depleted and remembered Zoë had set extras on the kitchen counter. She left Kelly to answer a question from Riki and headed toward the kitchen. When she pushed through the swinging door she saw Danny standing near the sink, staring out the window.

"Hey, Danny. Something I can help you find?"

Startled, he turned to face her. "Oh. No, thanks." A pensive look crossed his face. "Sam, I heard the guys say Beau used to be the sheriff here?"

"Yeah. Up until four years ago. I'm surprised he hasn't mentioned that. Well, maybe not. He's fully embracing the ranching life now." She found Zoë's second platter of sandwiches and busied herself removing the plastic wrap. "Why?"

Danny's feet shuffled. "I don't know … Well, something came to mind."

"Something you want to talk about?"

"I don't know …" He seemed to be formulating his thoughts. "I wonder if he'd have some advice on how to get someone to stop harassing you."

She let a long moment go by. "Someone's harassing you?"

His head waggled back and forth a little and he wouldn't quite meet her eyes.

"Danny, is it Lila?"

His glance shot upward. "How do you—?"

"I wasn't sure whether to bring this up. I was at Walmart earlier, getting a gift bag, and I saw you in the same area. There was a young woman talking to you and, well, you said her name." No way was she going to admit she'd spied at his phone screen the night before. "I would have said hello, but the conversation seemed kind of … intense."

His mouth twisted into nearly a smile. "Yeah—intense is a good word."

From the other room, excited kid shouts. Time to open the gifts.

"Do you need to—?" he asked.

"No problem. She won't miss me for a short while. We can talk, if you'd like."

"It's just that Lila got way too serious, way too soon. She wants to get married. I feel like I barely know her."

"You haven't been in town long. Did you just meet her here?"

"Oh, no. She's from San Antonio. Well, actually, that's where we met. She grew up in Nuevo Laredo. Anyway, she just kind of latched on to my set of friends and started hanging out with us, and before I knew it she's telling everyone I'm her boyfriend."

Sam busied herself putting things in the fridge and

wiping the countertop. He seemed more comfortable talking when she wasn't making a lot of eye contact.

"Did you know her very long there?"

"A few months. She's really pretty, super hot, and, um ..."

"You're a guy. You kind of succumbed to her charms."

"Well, yeah. So, I guess we did sort of become a couple. Then she starts sending me these texts, all times of day and night. 'We gotta plan the wedding' and that kind of stuff. So, I was all, like, what! And I told her no, we gotta take things slower. And she just doesn't let up."

"Had you actually proposed?"

"No!" He stared toward the window again. "Well, I don't think so. I'm pretty sure not. There was one night when we all got pretty wasted. I might have said something, but I don't remember it. I seriously do not think I would have asked her."

Poor guy.

"Did you move here to get away from her? I mean, to give yourself a little breathing space?"

"Yeah, actually, that's exactly why. I even changed my phone number, but now she's got my new number and tracked me down. I don't even know how she did that."

"You didn't tell her you were in Taos?"

"I didn't even say I'd left Texas, just that I'd got a job out of town and needed to take some time."

"Part of what she said this morning—sorry, I couldn't help but overhear. It was about getting together to talk. Maybe that's your chance to tell her what you're feeling."

Again, his gaze went to the floor. "I'm not sure I can ..."

"I'm sure you'll be able to work it out if you explain to

her what you want."

He looked skeptical.

Cheers and laughter came from the other room.

"I guess I'd better take these sandwiches out and then make an appearance for the gift opening. Join us?"

He nodded, but his situation was clearly still weighing on him.

Chapter 5

Sam and Beau spent a leisurely Sunday with waffles and fruit for brunch, pitching in together to give the furniture and rugs a once-over cleaning, then settling in with books to read near the fire with both dogs curled at their feet. When she stood near the French doors at the back of the house, looking toward the barn, she saw Danny's truck was gone and she wondered if he'd stayed with his plan to get together with Lila and talk things out. But then the kettle whistled in the kitchen and she became distracted with mugs and chocolate and whipped cream.

Monday morning Beau was up early, announcing that he and Danny were moving half a barn full of hay bales, shifting them around to make room for a pair of early spring calves that would need indoor space for their first few weeks. He buttoned a buffalo-checked flannel shirt over his thermal undershirt, and added a light fleece over that.

"Don't forget, Evan and Riki invited us over for an early supper at their place," he informed Sam. "I assume you girls already talked about it the other day at Kelly's?"

They hadn't. Somehow, Sam and Riki hadn't quite ended up in the same conversation at any point during that busy afternoon. But she said she would call and firm up the details. It turned out the little dinner party was to include Scott, Kelly and Ana, as well.

Arriving at Evan and Riki's place was like coming home. In fact, it was home, the same small house where Sam had raised Kelly, the very place Kelly and Scott had lived for a year before they moved into the Victorian. When the Richards' rented the house, Riki made the point that it would probably be short-term. Once they started a family, they would need bigger quarters. But there'd been no pregnancy yet, a subject that could either get testy or sad if brought up. Sam normally avoided it.

As always with this group, the easy friendships were so close that the conversation picked right up wherever it had last left off. And tonight the topic began with Ana's birthday party.

"I love the gifts Uncle Danny gave me," she said, a chicken leg in one hand that was looming dangerously near Kelly's hair. "A purple purse, purple socks, a purple headband, three purple markers … I hope purple keeps being my favorite color for awhile."

The adults laughed. "Good thing it is," Evan said, "'cause I saw a plate of cookies on the counter with purple icing on them."

"I hope the rest of us don't begin to hate purple before she reaches the end of this phase," Kelly said.

"I do *not* have phases," Ana insisted. "I have preferences." She sat back, looking smug. "Daddy, I want that
to be one of my spelling words this week. Preferences."

Scott smiled ruefully. "See what my day is like?"

Kelly elbowed him.

"Mommy, I found a weird spelling book yesterday,"
Ana said. "It has funny letters and I asked Daddy but he
said he can't read it."

Sam and Kelly both inhaled.

Scott shrugged. "I don't know where it came from. It
seemed vaguely familiar but it's not one of mine. Leather
cover that looks real old. Pages are kind of like parchment."

Sam spoke up. "Oh, *that's* where I left that old thing.
Remind me and I'll take it back home with me." She'd
never been great at bluffing, and with two law enforcement
men at the table—could she pull off the fib?

But Beau was busy adding more coleslaw to his plate,
and Evan seemed distracted by the buzzing of his phone
in his hip pocket. He took a look at the screen and stood
up.

"Yeah, Dixie?" he answered, walking toward the
bedroom.

Beau perked up at the name of his dispatcher. His
former dispatcher.

Sam patted his hand and asked for the coleslaw.

"Sorry, everybody, I gotta run," Evan said. "Bad traffic
pileup. I'll probably be late."

Riki placed two extra pieces of the fried chicken in a
sandwich bag. "In case you feel hungry later." She followed
him to the back door as he put on his heavy uniform jacket
and hat. "I love you," she called out.

Sam watched Beau's expression, but there was no hint

that he'd love to be leaving the dinner table to take an emergency call.

"And now we know the real reason I can't seem to get pregnant," Riki announced as she came back. "My darling husband is never home."

Kelly reached up and snagged her friend's hand, giving a sympathetic squeeze.

"Sorry, that wasn't polite of me," Riki said, forcing her smile to brighten. "What more do we need from the kitchen?"

"Cookies!" Ana announced. She had finished her chicken and most of the fries.

"You shall have some, my darling," Riki told her, "as soon as everyone is finished. *And* there is ice cream to go along with them."

Beau and Scott perked up at that news.

Sam's mind went back to the leather-bound book Ana had found. The book of magic, with its rune-like characters, had come into Kelly's possession near the time of Beau's shooting. It held the full story of the three carved boxes, the powers of each, and the implications of the boxes' combined power. Had Kelly recently been reading the book again?

The day of their cornflower experiment Sam had put the book on a high attic shelf. She caught her daughter's eye, but Kelly gave a slight shake of her head.

One thing for certain, the book was not something that should fall into the hands of a child, even one as precocious as Ana. *Especially* not one like Ana.

Chapter 6

Kelly tossed her purse into the car and then buckled Anastasia into her car seat in the back. Their appointment was in ten minutes, and somehow the morning had gotten away from her. One of those where the toast burned, Scott was harried because of his book deadline, Ana had been uncharacteristically indecisive about what to wear, and Kelly's hair wouldn't behave.

"Why did I think a second cup of coffee would be a good idea?" she muttered as she inserted her key and cranked the engine.

"Coffee is good, Mama. You like it."

Kelly rolled her eyes at the rearview mirror. Never say *anything* out loud that you don't want repeated back to you, not around this kid. They arrived at the pediatrician's office with one minute to spare.

Sam was already in the waiting room. "I signed you in already. The place was teeming with kids, all sniffling and coughing."

"Anastasia Porter," called the receptionist.

Kelly grabbed her daughter's hand and led her to follow the woman. "Don't touch anything," she murmured under her breath.

While Ana sat on the exam table, swinging her legs and looking at the colorful charts on the walls, Kelly and Sam finalized their plans for lunch.

"Beau and Danny were working in the barn when I left," Sam said. "Something about repairing the feed bin. Anyway, I have all afternoon if we decide to add some shopping to our day."

"Might be fun. Scott gets kind of testy when he's working on deadline, so the more we can stay out of his hair the better."

The doctor, a short woman with gray hair in a severe cut, stepped in just then. Ana giggled when the woman smiled, more because of her large teeth than out of any friendly reaction. The exam went quickly and everyone bore the immunization stoically.

"I'd say you're in the peak of health for a four-year-old," the doctor said, giving Ana a hand down from the table.

"I'm one," Ana said with pride.

But the woman was busy tapping notes on her tablet. Sam met Ana's eye and shrugged. Kelly paused to handle the billing and the three of them headed toward Kelly's car.

"Mama, that doctor doesn't even know about my birthday," Ana said as Sam strapped her into her car seat. "She didn't even listen when I told her."

Yeah, well, get used to it. "I'm sure she was just busy

making sure she wrote all nice things about you on your chart, honey."

"So, I'm thinking lunch at the Bent Street Café as a special treat and then we'll see if we're in the mood to check out the shops," Kelly said. "It's close enough that it's easy to bring you back to your car, Mom."

"Perfect." Sam settled into her seat and mentioned the bean soup, which was her favorite at the street-side café.

They walked in to the crowded, popular spot and a hostess showed them to the one empty table. Ana spotted a familiar face first.

"Uncle Danny!" she shouted, running toward him.

The dark-haired girl sitting with him seemed momentarily surprised. She wore skinny jeans, a tailored white shirt, coffee-colored blazer, and boots that must have cost a pretty penny.

Danny stood and greeted Ana with a smile, then looked toward Kelly and Sam. "Hey, ladies! Um, don't worry, Sam, I didn't leave Beau in the lurch. We nearly finished the bin, and he sent me to town for some more nails. And … I ran into Lila over at Randel Hardware."

He introduced everyone. "I did call Beau to let him know I'd be delayed a while."

Sam gave him a warm smile. "No need to apologize, Danny. I'm sure he's fine with it."

"A guy's gotta spend some time with his fiancée," said Lila. "I mean, we've had, like, *no* time together in the past couple weeks."

Kelly glanced toward Sam. *I thought he was going to break it off?* Sam lifted one shoulder in a tiny shrug.

"Well, we'll let you two get back to your lunch," Kelly said.

Their spot was two tables down the way from the couple's, too far to converse with them, but near enough to overhear bits, especially when the table between them vacated and no one immediately moved to take it.

Kelly helped Ana decide and they placed their orders, studiously avoiding eye contact with Danny and Lila. The conversation they'd interrupted seemed to have picked up where it left off.

"Danny, sweetheart, you're being *so* dramatic. I don't understand why you ran off like that." Lila talked with her beautifully manicured hands, waving and gesturing.

"Lila, I—"

"Seriously, you know you can *always* talk to me." Her voice went all tea-and-sympathy. "Why just leave? We can work out anything. But, honey, you have to answer my calls and texts. We can't talk if you won't pick up."

"I told you …" His voice dropped lower and Kelly lost the drift when the server arrived with their food.

She cut Ana's grilled cheese sandwich into quarters and then concentrated on her own bean soup. It seemed Danny and Lila were nearly finished eating anyway; he was pulling out his wallet and making definite signs of leaving the restaurant. Two women took the table between, and their flurry of activity cut off the view toward the younger couple. By the time Kelly could see past them, Danny and Lila were out the door and walking toward the street.

"So," she said, leaning toward Sam. "Do we honestly believe Lila just *happened* to be at the hardware store at the very moment Danny went there?"

"She doesn't look to me like a very hardware type of girl."

"Exactly. I wonder if she's been watching for his truck.

Does she know where your place is, or that he's living out there?"

Sam shrugged. "No idea. He might have told her."

"Maybe. Or she might be doing her research."

"His mother has family here, remember? Lila could have had the information before she ever left San Antonio." Sam's soup bowl was empty and she set her spoon aside. "I don't know what to think. She's definitely beautiful and seemed very polite toward us. I have to keep in mind that my ideas about her are filtered through what Danny has said about her. I don't know much at all, firsthand."

"Yeah, I don't know … it's subtle, but there was a lot of pressure on him in that little scrap of conversation just now."

Ana was beginning to squirm in her chair, so they paid their check and left. On the way back to where Sam's car waited at the doctor's parking lot, Sam brought up the subject again.

"I guess the one thing that puzzles me is why a girl like Lila has latched onto a guy like Danny. I mean, I see her as the prom queen, the beauty pageant contestant, and he's just a simple rancher. Don't get me wrong—he's as nice as can be, polite. That kid was raised with manners. But wouldn't Lila be after bigger fish?"

Kelly chewed at her lower lip for a moment. "Yeah, interesting. I suppose every high school has a Lila—the girl with the perfect hair, the perfect makeup. Like you said, the prom queen. Maybe Danny was skinny and pimply in school but sort of morphed into this muscled guy with a tiny waist, chiseled features and fantastic smile?" She glanced at her passenger. "Oh come on, Mom. The guy's a hunk now. I'm totally in love with my husband, but I'm not blind."

Sam laughed and sneaked a peek toward the back seat, where Ana had drifted off to sleep in her car seat.

Chapter 7

Sam folded the warm towels from the dryer, taking in the scent and savoring the late afternoon sun on the fields outside. Part of the deal with the furnished lodging for Danny Flores was the perk that Sam supplied clean sheets and towels each week, and it was a task she didn't mind doing.

Apparently, he'd driven straight back from town after lunch. His truck had been beside the casita when she arrived home. She set his towel and washcloth on top of the already folded sheets and picked up the small stack. She didn't bother with a jacket as the afternoon had turned warm and the small guesthouse was merely twenty yards away.

She tapped at the door, got no response, and tried the

handle. As she'd guessed, Danny and Beau must still be working in the barn. She set the stack of clean laundry on the bed and glanced around. A water-filled cereal bowl and spoon sat in the sink, and a coffee cup was rinsed and turned upside down on the drain board. No dirty clothes strewn about, no food wrappers or other trash that might be enticing to mice. They'd lucked out with their hired help and the housing arrangement.

She turned to go and that's when she spotted his cell phone on the tiny dinette table.

Hmm …

Almost on auto-pilot, her hand reached for it.

Stop it—this is personal.

But he did ask my advice about dealing with this girl. And I'm just gathering facts.

Sam! Drop it!

She looked out the window above the table, which faced the barn. Neither of the men was in sight.

One quick look. Just to get an idea if he's succeeded in getting through to Lila. Maybe he won't need my help anymore.

Yeah, right. You're just dying of curiosity.

She pressed the button and the screen lit up. *It probably has a password, and that's when I'm stopping.*

But the screen full of icons appeared, and the one for text messages showed new ones waiting. Her heart rate picked up as she checked the path to the barn again.

Okay, I'll only look at the ones he's already read.

Yeah, so he won't know you snooped.

She opened the app and found a thread from yesterday.

Lila: Hey baby, I've missed you. I'm in Taos and need to see you. Today?

Danny: Taos seriously? Sorry, I'm busy today.

Lila: Tonight then. I'm at the Fernandez Inn. Call me.

From the look of it, she was dictating what she wanted. And why was he apologizing to someone who'd shown up unannounced? Sam scrolled upward to the earlier part of the thread.

Danny: I can't talk about marriage right now. Look, we just don't know each other that well.

Lila: Baby, I know this is right. Like I said, I got a message from my guardian angel. It's God's will that we belong together.

Sam read that part twice. Angels relaying God's will? Really? Danny had said he'd only known Lila a few months. Still, she supposed, for some people the attraction is immediate—she and Beau had felt very strongly about each other right away. Except that the further back she scrolled, the more the messages showed that this whole marriage idea was definitely Lila's.

Danny: I need time and space to think.

Lila: You're overreacting, trying to throw me off track. We have wedding plans to make.

At the end of each day, she'd signed off with **Sweet dreams, baby.**

Poor Danny. And his attempt to get away had now failed. She thought back to the lunchtime encounter today. Lila had seemed animated as she talked and planned, while Danny had been a man of one-syllable responses.

A beam of sunlight came through the window as it began to set behind the trees on the far side of the pasture, reminding Sam of the time. She exited the texts and set the phone back exactly where she'd found it.

She stepped out the door and saw Danny walking toward her. *Oops—close.*

"Hey, Danny, I just dropped off your clean linens."

"Thanks, Sam."

"It was nice to meet Lila today. She seemed nice—and pretty too. Funny how we all ended up in town at the same time."

"Yeah, funny about that."

"Danny?"

"Well, how did she do it? *Happen* to arrive in Taos and then *happen* to be in the same hardware store at the moment I was sent there by Beau?"

Yeah, the same thought she and Kelly had shared on the way home. Could Lila have some method of tracking him?

"Anyway, yes, she was very nice at lunch today. She just seems so different at times. Like, she'll be super pushy, and then other times she seems to completely understand me. Maybe I'm just being too sensitive—do you think?"

What could she say without admitting she'd just sneaked into his private messages?

"I think you're wise to take your time to think about this. If a person's moods switch around a lot, I'd take that as a warning sign." The sun sank out of sight and the temperature immediately dropped. Sam crossed her arms and rubbed the chilly places.

"Thanks, Sam. I'll let you get back inside." His smile was genuinely grateful. For what, she didn't know. She felt as though she hadn't exactly offered any great epiphany for him.

She quick-stepped back to the house and pulled out the steak she planned to broil for Beau's dinner. The gist of those text messages ran through her mind as she chopped greens and tomatoes for the salad. Some kind of divine message had told Lila she should marry Danny?

Okay, lots of young women got starry-eyed ideas about

guys. And sometimes, the earlier in the relationship the more unrealistic the dreams. But this felt like something more. Danny's uncertainty about what he had actually promised Lila, versus what she claimed he said. And his apologizing for his own feelings. What type of relationship prompted those things?

Chapter 8

Kelly flipped the switch on the electric kettle and measured loose tea into a strainer, an afternoon habit she'd cherished since she and Scott spent their honeymoon in England. The attic room had come to hold the most interest for her, of any space in the old Victorian house. Here, she kept the carved box, Manichee, which had come into her possession also during that trip to England. Knowing the box had once belonged to her great uncle was a tie, of course, but learning of the box's power and how it was related to the one her mother owned—there was the magic.

As the kettle heated she opened the leather-bound book, which she kept on the highest shelf in the room. Golden sun filtered through one of the attic's dormer windows, where Eliza lay stretched out in feline contentment. Just outside the door, on the landing, Ana played contentedly with two dollies, serving them pretend tea from her little china tea set.

Through the window, Kelly saw Sam's new little SUV coming up the long driveway, disappearing behind one of the gables. Downstairs, the sounds of movement in the kitchen. The kettle clicked off. Kelly, following the English method for tea, swished the boiling water into the pot, poured it out in her small work sink, and then poured more water over the leaves in the strainer.

Sam arrived at the attic door just as the three-minute timer went off. She held a bakery box from Sweet's Sweets.

"Perfect timing." Kelly set the book aside and picked up the two tea mugs she'd purchased at Harrod's.

Sam pulled a stool up to the heavy wooden table Kelly was now using partly as a library table, sometimes for experiments and to test ideas she found in the book of runes, as they'd come to call the volume that they'd learned had once belonged to a Romanian witch—supposedly. Since the book and the two boxes had come into their lives, they'd learned to remain open to almost any possibility.

"So, I have a confession to make," Sam said as she opened the bakery box to reveal a dozen decorated Easter egg cookies.

"You're hitting Easter early?"

"Becky's idea. They're selling well, so who cares if the holiday is more than three weeks away." Sam took one to Ana, who proceeded to break it into small enough pieces so her dolls could eat some.

Eliza joined the little party on the landing, and Ana proceeded to explain why cats don't generally like tea. Eliza watched her hostess with head cocked, ears perked forward.

Sam started to sip her tea but backed away when it proved too hot. She pointed to the book. "Do you suppose this has spells or potions or something to fix relationships?"

"That's your confession? Is there something at home you're not telling me?"

Sam laughed. "Guess I'd better start over. My confession is that I snooped on Danny's phone. My question stems from my suspicion that things are seriously messed up between him and Lila."

"Really? What was your first clue?" Kelly said, giving her mom the dagger eyes.

"Do you believe a person can receive a divine sign that they are meant to be with someone?"

"What, like lightning strikes them or something?"

Sam told her about the messages on the young man's phone, quoting several.

"So, which was it—God or an angel that gave Lila this edict from heaven?" Kelly was smirking into her mug.

"I know, right? And then ... saddest thing is that he's apologizing to her! She gets him thinking it's somehow his fault that he doesn't want to commit to marriage after knowing her just a few months. I tell you, the lady is unbalanced."

Kelly held up an index finger. "Hang on ... I've read something about this. It's a thing."

She set her mug down and picked up her tablet. With a few clicks, she had come up with an article.

"Does Danny seem to be second-guessing things he knows to be true?" she asked after a couple of minutes.

"I'd say so. I watch him around Beau and he's confident and assured. When we've had conversations, he seems to know what he wants, knows he wants to break it off with her. But then she says something—like that whole heavenly message bit—and he's dithering again. He asked me if I thought he was being too sensitive, but from what I've seen she completely ignores his wishes. Her messages just sort of talk right over him, telling him what's going to happen despite what he states to her."

"So he's questioning his own decisions?"

"Yeah, I think he's even questioning what his actual words were. He says he never proposed to her, but she's almost convinced him that he did."

"Yeah, that's what I'm finding here. Her social media pages are all full of claims about him and their plans together. She puts incredibly personal stuff out there for the world to see." She held up the screen for Sam to take a look. "And now, in these recent posts she's going on about how much she loves him and how it's breaking her heart that he wants to delay the wedding, as if it was all set."

"What wedding? The girl is off her rocker."

"Yeah, this stuff is over the top," Kelly murmured, switching to another screen. "Okay, here's the article I read a while back. Gaslighting. That's what this is called, quote 'when a person manipulates or controls someone else in ways that make them question their memory of events or even their sanity'."

"*Gaslight*, that old movie with Ingrid Bergman ... Wow. That was powerful stuff."

"Exactly. The husband gradually drove her crazy by playing little tricks and then telling her she was imagining everything. That's what happens. Lila's got all their friends believing they are this super close couple, the fairytale romance, and the wedding will be happening soon, and Danny's caught up in wondering if he did actually propose and agree to all this."

"Can we do anything to help him?" Sam wondered.

Kelly shook her head slowly. "I don't know. How often does anyone believe what outsiders are telling them about their relationships? He may just have to figure this out for himself."

"If the genders were switched—if this was a woman friend being manipulated by a man, I wouldn't have any trouble speaking up and suggesting she get herself out of there. But with a guy, I just don't know how much to say. They've got their pride."

"I'll print this page and maybe you can find someplace to leave it for him—his truck or in the casita. What do you think?"

"He's already tried to get himself away from her, but maybe if he sees it spelled out in black and white … Anyway, it's worth a try."

Sure. What could go wrong with that?

Chapter 9

Sam decided not to say anything to Beau about what she and Kelly had found. The texts, the social media posts, and Danny's distress over Lila showing up were all pretty compelling, but at the end of the day it was Danny's problem to solve. Beau would give her a hard stare and tell her it was none of their business.

So she did what most wives would do and kept the printed page from Kelly's research a secret. The folded paper, left inconspicuously on the casita's kitchenette countertop, might at least give Danny the knowledge that he wasn't alone, that others had experienced similar problems. Sam was tempted to jot a note to suggest he block Lila's calls and messages so he wouldn't even see them, but she felt sure he'd already thought of that. He had gone so far as to move to another state to get away from her. She wasn't sure what else to advise, so she went to bed that night determined to put everything out of her mind.

Beau was reading a biography of the frontiersman Kit Carson when the distinctive sound of tires on gravel sounded outside. Sam watched him set his book aside and step over to the window that overlooked the front of the property.

"Someone coming up the driveway," he said. "It looks like a small sedan—we know anyone like that?"

"No one I'd be expecting after ten o'clock at night."

"It's heading for the casita. Stopping beside Danny's truck."

Sam had a bad feeling about this. She jumped out of bed and joined him. By the casita's porch light she saw a woman with long dark hair, wearing jeans and puffy jacket, step out of the car and approach the door. More than a minute passed and Danny didn't open up. Then they caught the sound of Lila pounding on the door. It opened suddenly.

"Doesn't look like he's gotten through to her yet," Sam said.

Raised voices, then Lila went into the casita and the door closed.

"Sam ... you gotta leave this alone. Danny has to figure it out for himself." Exactly what she'd known he would say.

"I know."

They crawled back into bed and turned out the bedside lamps. But Sam couldn't take her eyes off the numerals on the clock. She imagined herself casting a spell, flinging lightning bolts from her fingertips to chase away the unwanted visitor. As if she actually knew how to do such a thing. But the image comforted her, made her feel useful.

Fifteen minutes passed, and then she heard the sound of the car driving away.

In the morning Beau called Danny. "Come up to the house. I need to give you some cash to pick up our order at the feed store."

Sam was at the kitchen window when the ranch hand arrived. He stood on the front porch, stroking the sideburn on the left side of his face. Beau went out and she watched him hand Danny a piece of paper and some money. When he reached out to take the cash, Sam saw marks on his face.

"What happened to Danny's face?" she asked Beau two minutes later, when he came inside.

"He didn't explain and I didn't ask. Looked like scratches."

They exchanged a look, both thinking the same thing. Lila.

"Beau, if this is getting physical, shouldn't we say something?"

"Sam, leave it. He'll figure it out." Beau put on his work jacket and headed out toward the barn, and she saw Danny's truck pull out onto the county road.

But she couldn't get the image of those red lines out of her mind. She took a long breath. Today was her morning at the bakery, with an important wedding cake to finish. She needed to follow Beau's advice and just get on with her own business.

The drive into town calmed her. Spring was in the air and, although she knew the weather could turn any direction at this time of year, she savored the clear sky and noticed the tender buds on the trees. Coming in on Camino de la Placita, she slowed to look at the front of her pastry shop.

Sweet's Sweets had been her dream for many years and now it had become exactly what she wanted, the place to stretch her creative baker's muscles, although not with the intensity of the early years when she'd worked nearly around the clock. The purple awning and attractive window display brought customers off the street, as well as her diehard loyal fans.

She had just slowed for the stop sign at the corner when she spotted a woman leaving the shop—dark hair, puffy jacket, and those expensive boots. Lila got into a white sedan that screamed *rental*, and backed out. This didn't seem like a coincidence. Sam debated following, but didn't see the point. Plus, she had a wedding cake with a deadline. She pulled into her normal spot in the alley behind the bakery and went into the kitchen.

"Hey, Sam." Julio, her star baker, was dumping flour into the big Hobart mixer. "The layers for that big cake are ready."

"Thanks. I'm going to grab a coffee up front." Sam pushed through the curtain that separated the kitchen from the sales room, not even pausing to take off her coat first.

Jen was alone, taking a moment between customers to wipe down the bistro tables.

"That young woman who was just in here …" Sam said, approaching the beverage bar. "What did she want?"

Jen's forehead furrowed for a moment. "Long, dark hair, pretty, about twenty-five?"

"I saw her leaving."

"Yeah, she was looking at the wedding cakes in the window display, asking prices and stuff."

"Did she actually order a cake?"

"Oh, no. Said she was just gathering information, real

preliminary questions. You know the type."

Sam nodded. "Did she mention me or Beau? I wonder if she knew this was my shop?"

"Nope, not at all. Like I said, just general questions. She ended up buying one cupcake, a triple chocolate." Jen chuckled. "Admitted to being a real chocoholic and we laughed over that. She seemed nice."

Sam nodded as she poured a mug of her signature blend coffee for herself. "Okay, thanks." So, maybe there were coincidences after all.

In the kitchen she hung up her coat, washed her hands, and took out the layers for the new cake, a four-tier confection in pink and burgundy. She began by rolling rose-pink fondant and draping the tiers with it, then creating swags and ruffles tinted a slightly darker shade. It was the type of work she loved getting lost in, the draping and shaping of the swags.

At some point Becky informed her she was taking the bakery van to make a couple of deliveries and asked if Sam wanted her to bring back something for lunch. Had the morning slipped by so effortlessly?

A familiar male voice joked with Jen in the front room, and within a minute or so her friend Rupert Penrick walked through to the kitchen.

"Greetings, my dear," he said, sweeping in and planting a kiss on Sam's cheek. Today's outfit consisted of flowing purple pants and bright yellow tunic, a purple beret, and a flowered scarf. If she had to bet, he had a new boyfriend. Or his work was going really well.

"You're in a great mood. Must have finished that book you were agonizing over when we talked at Ana's birthday party?"

"I have, and it's the most glorious feeling. Typing 'the end' must be for me somewhat like placing the topper on that fabulous cake will be for you. A creative endeavor well done, and happily so."

Sam laughed. He was so right.

"So, what's this one about?" she asked.

"About? What they're always about—love and romance. There are times I feel like killing off a character, but my audience buys them for the happily-ever-after ending." He was always so modest about the fact that every one of his books, written under the pen name Victoria DeVane, was a top bestseller before even hitting the stores.

"Have you ever written a plot about gaslighting?" She worked as they talked, kneading color paste into a ball of modeling chocolate, tinting it deep burgundy for the orchids that would adorn the top of the big cake.

"Ah, the ever-popular theme of the evil lover manipulating the innocent heroine by convincing her she's insane. Usually wanting her to be insane enough to hand over her vast fortune to him. Yes, actually, I've written one or two. Of course, I must always add the heroic-but-poor man who will step in to save her from such nefarious doings." He picked up one of the small pearlized spheres Sam had made, the representation of champagne bubbles she would add between the swags, and popped it into his mouth. "Why? You looking for a good read that will keep you up at night?"

Sam chuckled. "Not exactly."

"You know someone it's happening to! Ohmygod, tell me more." Rupert always was one to dish gossip, but Sam wasn't about to name names.

"I'll only say that it appears it's not always the innocent

young girl and the despicable man."

"Role reversal—I love it. The male is the innocent and the female is predatory." He picked up another of the champagne bubbles, waving his hand as he talked. "Not for my audience, most likely, but something to think about."

He rolled the candy around on his tongue. "Ahhh, wait a second. You want to know how the good guy stops the bad guy in these things. That's it, right?"

Sam tilted her head, not sure where he was going with this, but open to any ideas.

"In a historical romance, I just throw in a duel or something and the cad gets run through or shot or shoved from a cliff … but I'm guessing those aren't options in the present-day scenario."

"'Fraid not. But we'll think of something."

He got a sly look. "So there is a *we*, and *we* are thinking of a plan …"

Sam realized she'd said too much. "It'll work itself out. I'm sure it will."

His wide shoulders slumped. "All right. But keep me in mind if a plan does develop. You know how good I am."

A vision popped into her head, one where Rupert had dressed her up as a wealthy art patron to fool the owner of a high-end gallery. His statement was correct—he was good at that sort of thing. "I'll keep you in mind. Now quit eating all my champagne bubbles."

He laughed and pecked her forehead. "Happy decorating, love."

For the next two hours she lost herself in forming swirl-roses and the placement, one by one, of candy bubbles around the cake. The work nearly made her forget about the situation with her ranch hand.

Chapter 10

Sam stashed the finished wedding cake in the walk-in fridge, checked in quickly with Kelly to see how her day had gone (quietly, now that Scott was out of hibernation and was schooling Ana again), and headed home with the idea of making spaghetti and meatballs for dinner.

She pulled off the highway and turned onto their long driveway, parking in front of the house as the two dogs raced from the barn area to greet her. Ranger, the Lab, was moving slower these days but he came to her and nuzzled his graying face against her leg. Nellie circled them both, then ran back to Danny, who was coming down the path with a basket in his hands. The dog led him straight to Sam.

"Hey, Sam. Beau wanted to be sure these got safely to the house." He waited a moment while she hitched the strap of her backpack over a shoulder, then handed her the fresh eggs.

Several long scratches were visible on his left cheek.

"Thanks for bringing these," she said. "Everything okay? We saw Lila drive up to the casita late last night."

His hand automatically went to his face, confirming the source of the injury.

"Yeah, sorry about that. I didn't invite her. I would never have someone over late, when they might wake you up."

"We were just reading. No problem." She stared out toward the pasture. "You said you tried blocking her number. Is that why she decided to come out here?"

"I suppose so. She even went out and got a new sim card and called from a different number so I wouldn't recognize hers. And the texts aren't letting up at all. I told her we're not getting married and she should leave Taos. That didn't work."

"Did you talk to Beau about this? Or Sheriff Richards?"

He shook his head. "It's not the kind of thing a guy wants to mention to his boss."

Sam nodded. Beau had already told her the answer was to let Danny figure this out for himself. He wouldn't ever interfere.

"Well, you need to treat those scratches—they're pretty inflamed. I've got some antibiotic ointment in the house. Hang on and I'll grab it for you."

Inside, she set the egg basket on a side table and dropped her pack on the sofa before heading upstairs. The carved box sat on her bathroom vanity and she picked it up for a minute, hoping some brilliant idea would come to her, the exactly right thing to say to Danny. But although the box warmed slightly, no words of wisdom popped into her head. She set the box down and reached into a drawer for the tube of ointment.

"Here," she said, handing it to him when she got back to the porch. "A little bit of this, couple times a day, ought to keep that from getting infected."

"Thanks, Sam. Look, I'm sorry about all this. She won't be coming out here again."

He dropped the tube into his shirt pocket, murmured something about finishing his chores, and turned away, thanking her again for the ointment. His eyes were downcast, his words soft, but she could see a distinct muddy orange aura around him. He was harboring a lot of anger.

At least he said Lila wouldn't be coming out here again. He must have been firm with his orders this time.

* * *

Over dinner, Beau was full of stories about the two new calves and how the two men had made a special pen inside the barn for them, so Sam tucked her concerns over Danny and Lila's situation into the back of her mind. Beau was right—Danny would work this out somehow. But the orange aura surrounding him nagged at her. As the night grew silent, she found herself listening for the sound of a vehicle on the property.

In the morning Sam decided to get an early start. She would drop by Kelly's for a short visit before going back to the bakery to put the final touches on the champagne bubbles wedding cake. She tidied the kitchen and gathered her pack and coat before heading out into the bright, clear day.

At the end of the driveway she spotted Danny's truck

making the turn onto the county road. A white sedan emerged from behind a huge chamisa bush and followed.

"I don't believe it." Her first instinct was to race after them both—to warn Danny or stop Lila. But would she actually accomplish anything?

Let them work it out, came Beau's words.

She backed her SUV around and headed out. Within a mile she was behind the two other vehicles, and the situation was eating at her again.

Leave it, Sam. Just leave it.

She made the right-hand turn toward the Victorian and concentrated on the winding road lined with winter-bare trees. The large blue-gray house loomed ahead and Sam turned in, finding Kelly in the spacious kitchen.

"Hey there, want some coffee?" Kelly looked cozy in blue leggings and a thick cream-colored sweater. Eliza was lapping water from her bowl near the fridge.

Sam waved away the coffee; she was already edgy enough.

"So, what's bugging you, Mom? I know that look." Kelly held out a plate of cinnamon roll nuggets left from breakfast.

Sam paced to the window above the sink. "Oh, it's still about Danny and that girl. Two nights ago, she showed up late and today he's got these scratches on his face."

Kelly stopped in mid-chew on her cinnamon roll. "So now the battle is getting physical?"

"He didn't inflict those scratches on himself."

"I wonder what he said or did …"

Sam repeated what Danny had told her. "He doesn't want to bring it up with Beau or Evan. I guess that's not considered manly."

"Beau would probably advise him to get a restraining order, but you don't honestly think a piece of paper would stop her, do you?"

Sam slumped against the counter. "No, not really."

"So, we just need Lila to fall out of love with him. If she simply didn't care anymore, she'd go away, right?"

"One could hope."

Kelly's gaze went upward toward the ceiling. "I'll bet our book has a love potion or two. It's a universal thing ..."

"Um, we want her *out* of love, not falling harder."

"Right. But if there's a potion, there must be an antidote. We already know she's in love, so we make the antidote for that and—" Kelly looked at Sam. "What? It'll totally work."

"Well ... it could be the best way to get her to leave town. But we have to be sure it's not going to harm her."

Eliza had sat on a chair, watching the whole conversation. Now, with a strident *meow*, she jumped down and ran toward the stairs, leading the way.

Kelly put down the half-eaten piece of sweet roll and dusted her hands. "Come on, no time like the present. Scott's got Ana out on a nature walk this morning—she's probably going to be into advanced botany before we know it. Anyway, it's the perfect time for us to play around in the attic and see what we can come up with."

Sam followed up the main staircase, toward the back of the house, and up to the third floor. *What on earth am I getting myself into?*

Chapter 11

Kelly pulled two stools up to the big wooden table in the center of the room, then brought the leather-bound book from the shelf. The cat jumped up to the table and watched in fascination. Kelly stared at the first page for a moment before remembering that she had to handle the wooden box before the rune-like characters would make sense. The lower sections of the bookcase were enclosed and one of those was equipped with a lock. She pulled a silver chain with a key from beneath her sweater and unlocked the door to it.

Within moments of handling the box it began to glow and her hands began to feel warm. The cat's orange ear twitched, then the black one.

"Okay, that should help. Did you bring Virtu with you?"

"No, sorry, I had no clue we'd be going in this direction." Each of them could read the book, but only after handling her specific carved magic box. No other method had yet worked for them.

"That's fine. I'll see what I can find." Kelly laid the ancient book on the table and paged through it slowly, handling the old parchment carefully.

From the beginning, when the book had been handed to Kelly by their quirky Romanian chocolatier friend, Bobul, the two women had noticed oddities about it. Unlike a normal book, this one didn't appear to have been printed or bound in the usual way. Some pages were parchment, some appeared to be as thin as rice paper, some were yellowed with age, others crisp and much newer. And the edges had not been trimmed to match up. Smaller sheets were inserted at random places. Some larger pages extended slightly beyond the covers. And they'd yet to discover a table of contents or index.

"I wish I'd taken more time with this," Kelly mumbled. "I might have discovered if there was some rhyme or reason to the way it's organized."

Sam smiled at her daughter's fierce concentration. "There's not a section called Relationship Problems?"

"I wish."

"Okay, so let's say we do discover some 'anti-love' potion ... How will we get Lila to take it? I can't see either of us approaching her with a vial, or her falling for the Drink Me label if we could leave it in her car."

"We have to find something she loves to eat and we'll put it in that," Kelly said, turning another page and staring at the writing on it.

An idea flashed through Sam's mind. "Jen met her. Lila stopped in at the bakery one day and Jen said she bought a triple-chocolate cupcake. Lila admitted she's a real chocoholic."

Kelly looked up with a huge grin. "That's it, then! We give her a spiked cupcake."

"Um, we need to think this through. She might trust me more with a cupcake than a vial, but what if she doesn't?" Sam paced the length of the big, open space. "And we probably need to witness her eating it. What if she gave it to Danny? I mean, the guy couldn't be much more not-in-love than he already is. A potion could take him from apathy to downright hatred and I wouldn't want to see where that could lead."

"Hm, you're right about that." Kelly drummed her fingers on the table for a moment. "Well, we just have to hope that the potion recipe comes with directions."

Kelly was a fraction of the way into the book, and Sam could feel her bakery order calling. "Look, I'll leave you to it. Call me when you find something, but don't actually stir up anything on your own. Let's do that part together."

"Right. First things first—we have to hope the ingredients are something we can actually get our hands on. If it requires eye of newt or shavings from a witch's fingernails, I'm not sure what we'll do."

"Meow," said Eliza, tapping the open book with a white paw.

Sam came around the table and gave her daughter a hug. "If we get lucky, Lila will just leave town on her own. But I'm not counting on that."

"Nope. That one's like a bad rash."

Sam grinned. "Which, if we can't find the potion we want, would be another avenue. We come up with something that gives Lila a miserable rash and she'll leave

Danny alone because she won't want him to see it."

"Oh, Mom, you're starting to think like your devious daughter."

* * *

The bakery felt quiet when Sam arrived. Julio was pulling a tray of cupcakes from the big bake oven. Triple chocolate. She imagined the rich devil's food cake, the molten center filling, and the decadent pile of chocolate buttercream frosting that would go on top. Which of those would provide the best cover for the potion? It would depend on the taste of the magical ingredients. The molten center could conceal the texture and flavor, but if the ingredients wouldn't stand up to heat, it would have to go into the frosting. Besides, what part of a cupcake could no one resist—the icing!

What am I thinking? This plan is so over the top—

"Sam?"

She snapped to attention. "Sorry, Julio?"

"I asked if you wanted me to bring that wedding cake out of the cooler. I'm putting this inside."

"Oh, yes, please." She hung up her coat, donned her bakery jacket, and washed her hands.

The tall pink and burgundy cake was a confectioner's delight, Sam had to admit. She didn't remember whether Jen had suggested the champagne bubbles theme, or if that had been the customer's idea, but they set off the draped fondant and the roses around the lower edge so well. All it needed now was a dusting of edible pearlized powder.

Sam found a clean brush, similar to one from a makeup kit, large and fluffy. She dipped it in the pearlescent dust and tapped off the excess, then swished the brush over the clusters of little spheres she'd made yesterday. Instantly, they took on the glow of pearls, the iridescence of liquid bubbles. She stood back for a look, and decided the roses could benefit from a dewy glow as well. A few more flicks of the brush, and the cake was perfect.

Becky stopped in the middle of her Easter bunny cookies. "Wow, Sam. That's one of your best. It's spectacular."

"It's ready to go, whenever. The order says it needs to arrive at the church between three and five this afternoon."

"I'll take it," Becky offered. "I have two birthday cakes to deliver as well. One is done, and I'll finish the other one right after lunch."

Sam walked to the sales room. Two women sat at one of the bistro tables, chatting and nursing cups of coffee. An empty plate with a few crumbs sat in front of each.

"Busy breakfast and morning rush," Jen said, bending to reach inside the display case. "We have a few muffins left for the teatime crowd, and I'm about to add cheesecake and cupcakes as soon as Julio has them ready."

"He's nearly there. Just took triple chocolates out of the oven, so as soon as they've cooled and Becky adds the frosting. Plus, she's got more seasonal cookies decorated for the after-school kids."

"Good. We've kind of had a rush on triple chocolate this week. Not sure why."

"You mentioned a young woman a day or two ago … has she been back?"

"Twice. She's clearly addicted."

The door bells tinkled and an older man walked in, his eye on the last blueberry muffin. Sam left Jen to tend to the sale.

So, Lila was hooked on the triple-chocolate cupcakes. Interesting.

Sam's phone vibrated in her pocket just as she reached the kitchen. Kelly.

"Can you stop by on your way home? I think Eliza found us just the potion we need."

Chapter 12

A small paper bag with the logo of Blue Sky Herbs & Things sat on the big table in the attic. The book of runes lay open beside it.

"I had a small shopping list," Kelly explained. She pulled two tiny bottles and a stick of incense from the bag. "To go along with *these* handy kitchen items."

"You said Eliza found the recipe?" Sam glanced at the window seat where the cat was licking one paw daintily. She walked over and rubbed the cat's ears.

"She was sitting on the table when you were here—remember? Well, when I turned around, she had laid down on the open book and her paw was pointing right to the spot."

"Good kitty," Sam said.

The cat flicked her head away from Sam's hand.

"I don't think she likes 'kitty' much. She hissed at me the first time I called her that."

"Sorry, Eliza. You have too much class for nicknames, right?"

"*Mrroww.*" Eliza sat tall and statuesque.

Sam turned her attention back to Kelly.

On the table sat a cinnamon stick, a piece of ginger root, and a bottle of cardamom, alongside a small metal dish and some tea light candles. Sam watched as Kelly consulted the book, then lit the incense and passed each of the utensils and ingredients through the smoke.

"To cleanse them," she explained. "Now we heat the metal dish over the candles and start cooking." She grated a small amount of the ginger into the dish and sprinkled cardamom over it, then stirred the mixture with the cinnamon stick. As the spices began to emit their scent, she took the bottles and uncapped them. "Essence of roses and just one tiny drop of jasmine oil. As I let the drops fall, take the cinnamon stick and stir everything together, counterclockwise."

A lovely smell of flowers and spice filled the air as the ingredients blended.

"Okay, let's get it off the heat before it burns." Kelly grabbed a towel to pick up the metal dish, blowing out the candles as she set the bowl aside.

"Now, the important part of the spell is that this has to be given by the object of the person's affections. Danny is going to have to give it to her, and he has to say specific words when he does. The love potion is exactly the same ingredients—but the process is different. To make someone fall in love, the spices and oils are blended in water and consumed as a tea. This one is the reverse spell, to make someone fall out of love, and it's prepared over fire. Opposites—fire and water. Anyway, it made sense to me."

Sam nodded and stared at the mix. "Well, it's all edible stuff. And it smells enticing. I think we can get it into the cupcake icing, no problem."

"You said Lila is hooked on your triple chocolate cupcakes. She may notice the difference in taste."

"I thought of that," Sam said. "I'm going to bring home the cupcake and tell Danny it's for Lila. I'll say we're testing a new recipe and want her opinion on it."

"Oh, great plan!" Kelly scooped the potion into a small glass jar, capped it, and handed it to Sam.

"Now I just have to get him to go along with it." As if there was a logical way to explain all this? Sam had her doubts but Eliza purred approvingly.

Sam's chance came sooner than she'd imagined. Beau and Danny were out on the back deck, hammering at the planks, making repairs to a few of the winter-damaged redwood boards. It seemed natural enough to say she had some steaks thawing and to invite Danny to join them for dinner. Both men lit up at the word *steak*.

All she had to do now was figure out how to work cupcakes into the conversation. And preferably at a time Beau wasn't in the room, considering how he'd told her twice to back away and let Danny and Lila solve their own problems.

Lila herself provided the perfect lead-in to her mission. Beau was outside, turning the steaks, and Danny had offered to carry the large salad bowl and a platter of garlic bread to the table for Sam when the text pinged his phone.

"I'm reaching my limit," he muttered, shutting off the sound on his phone.

"She's still doing it, huh."

"Yeah, nearly nonstop." A muscle in his jaw twitched and his dark eyes were smoldering. "And, you wouldn't believe this. She followed my truck when I went to town this morning. People think of men as stalkers, but this girl has all the moves down pat."

Sam glanced out the windows at Beau, who still seemed occupied.

"Would you be willing to try an experiment? I'm not going to say it's magic or anything …"

"Is it something a *curandera* would do? Abuela told me last weekend I should talk to a *curandera*."

"Yes! Exactly. I know someone, and I can probably—"

Beau opened the back door and stepped inside, balancing a platter of steaks with his right hand. "You guys had better get to the table," he announced.

Sam mouthed *shh* at Danny, and he gave her a subtle wink.

The steaks were a hit, and Danny's mood visibly improved during the meal. Sam found herself breathing easier about the plan.

* * *

As she'd envisioned, chocolate buttercream frosting was the ideal medium for the potion; it mixed in without a trace. Sam had come into the bakery early, planning to avoid questions from the rest of the staff. Julio was there alone and he kept to himself, wrapped up in his own little world of muffin batter and streusel coffee cake.

Sam confiscated two cupcakes from the tray that would soon be on its way to the sales room, one triple-chocolate, one apple spice. She left the apple one alone; for the chocolate one, she scraped off the existing icing and picked up the small bowl in which she'd mixed the separate batch of special buttercream. Quickly filling a pastry bag, she piped an elaborate swirl on the cupcake. A deft sprinkling of tiny chocolate chips denoted this as the custom-made dessert.

She picked up the gift box she had set aside, fitted the two cupcakes into the slots that would keep them from touching, and closed the lid.

"Woo-hoo, anyone here?" came a voice from the back door.

"Rupert! What a surprise. You aren't normally such an early riser."

Her purple-clad friend stepped in and closed the door. "Once in awhile I even surprise myself," he said. "Actually, I'm having breakfast with someone special, and I thought I'd see if there were any extra fantastic goodies baked already, something I can take along as a little gift."

His eyes fell on the gift box. "Ooh, what's this? It looks perfect."

"Ahh—no, no. Sorry, this one is spoken for." She grabbed the box and carried it to the safety of her desk. *Close call!*

She studied the cooling racks for ideas. Something ready to go, something quick. "How about an assortment of muffins—I can make up a basket, add a packet of my signature coffee?"

"Umm, normally I'm not big on chocolate in the morning, but this is to die for," said Rupert.

Sam turned and saw him swiping his finger inside the frosting bowl for a second taste.

"Whoa! Wait!" Sam felt her eyes go wide.

"What? It's marvelous."

"What if I told you that one contains a secret love potion formula?" she said, reaching for the bowl and getting it out of his grasp.

"All the better. The man I'm meeting for breakfast—well, I'd be fine with it if he turns out to be the one. Wait—you're not saying this is going to make me fall for *you*?"

"No, no. It only takes effect if you're with your intended." Sam felt her palms go sweaty. Would the small amount of the potion be enough to wreck Rupert's chances?

Well, it was a done deed now.

Chapter 13

Sam ran through Kelly's instructions in her head as she approached the casita. This felt so sneaky, starting with the fact that she'd waited until Beau got in the shower so he wouldn't know what she was up to. Through the window she could see Danny pacing the floor, his fists clenching and unclenching at his sides. She clutched the bakery box in one hand and tapped on the door with the other.

It flew open with a vengeance.

"Oh, Sam. I'm so glad it's you." He stepped aside and ushered her in. Before she got the chance to speak, his phone pinged from the dining table. He rolled his eyes and turned his back on it. "Again!"

She held the box out to him. "This is what we talked about ..."

"From your *curandera* friend."

That works. "Yes. Now there are specific instructions, and I need to be quick. Inside are two cupcakes. You need to get together with Lila at a time when you'll both eat them together. Hers is the chocolate one, yours is the apple spice. If she says anything about hers tasting different than usual, it's because I've asked you both to be part of a customer survey about a new flavor we're trying out. Got it?"

"I need to see her eat the cupcake; it's a new flavor you're testing."

"Right. And … this part is very important. The moment she finishes her chocolate cupcake you have to look her in the eyes and say 'Lila, you don't love me.' Exactly those words at exactly that time. Repeat it back?"

"Lila, you don't love me. Right when she's eaten the cupcake."

"Exactly. Any questions?"

"What do I do next, run for my life?" His mouth twisted in a wonky grin.

"That might not be a bad idea." She reached out to pat his shoulder, and her phone buzzed down inside her pocket.

"Go ahead," Danny said. "I got this. Lila wants to meet in an hour for a drink. I'm going to suggest coffee instead and tell her I'm bringing dessert."

Another buzz from Sam's phone.

"Sounds good. Let me know how it goes." She pulled the phone from her pocket and saw that it was Rupert.

She tapped the phone and headed down the path toward the house.

"Sam, what the hell?"

"Rupe? What's the matter?"

"I cannot believe what I just did. You must help me."

"Slow down a second. What's the matter?"

She could hear him take a deep breath. "Jimmy and I were supposed to have breakfast this morning, but he called to cancel. So, okay, it didn't matter to me—we could get together any time, but I didn't say that. What I said— well, I'm not going to repeat it. Bottom line is that I started a stupid argument over a stupid subject. I'm not sure he'll ever talk to me again."

"And …"

"And your stupid love potion icing completely backfired. I thought I would have my mojo completely together after I ate it. But no … Now my budding relationship is probably toast."

Sam pulled a *Yes!* with a fist. The anti-love potion had worked.

"Rupe, I didn't want you to eat that stuff, if you'll recall."

"You didn't stop me."

I had my back turned when you stuck your greedy finger in the bowl. But arguing with a friend wasn't solving anything for either of them.

"I have an idea. Call me in the morning and we'll see what we can do."

"Sam … this had better be good."

"Just get some rest tonight. Things will look better in the morning." She hung up before he could respond, then she dialed Kelly.

"Small tragedy. We have to brew up some of the real love potion as an antidote," she said, explaining how Rupert had helped himself to the icing.

"I can do that," Kelly said, not sounding the least bit worried.

"I'll pick it up on my way to the bakery in the morning."

"This is *so* exciting!" Kelly's voice changed timbre. She must have walked into another room, away from Scott and Ana. "It worked! Our first potion really worked!"

Through the windows, Sam could see Beau coming down the stairs, looking around the living room for her.

"Congratulations, fledgling magician. You did it!" She said goodbye and walked into the house.

Now it was all up to Danny. It would be nice to see him without that harried look on his face.

* * *

Kelly stepped out her kitchen door and handed Sam a pint jar of pale brown liquid. "The turn-on version of the spell. Tell Rupert he can drink this tea hot or cold, it doesn't matter."

Sam laughed. "Luckily, you found the love potion right away."

"Remember, the two were side by side in the book. I suppose even the old Romanian witches wanted to be sure they could reverse something they'd set in motion." She pulled her thin sweater more tightly around herself as a breeze channeled under the portico.

"Get inside where it's warm. I'll call Rupert."

They met at the plaza, near the gazebo, where no one would overhear their conversation. Sam pulled the tea jar from her large coat pocket and relayed Kelly's instructions.

"Pour the tea in a cup and get in a comfortable place. Envision the person you want to attract and hold that picture firmly in your mind as you say the words 'Love, come to me' as you drink the tea. Keep loving thoughts toward that person, and he will call you." She raised her eyebrows. "Or so they say."

Rupert stared at the liquid in the jar. "Well, if it works anything like the other one did, we'll be together before nightfall."

"Oh—one other thing. The instructions caution against envisioning a love that lasts forever. If you ever want to break it off, you'll never be able to get rid of him. You'll be calling me in a panic to get more of the first version. I'm not sure we can just make these turn-on, turn-off potions on a whim."

He reached an arm around her shoulders and squeezed hard. "Thanks, Samantha. I owe you."

"Just be careful."

"One of these days, this will very likely end up in a book."

"So long as you don't name names, okay? Beau doesn't exactly know about all of what he would call my shenanigans."

Rupert gave her a thumbs-up and headed for his car. Sam sighed, hoping this would straighten out the mess for him. All in all, it had been a fairly harmless experiment.

She headed to Sweet's Sweets to settle in for a routine day of cupcake-making—the regular kind.

Chapter 14

Two days passed and Sam hadn't had the chance to talk to Danny. When she'd casually asked Beau how things were, she got an oblivious "fine." She started watching for the ranch hand and finally caught up with him late that afternoon as she was getting home from the bakery.

Danny was carrying a saddle toward the barn and Sam called out a hello. He paused for her to catch up and they walked along together.

"So? How's it going? I have to admit I'm dying of curiosity about how Lila liked the cupcake."

"Yeah, she raved about it. She didn't stop by and give her report?" he asked. "I did like you said and told her it was a new recipe and you wanted feedback."

"We haven't seen her, and I'm pretty sure Jen would have mentioned something."

"Hm."

"And what about your situation? The calls, the texts?"

"You know … I haven't heard a word. Beau's kept me busy around here, and I guess I didn't realize. It's been the longest quiet spell since I met her." He hefted the saddle over the fence rail, to take the load off.

Sam smiled. "Then it worked. The, um, *curandera's* cure."

A grin spread across his face. "It did! Wow. Thanks, Sam."

"Well, keep your guard up for awhile. Hopefully, she just gave up on you and went back home, but it could be that she's lying low and planning something." *Why did I have to say that?* "Let's just stick with the positive. She's gone once and for all."

"Let's hope so. My family will be happy to hear it." His expression changed. "But don't worry. I'm not quitting the ranch to go back to the city. I really like it here."

"Beau is happy to have your help. And don't worry— some day you'll meet the right girl and things will work out great for you."

He gave a glance toward the barn, eager to get back to work.

Sam hitched her pack onto her shoulder and walked toward the ranch house. Beau was in the kitchen, staring into the fridge, finally choosing a beer before turning to give her a kiss.

"You have a good day?" he asked.

"Yeah, very." She scooped kibble into two bowls for the dogs, who were dancing around in anticipation. "I was thinking of warming up that chicken casserole we had yesterday, making a salad to go along with it."

"Sounds great. I'm taking my beer and settling in with the paper I picked up in town today."

Sam turned on the oven, placed the casserole inside, and set a timer. The salad came together quickly and she still had time to sit down. With a glass of water in hand, she joined Beau in the living room. He held the sports section of the *Taos News* and the front page lay draped over the sofa arm.

When Sam saw the headline below the fold, she nearly dropped her glass.

Texas Woman Dies, Police Investigate as Homicide

The body of a young woman was found yesterday afternoon in a local hotel room. The Taos visitor, whose name is being withheld until notification of next of kin, was identified only as a 25-year-old from San Antonio, Texas. She was the lone registered occupant of the room at the historic Fernandez Inn, and the Taos County Sheriff's Department is investigating the death as a homicide. No further information has been released, but Sheriff Evan Richards has promised to pursue every lead and seek a quick arrest in the case.

Holy crap! Sam felt panic rise in her chest. What if the cupcake had poisoned her?

She bolted from the couch and dashed to the coat rack, where she'd left her phone in her coat pocket. Punching a number, she walked into the kitchen and let the door swing shut behind her.

"Kelly! Have you seen the newspaper?"

"Um, no, Mom ... I rarely get one. Why? What's up?"

Sam relayed what she had read.

"Oh shit! Do you think—"

"It has to be Lila. Twenty-five years old, from San Antonio, staying at the Fernandez Inn." Sam had paced the width of the room three times. "Kel, what if we poisoned her!"

There was a long beat of silence. "Okay, let's think a minute. Does the report say it was poison? No, wait, what am I saying. It can't be. Everything we put in there was stuff right out of anyone's kitchen. I mean, unless she had a severe allergy to ginger or cinnamon or—"

"Maybe she got too much of it, ate it too fast ... I don't know." Sam bumped into one of the chairs and it toppled over with a crash.

"Everything okay in there?" Beau called out.

"Yeah, fine," she shouted.

"Mom? What should we do?"

"We need to find out for sure. But I don't want to just call Evan and ask straight out. He'll ask, and then he'll find out Danny gave her the cupcake. Let me think." With a calm she didn't feel, she opened the oven door and looked at the casserole. It was looking nice and bubbly so she switched off the oven. "I can get into the department offices and find the autopsy report. That'll tell us something."

"Mom, if she did die as a reaction to the potion, we'll have to 'fess up. It was an accident. There's no way we could have known ..."

"You're right. If we don't say anything, then the trail will lead to Danny."

"Mom, it's probably going to lead to him anyway. He's the reason she came here."

"True. But let's take one thing at a time. First, I have to be sure we didn't do anything harmful." She heard Beau's footsteps coming toward the kitchen. "Gotta go."

"Hey, everything okay in here? Were you on the phone?"

"Kelly called. There's a small emergency and I need to get over there and help. Casserole and salad are ready. Just dish yourself up a plate, and I'll eat when I get back."

She was already on her way toward the front door.

"Anything I can do to help? Is anyone hurt?"

"It'll be fine. Just a little mom-daughter thing."

"Okay … Keep me posted."

Sam talked herself down as she got in the car and headed toward the road. Keep calm, just look for the facts. Fact: she still remembered the keypad code for the back door at the sheriff's office. Fact: the dinner hour was normally pretty quiet there. Fact: if she could just get a look at the medical investigator's report, it would ease her mind. Surely nothing in the potion could have harmed Lila, but she had to know.

Fifteen minutes later she was parking on the street outside the walled Sheriff's Department parking area. She pulled up the hood on her jacket and locked her SUV, actually walking on tiptoes toward the driveway entrance and repeating the keypad numbers in her head. She could only hope and pray Evan hadn't changed the code when he took office.

She was a scant five feet from the back door when headlights swept across her. Oh crap. Caught in the act.

"Sam?" said a familiar voice. She spun to face the cruiser that had parked right next to her.

"Rico! Hey, I didn't know you'd be here." *Obviously.*

"What're you doing at the back door? You could have come in the front. Or—is there a problem? Is Beau okay?" The young deputy had scrambled out of his car and was approaching her with concern on his face.

"Everything's fine. I just—" She cleared her throat. "I was just on my way home from the bakery … and I … um, well I saw today's news about the homicide at the Fernandez Inn. I'm kind of worried that it might be a girl I met a few days ago. You know anything about the case?"

"Well, yeah, the whole department's working on it, although we don't have a lot to go on yet."

"Was her name Lila?"

"Lila Contreras, yes, I'm afraid so. You do understand we aren't releasing that publicly yet, right?"

"Oh, definitely. Hey, I was once a deputy, remember? I can stay quiet about it." She shuffled her feet on the chilly pavement. "Have you established the cause of death yet?"

Please don't let it be cinnamon or ginger.

Rico shook his head, probably wondering why Sam cared about this. "No, nothing for certain. The OMI hasn't released the autopsy report yet."

There wasn't a whole lot more she could ask without raising too many questions about her interest in the case. *Oh, was she poisoned by a cupcake?* That would surely lead to a long evening in the interrogation room. Sam couldn't think of what else to say so she wished Rico a good evening and sent her best wishes to his family, and then she scurried out of there like a bug when the lights come on.

Chapter 15

Beau was deep into an action movie when she got home. Over the back of his recliner she kissed the top of his head and went to the kitchen to get a small plate of the leftover dinner. As long as he saw she wasn't visibly upset, he would assume all was well at Kelly's and not ask too many questions. Thank goodness he was completely into ranching now and not his old law enforcement mode.

The casserole didn't settle well. Sam pleaded tiredness and went upstairs to chomp down a couple of Tums. She called Kelly to report that she essentially knew nothing, other than having confirmed that the victim was Lila.

"Surely, by tomorrow we'll learn something more," she said, wishing her daughter a good night, knowing she'd have a devil of a time sleeping, herself.

No surprise, she was wide awake at four a.m.

She went down to the kitchen where she made a cup of hot chocolate because it seemed like better comfort food than coffee at that hour. Beau walked up behind her at the kitchen table a bit after five-thirty.

"I'm guessing you could use a hearty breakfast this morning," he said, massaging her shoulders.

"The tossing and turning was obvious, huh?"

"A little." He bent low and gave her a kiss. "I saw your calendar. The dogs have a bath appointment at Riki's place today. So, how about if we both take them in, then we'll go have a burrito at Taoseño?"

She couldn't very well turn that down. Their favorite breakfast and help to load the dogs in and out of the car—couldn't ask for a much better morning.

"And maybe by the time we've got some green chile in us you'll feel like telling me about whatever's bugging you."

And she thought she'd been so smooth about last night's drama. She smiled up at him. "Rest assured it's nothing to do with you and me. But yeah, it's a deal."

While he went out to start the morning chores, Sam showered and dressed. Ranger and Nellie gobbled their breakfast, but they hung close to Sam afterward. The minute she'd set their leashes next to her coat, they knew something was up.

It was a few minutes after eight when they pulled up at Puppy Chic, and the dogs quivered with excitement when they realized where they were. Riki was one of their favorite humans because she handed out treats very liberally. They dashed to the door with Sam and Beau on their heels.

"Good morning, my canine lovelies," Riki said, coming around the front of her desk to give each dog an affectionate ruffle of the ears. "Let's get you two settled."

Ranger, the Lab, loved his bath—anything involving water was on his top ten list. Nellie, on the other hand, bore it grudgingly, mainly because her long coat required a long time under the dryer and a great deal of brushing afterward.

"They should be ready around noon," Riki said to Sam and Beau. "Or shall I just give you a call?"

"If Kelly's coming in today, she can bring them home whenever she leaves."

A thumbs-up. "Perfect."

They turned to leave, visions of a breakfast burrito filling Sam's head. Until she saw a sheriff's department cruiser pull up next to her car. Evan climbed out, placed his Stetson on his head, and adjusted the heavy belt of gear at his waist. She and Beau halted on the sidewalk, the two men greeting each other with a warm handshake, and Beau asked Evan how everything was going.

"Well, it had been pretty quiet for a couple months— just the normal stuff tourists and skiers get themselves into over the winter. But now, we've got this murder."

Sam felt her insides tense up.

"I saw the blurb in the paper," Beau said. "It's the woman from San Antonio?"

"Yeah. We pretty much guessed the cause of death, but needed it confirmed by the MI's office. Never know when there might be underlying or hidden causes."

Beau nodded. *Isn't he going to ask?* It was all Sam could do not to bounce on her toes.

"Yep. Strangulation. It's official."

"Any suspects?"

"Possibly. I think the unrevealed evidence is going to be key here. It's a strange bit."

There was always a clue or two that was not given out to the press or the public, something the law enforcement agencies could use to know whether they were talking to the real killer versus someone who might confess just to get media attention. *Please don't let it be that her last meal was a chocolate cupcake...*

Beau tilted his head, his expression curious.

Evan stepped in somewhat closer. "The vic had words cut into her forehead. Sweet Dreams, it said."

Sam felt the blood drain from her face. The same phrase Lila always used in her texts to Danny. This was looking bad for their friend.

Beau was talking. "You're right, that is an odd one." He glanced toward Sam. "My wife is looking a little peaked, Evan, and I promised her breakfast out this morning. Guess we'd better get going."

Evan tipped his hat and said goodbye before walking into Puppy Chic.

"Want me to drive, darlin'? You're kind of pale."

Sam cleared her throat and stood up straighter. "No, I'll be fine." She took two long, slow breaths as she started the car. *What the hell!*

Her first instinct was a desire to call Danny and ask him straight out. What went on between him and Lila when he last saw her? She thought back to what he had said— Lila enjoyed the cupcake, she left, she hadn't contacted him again since. And now Sam knew why. But would the sheriff see it the same way? The fact was, Lila knew hardly anyone in town. And what were the odds any of her casual acquaintances knew about the goodnight phrase she used with her boyfriend—practically nil, Sam would guess.

She nearly missed the turn at the Taoseño driveway

and made a sudden move to correct. Beau gave her another sideways glance but didn't say anything.

Thirty minutes later Beau had polished off his burrito and Sam was still picking at hers.

"Okay, something's not right," he said, wiping his mouth and setting his napkin aside. "Unless you want me to haul you to the doctor, you need to tell me."

Sam put her fork down. "It's what Evan said back there. I'm worried Danny might be involved."

"Okay ... and why is that?"

She glanced around at the crowded restaurant. "Can we talk about it on the way home?"

"Sure. Don't you want to finish your breakfast first?"

She asked the waitress to box up the remains of her meal. Once she got this idea out of her head, maybe her appetite would return. Or not. She really needed answers.

Beau drove and Sam told him about the sweet dreams connection, how Danny had confided that the phrase was one Lila used with him all the time. "I know he planned to see her that evening." She didn't go into details about the cupcakes.

"You're right—it's looking scary for him. It won't take Evan any time at all to go through Lila's phone and find those texts."

"So, what would you advise?" Sam twisted in her seat to look directly at him. "I'm sorry, Beau. I know you don't want anything to do with law enforcement, now that the ranch is your life."

"True. And I'm not going to get involved."

"Do you mind if I talk to Danny about it? Maybe he'll have some ideas, somebody back home I could talk to that would lead to another suspect. I know you like Evan a lot, and you respect his law enforcement knowledge, but I have a feeling once he zeros in on Danny he won't be looking a whole lot further."

He looked at her and gave a crooked little grin. "Would it matter if I minded? You're going to do it anyway."

But he reached over and took her hand. A gentle squeeze told her he was okay with her idea. He had, after all, deputized her at one point precisely because he trusted her instincts on his cases.

He parked her car in its normal spot. "So, shall I invite Danny to come over for dinner? I won't tell him the one thing getting grilled is him."

Sam gave him a light punch on the shoulder. "No, thank you. I'll catch up with him before then." She didn't say it, but her big fear was that Evan would come rolling along at any time and take Danny away before she got the chance to talk to him. "I'll put my breakfast in the fridge and then come out to the barn. You can join me if you want."

He shook his head and handed Sam her keys. "Nope, not this time. He might feel like we're ganging up on him, and I don't want to scare away my best ranch hand."

While Beau sauntered toward the barn, Sam went into the house. Upstairs, she headed straight for her most trusted ally—the carved box. Long experience had taught her she could rely on the insights she gained from it. She picked up the box and stroked the lid with one hand. The wood began to lighten and glow, and the colored stones started to sparkle. When the box became almost too warm for comfort, she set it down and took a deep breath. Now or never.

She walked out the back door and looked toward the

barn for Danny. She spotted him walking into the casita and hurried to catch up.

"Hey, Sam. Beau told me you might be stopping by. Something I can do for you? I'm glad to help around the house, too, you know."

"Oh, no, nothing like that. Did he mention that we ran into Evan Richards this morning?" She carefully watched his aura. Clear white—open and trusting.

"Maybe we should go inside," she suggested. "I have some bad news."

A small furrow formed between his brows, but she didn't get any vibe that he was hiding anything.

"You haven't seen the newspaper, I guess?" She walked into the one-room space.

He shook his head. "I'm not much on following the news, other than how the weather is going to affect our work. Lila used to read me my horoscope every day but that never seemed very useful."

"Well, it's about Lila, Danny. There was a small news story yesterday about a Texas woman dying here in Taos. This morning Evan confirmed it's Lila."

"What!" His shock seemed genuine. His eyes darted around the room, not finding focus on any particular thing. His clear aura went fuzzy at the edges. "My god, what happened?"

"She was strangled in her hotel room." She picked up a pen that was lying on the kitchenette counter, mainly to give her hands something to do. "Danny, I'm afraid the sheriff may come around and want to talk to you. Lila didn't know many people here. You're likely to be a suspect."

He tossed his Stetson on the bed and sat down hard, raking his fingers through his hair. His face had lost a few shades of color and his aura was now pulsing. But it hadn't changed its essential color, Sam noticed.

"Could I ask you some questions, some things the authorities might want to know?" Yes, she realized she was preparing him, giving him time to come up with the 'right' answers rather than letting Evan take him by surprise. Was that ethical? She didn't know.

He nodded.

"How much do you know about Lila's background?"

"I think I've already mentioned that I knew her for just a few months," Danny said. "She told me her parents had split and she moved from Nuevo Laredo to San Antonio with her dad. Her mom stayed there. I got the impression there was another man involved. But I never met either of her parents."

"What about siblings? Other friends? Did you meet anyone else connected to Lila?" Sam asked.

"We mainly hung with my friends from high school. Some went on to college and they'd be around now and then. Chad Smith, Josh and Devon Miller—they're twins. And of course Sergio Sandoval, my best friend from, like, the first grade on. Jacob Brown, Michael Montoya, Matthew Naranjo."

"Any girls, besides Devon?" She found a blank sheet of paper and started jotting the names.

"Lila got pretty chummy with my sister, Patsy. She's in law school and just got her first apartment, but she's a couple years older and pretty busy. Most of the girls kind of came along with the guys. Emily was Michael's girlfriend, Abby's a real brain, studies a lot, didn't date much, but Taylor was popular. She and Matthew hit it off senior year."

"Sounds like a big group," Sam said. "Everyone close?"

"Pretty much. You know, the usual little rumbles, but we all got along."

"So, among the friends, who knew you came here, and who might have told Lila?"

"Well, Patsy and my mom knew, for sure. But I told them the reason I was getting away for a while, that Lila was freaking me out. I doubt either of them would have told her where I went. The guys ... yeah, Sergio knew, but he wouldn't tell her. He, um ... how to explain it ... he just kept his distance. I asked him once and he just said she wore too much perfume. He didn't want to come right out and say he didn't like her. You know, don't diss your best friend's girl, or something."

"How much did he dislike her?"

"Like, enough to hurt her? Oh, nothing like that. Serg would never hurt anyone. Seriously, the guy doesn't even set mousetraps."

Sam nodded. "When Lila contacted you here, did she say how she knew where you were?"

He shook his head. "Just the usual. She started up with the texts about how much she'd missed me, how we were meant to be together. Always stuck on a bunch of heart emojis or said how she loved me. She had this irritating way of sending one final text at night. I don't know—at first I thought it was sweet and thoughtful, but after a while it just felt creepy."

He rubbed his palms against his jeans on the thighs. "Anyway, when I didn't answer the texts she started calling. Saying things that got me questioning my own memories. I mean, I seriously began to ask myself whether I actually *had* proposed to her. She knew about *Abuela's* ring, described it perfectly, and I got scared that maybe I really had given it to her."

Another thought came to her. "Danny, you'd better prepare yourself to answer questions about all the text messages Lila sent and whatever your responses were. Once her personal possessions are collected as evidence, it won't take the sheriff long to go through those messages on her phone."

"Oh, shit!" Danny jumped up from the bed and paced to the far side of the small room.

"Danny?"

His eyes were wide. "I-I have her phone. I completely forgot."

"What …?" Sam felt a moment's confusion.

"When we met at Java Joe's for coffee and the cupcakes, it went pretty much the way I had hoped. I said the words you told me—'Lila, you don't love me.' And she just looked at me kind of funny, almost like she didn't know me anymore, and then she got up and left. Just like that."

"Right. But the phone …"

"I waited until she got in her car and drove off, and then I got up to leave. Her phone was on the floor. I guess she dropped it." He fidgeted with an apple from the fruit bowl on his table. "I was going to return it, honest. In fact, I could have followed and taken it to her hotel right then. But … honestly, it was so nice not hearing from her six times over the evening … I just put it off. I had no idea something had happened to her."

Sam believed him. The aura was clear and clean again. "Where is her phone now?"

He thought hard for a minute. "I guess it's still in my truck. I haven't driven anywhere—been busy around here."

"You really should turn it in to the sheriff, Danny."

He set the apple down and nodded. "I will."

"Do it sooner rather than later. As soon as they release her name—or even before that. Tell them what you just told me about her leaving it behind. Okay, you can probably leave out the cupcakes." Her smile lightened the mood.

"Thanks, Sam. I appreciate the advice."

"Beau and I are on your side. You can come to either of us." She left the casita, feeling better about Danny and his story, suddenly hungry for the burrito in the fridge.

Chapter 16

It was shortly after noon when Kelly drove up to the ranch house. With shining coats and big smiles, Ranger and Nellie bounded from the back of her car and raced to the door. Sam sat at the dining table with her sewing machine.

"I swear, I don't know how every one of Beau's flannel shirts manages to rip itself out there in the barn." She laid the shirt aside and turned to Kelly.

Both dogs sat back on their haunches, fixing her with eager stares.

"Don't believe them," Kelly said. "Riki and I both gave them treats when we complimented them on how pretty they look."

Sam stroked their heads and sent them away. "Can you make time for a cup of tea? I'm tired of mending and could use a break."

In answer, Kelly dropped her jacket on the couch and held up a small bag from Sweet's Sweets. "I was *so* hoping you'd suggest that. I brought butter spritz."

Sam put the kettle on and pulled two of their favorite mugs from the cupboard while she briefly told Kelly what she'd learned about Lila's death.

"Oh, good, it didn't have anything to do with our anti-love potion."

"Thankfully, no. I'm still worried about Danny though. Evan's going to make the connection eventually, and I'm sure he's in for some questions."

"But he didn't—"

"No. I'm sure he's innocent." *Unless my aura detection skills have tanked, I'm sure.*

"Do you think he'll go back to Texas or stay here?"

"He says he loves working on the ranch, so my guess is he'll stay."

"So, he's single again ..."

"Kel ... what are you thinking?"

Kelly opened the cookie bag and reached for one. "I'm thinking that Jen has a younger sister who would be so perfect for him."

"You've had this in mind for a while, haven't you?"

A tiny shrug. "Maybe a week or so. Since the birthday party, actually."

The kettle screeched and Sam shifted her attention to the teabags and hot water. Handing Kelly a cup she said, "Okay, little miss matchmaker. First off, let's make sure he's perhaps slightly interested in dating again. He got badly burned last time."

"Oh, right. And we'll need to be sure he doesn't actually

end up in trouble with the law. I can't see setting Crystal up, knowing she'd be visiting a felon on death row."

"Kelly! Don't even joke about it."

"Sorry. That was in really bad taste."

"He's not a felon, and he won't be in trouble with the law. He just needs the chance to talk to Evan and clear his name."

But what if the evidence was way too strong against him? Sam had no idea what the department had gathered at the crime scene. And how damning would those text messages on Lila's phone appear?

Chapter 17

Sam stood near the French doors at the back of the house the next morning, sipping her first cup of coffee. Beau had actually slept past sunrise and by the time they came downstairs, she could see Danny out at the barn with the feed bucket for the two horses. Their breath made white clouds in the morning air as he dumped feed into the trough for them, and he stood by as they began to eat, stroking each of their foreheads in turn. She smiled at his kindness toward the animals.

"I toasted you an English muffin," Beau said, walking up behind her.

"Did you get something?" She took the plate from his hand.

"Oatmeal. That should hold me for the morning. I'd better grab my coat and get outside." He ruffled her hair and gave her a kiss.

She set her plate and cup on the dining table, thinking about the day ahead and how, for once, she didn't have a half-dozen duties awaiting her attention.

"Huh." Beau's attention was drawn to the driveway out front. "One of my guys is here."

Sam turned and spotted the blue lightbar of a sheriff's department vehicle. She smiled at Beau's words. Despite his adamant claims that he'd completely given up law enforcement, he would always think of the deputies as 'his guys.'

But this time it was Sheriff Evan who stepped out of the cruiser and walked up the porch steps. Beau had the door open before the knock came.

"Hey, Sheriff."

"Hey, Sheriff." Beau smiled at Evan's acknowledgment of his old status. "Come on in."

Evan stomped his boots on the doormat and walked in, smiling at Sam across the room. He and Beau shook hands before he spoke. "Unfortunately, folks, this isn't a social call."

"What's happened?" Sam had crossed the room, prepared to take Evan's jacket and offer coffee.

"The new murder case—the victim, Lila Contreras, has direct ties to Danny Flores. I need to talk to him about her. Based on items we found in her hotel room—including a map and directions to your place and a phone number she'd jotted down, she was in touch with your ranch hand."

So, here it was, the interview. She'd done her best to warn Danny. The way Evan presented the news, Sam guessed Danny hadn't yet gone forward with Lila's phone. Now, he would have to simply tell the truth, and she could hope he didn't implicate himself.

"It's cold out there," she said. "Shall I invite him inside?"

"Not necessary," Evan said. "I'm dressed for it, so I'll just step out back and find him."

Beau was already putting on his own coat. "He should be in the barn."

Sam stayed behind. No need to overwhelm Danny now. She would simply have to grill Beau later about the interview. She closed the French door and watched anxiously through the glass.

Danny stepped out of the barn as the two men approached. When he saw Evan's uniform, he halted in his tracks and watched them.

It took all she had to turn away, but Sam couldn't be of help by staring out the windows. She went into the kitchen to clean up the breakfast dishes and check the coffee supply. If Evan lingered, coffee would be a way to keep him around long enough to ask questions.

As it turned out, she had no such luck. Less than ten minutes later, Beau was back in the house and Evan was driving away. She cornered her husband at the coat rack.

"So? What happened? What did Danny say?"

He kept his coat on and reached for his Stetson. "Not much. He gave Evan her cell phone, which he said she left behind at a coffee place where they'd met for dessert. Evan asked him about the relationship. Danny admitted knowing her, said they had a relationship for a short time before he came here. He said he'd been very surprised that she tracked him and came to Taos, but he agreed to meet her for coffee and talk things over. He says he told her, quote, 'Once and for all, Lila, it's over between us.' He says she took it well, and he told her she ought to just go home and pick up her life. Then he says she left."

Other than the direct quote, it went along with what Danny had told Sam. She pondered it all as Beau went back outside to begin his day's work.

Back in the kitchen, she hung the dish towel over the handle on the stove. All she could do at this point was trust that Evan would find all the facts and they would match with Danny's actions that evening. For now, she had other work to attend to. She picked up her coat, locked the front door, and went out to her SUV.

Since the big scare when she nearly lost Beau, Sam had sold her fine-chocolates business and curtailed her hours in the bakery. Becky was a skilled decorator now, and she handled nearly all the custom orders. During wedding season and busy holidays she called in a couple of extra helpers. Jen met with clients and helped design their cakes, as well as running the front sales counter with speed and efficiency. Julio, the Harley-riding baker, remained a man of few words but the man could turn out every one of Sam's recipes as well as she could do them herself.

Her routine, nowadays, was to check in with the crew a couple of times a week, take care of a select few of her old-time clients who insisted she be the one to make their cakes and pastries, and afterward pick up a new book for Ana at the bookshop next to the bakery. It had been going this way nearly four years, and Sam was only now beginning to feel a hint of discontent. She needed to stay busy.

A chill March wind channeled down the alley behind Sweet's Sweets, gripping Sam's ankles as she got out of the car. She picked up her pack and whisked up the two steps as quickly as possible. The warm kitchen smelled of cinnamon and chocolate, comfort scents that counteracted the harsh breeze outside.

"What have we got?" she asked, automatically, as she crossed the kitchen area and hung her jacket on a peg near her desk.

"The Salazar wedding is your big job of the week," Becky said, not raising her eyes from the intricate white lace she was piping onto a background of yellow. "I've got this bridal shower under control. The party is tomorrow but they want to pick up the cake this afternoon."

She attached the end of the delicate icing strand in place, then straightened her shoulders and glanced at the stack of orders on the corner of the heavy stainless worktable.

"Two kid birthdays and one for a great-grandmother tomorrow. That should be easy enough." She picked up an order sheet from the stack and handed it to Sam.

Sam looked at the Salazar order's specifications. Five tiers, basic ivory fondant coating, spring flowers in ivory, peach, and yellow. She could pre-make the daffodils and lilies so they had plenty of time to set up. The wedding was in three days—Julio would bake the cake layers tomorrow, and Sam could assemble and decorate it the next day. A reasonable schedule. She could remember a whole bunch of times she'd had to work on three or four cakes of this magnitude, with a lot less time to finish them.

Yeah, and I turned to the magic box a lot of those times, too.

She tamped down that thought and went to wash her hands.

Two hours later, Sam set the last of the flowers aside, checked on the sales room, said goodbye to the crew, and headed home with a sense of satisfaction.

Her peace was shattered when she pulled up to the

ranch house to discover a cruiser out front with lights flashing. *What the hell?* She practically leaped out of her SUV before it had rolled to a stop.

The front door opened and out came Deputy Rico, escorting Danny Flores by the arm.

Chapter 18

Rico! What on earth?" she called out. "Did you actually drive up here with lights and siren?"

Rico put Danny in the back seat before he turned to her.

"Hey, Sam," he said with a smile.

"Don't 'hey Sam' me. What's going on?"

"I was sent out to pick up a suspect." He glanced at the car and looked somewhat embarrassed. "Okay, I could have left off the lights."

Beau stepped out to the porch just then, pulling his coat over his arms. "There's been another development, sweetheart."

"Beau, we should go along. He doesn't have anyone else."

There was a short discussion when they got to the

sheriff's department, but out of respect Evan allowed Beau and Sam to watch from the observation room as he began to interrogate Danny. Beau admitted the tone was far more serious this time.

"Am I under arrest?" Danny asked before Evan had hardly settled into the chair opposite him.

"At this point we're just asking questions, clarifying a few things." Evan leaned back in his chair. "Some things you told me last time didn't quite match up with the evidence."

Danny squirmed a little.

"For instance, you said you met Lila Contreras for coffee at Java Joe's, but we've learned that you also met her in the hotel bar for a drink and you two talked. This was the night before she was murdered."

"Right. Well, she had a drink. I didn't want anything."

"Yes, the server remembered that." Evan had his pocket notebook out and flipped back a page or two. "She also remembered the two of you leaving together, walking toward the elevators."

"Yeah, uh, I told Lila it was over between us and then I left."

"Danny, your fingerprints were in her room. How do you explain that?"

Sam felt herself swallowing hard, mirroring Danny's reaction to the statement. He had not told her about any of this. Evan never took his eyes off Danny's face.

"Well? Obviously, you went up to her room. Once you two were alone, I'm guessing the conversation went a different direction."

"I never laid a hand on her!"

"So, then tell me about it." Evan's tone was skeptical

and Danny fidgeted some more.

"Down in the bar, I was getting up to leave. I'd said all I had to say. And at first Lila seemed to accept what I told her. But as I was standing up she said, 'Oh, by the way. I have your grandmother's ring, the one you gave me.' And I was all shocked, because I never gave her a ring. But she described it exactly, a ring that's been in my family a long time. And then she tells me if I want it back, I'll have to come up to her room to get it."

Another thing Danny hadn't told her. Sam looked at Beau. "Had he ever mentioned this?"

He shook his head.

"So you did go up to her room?" Evan asked.

"I wasn't even going to go inside. In the elevator, I told her to just go in the room and get the ring. I wanted to see it for myself 'cause I didn't believe she had it."

"So you got to the room and what happened?"

Danny took a deep breath. "She handed me her keycard and had me unlock the door, and then she reaches over and takes my hand and pulls me inside. It was the same old Lila all over again, rubbing up against me, telling me how much she loves me, begging me to change my mind."

"And you did what?"

Danny rubbed his temples. "I couldn't listen to her. She always got to me. So I just pushed her hands off my shoulders and asked where the ring was. I went over to her suitcase and pulled some clothes out, looking for it. She laughed. In the bathroom, her makeup and stuff was all over the counter, but no ring. I said I'd never given it to her and she laughed even more."

"Getting tricked by a woman. That must have made you furious."

Danny could see where this was going. "I was pissed, yeah. But all I did was walk out. I took the stairs and went out the side door to my truck and got the hell out of there. That's it, that's all the contact we had."

Sam waited for the other shoe to drop, for Evan to say there was more evidence that Danny had stayed longer, maybe he and Lila had ended up in bed. But Evan merely stuck his notebook back in his pocket.

"Okay, then. We're still processing evidence, going through her phone data, and we'll probably have more questions before we're done. Don't leave town." He held the door open and let Danny walk out.

Sam and Beau joined him in the lobby a couple of minutes later and offered a ride home.

"You heard all that?" Danny asked, once they had settled in Beau's truck.

Sam nodded. "It doesn't sound like they have much against you."

"I took the sheriff aside for a minute after he spoke with you. He says the places they found your fingerprints in the room were consistent with what you told him just now. That's good."

Danny relaxed a bit into his seat. "After I left the hotel that night, I went back to the ranch and called my mother in San Antonio. She looked around and found my *abuela's* ring with some other stuff I had packed and stored at her place when I came here. I knew I hadn't given it away. Lila was just baiting me."

"Sounds like she did that a lot," Sam said quietly. The rest of the ride went by in silence.

When they reached the ranch, Beau sent Danny out to make sure there was no ice on the horses' water trough.

"There's more, isn't there?" Sam asked.

"There was a message to Danny on Lila's phone, setting up the meeting at the hotel that Evan was asking him about."

"Only one? I—" *I am not going to admit to Beau that I peeked at the phone message thread and there were dozens.* Instead, she said, "He went so far as to change his number, and he didn't tell her about his move to Taos, and she still tracked him down."

"A *Fatal Attraction* kind of thing?"

"Maybe. But there's a weirder element. Danny told me she insisted they were supposed to be together because God told her so. Or sometimes it was an angel. She fully believed some universal force brought them together and she wasn't going to let him go."

"Wow."

"Yeah, creepy."

Beau opened the refrigerator door and stared inside.

Sam stepped over and edged him aside. "You're getting hungry because I'll bet you skipped lunch. Let's warm up the chile from the other night, and you can invite Danny again, if you want to. There's plenty." She pulled out the storage container and found a large saucepan.

"So, did you get the impression from Evan that Danny's no longer a suspect?" she asked.

He shook his head. "The opposite. Lila's continual harassment—almost stalking—the lies, the fact of her tracking him down multiple times … If anything, they think that gives Danny a stronger motive than anyone else. Not to mention, Lila seemingly knew no one else here in Taos. Danny's high on their radar, Sam."

It didn't look good. Someone had erased Lila's messages

to Danny—except that he or she had missed one, a very critical one. Sam nibbled at her lip, not wanting to think Danny had done that himself, but he was the one with access to the phone. She still wanted to believe her gut on this, but if Danny didn't kill his girlfriend, who did?

Chapter 19

The next afternoon Kelly stood at her kitchen island, poring over the rune book. She'd handled the wooden box earlier, up in the attic, and was now searching for a cure. Why hadn't someone, over the years, thought to index this thing? Finding any particular topic was like a computer search without the aid of Google. And this time Eliza was no help. She'd taken a casual look at the book, lifted her tail haughtily, and left the room.

Movement outside the back door caught Kelly's attention, just before Sam let herself in.

"Hey there, what's up, Mom?"

Sam hung up her coat and pack.

"Something's wrong," Kelly said, setting the book aside.

"Evan and Rico have questioned Danny twice now.

They've got some pretty incriminating evidence, things Danny never mentioned to me."

"Mom." Kelly fixed a stare at her. "A person has a right to some secrets. You didn't actually think he was pouring out his whole heart to you?"

A sigh. "No, not really. Okay, no, not at all. It's just that he asked advice on what to do, so I thought he would at least give me the facts."

"So he lied?"

"More like omitted. Huge, big omissions."

Again, the fixed stare.

"All right. I get it. I'm dropping it." Sam noticed the open book on the countertop. "So, whatcha up to?"

Kelly rolled her eyes. "Hoping to find some quickie cure. Scott has this nasty boil on his—" She cleared her throat. "Never mind. Right to have secrets. Anyway, I was just wishing the book had some sort of order—chapters, sections, an index. I've been through spells for conjuring up rain, a blessing for bountiful crops, and how to control an unruly child—any of which could come in handy at some point, but they aren't what I need today."

"Want me to take a look?"

"Sure. Go for it."

Sam went to her backpack and pulled out the box she'd begun carrying with her whenever she visited Kelly. She gave it a reassuring pat when it began to warm up, then stuck it back in the bag.

"Okay, let's see how this goes." She closed the book, held it between her palms with the spine resting on the counter, then let it fall open to a random page. "Hmm … we might be in the right section. Here's how to remove carbuncles. I have no idea what those actually are, but it might be close."

Kelly leaned in to read. "Could be. What's the cure, and is it anything feasible to make at home? Otherwise, I'll just try to get him a doctor's appointment."

Heavy footsteps pounded through the dining room and the kitchen door swung open. Ana burst in. "Grammy! Eliza told me you were here."

Sure enough, the cat trotted along behind Ana. Sam turned her attention and swept her granddaughter up in a hug.

Ana's eyes went to the open book on the table. "Whatcha reading? I finished my whole spelling list today and Daddy has a new book for me to read tonight. I know lots of words now."

She pointed to the page. "… in … a … bowl." She looked up at Sam expectantly.

"You can read those words?"

Ana nodded vigorously. Sam and Kelly exchanged a look. Neither of them could read the symbols in the book unless they handled one of the wooden boxes first. And each box worked only for its particular owner—Virtu for Sam, Manichee for Kelly.

"Baby, did you go into my attic room today?" Kelly asked.

Ana shook her head. "Huh-uh. The door is closed."

"Okay, good. That's the rule. When the door's closed no one can go in but Mommy."

"Right. Got it."

Sam laughed at the toddler's grown-up attitude. "Let's find you a snack since you've worked so hard on your lessons."

She set Ana on her feet and they walked to the fridge where Ana reached for the plastic container of approved snacks. She chose two apple slices.

Scott's voice came from the other room. "Anastasia Porter ... paging Miss Anastasia Porter ... we have one more story to read before dinnertime."

He came into the kitchen and spotted her. "Aha!" he teased. "I thought this might be where you vanished to."

He greeted Sam with a hug and noticed the book on the table. "Still trying to figure out the code, huh?"

He'd recommended a linguist professor from the university when the book first came into Kelly's hands, thinking the expert might recognize the language filling the pages. But no luck. The man had told them it appeared to be a coded combination of rune-like symbols, some Cyrillic lettering, and a couple of ancient, obsolete languages. One would need a code key in order to decipher it, he'd said. Kelly and Sam had agreed that it was best not to acknowledge the somewhat supernatural effects they experienced from the wooden boxes.

"I can read it, Daddy," Ana piped up. "It said to mix some stuff in a bowl."

"Ah, like a recipe," he said, his eyebrows arched upward. "Very good. Miss Maddie just might borrow your special skill in our next story."

Maddie Plimpton was the ten-year-old fictional character in Scott's bestselling series of children's mystery novels. After moderate success with a biography of the Victorian house's previous owner, the writer Eliza Nalespar, Scott had taken inspiration from being a stay-at-home dad to Ana and had come up with the concept for the novels. He jokingly said his degree in history and his tenure as a university professor had been excellent training for the career that brought his real success.

"And speaking of Maddie, I need to knock out another

chapter in the new one after dinner tonight," he told Kelly.

"I get the hint," Sam said with a laugh. "I'll leave you all to your evening. I've got to get home anyway."

"Take your time," he said, picking up Ana. "We're going to finish a reading lesson and then it's time for some relaxation with a video game."

Kelly stuck a folded paper napkin in the book and closed it, marking the page Sam had found. "I'm sorry, Mom. I know you came over wanting to talk about Danny's situation."

"It just happened to come up. I came to see all of you and I've done that. Unless you want some help with dinner, I'll get out of the way." She headed toward the coat hooks near the back door.

"Mom—I really do hope everything turns out okay for Danny. He's a nice guy and he can't possibly be guilty of what they're saying."

"I think you're right. I'm just worried that they'll keep finding these little secrets, and if they do arrest him, they'll quit looking for anyone else. If we're going to help him, we have to figure out who is the real killer."

She gave Kelly a hug and walked out to her car, but the question continued to nag as she drove home. And as she prepared chicken enchiladas for dinner, and as she pretended to be interested in the TV show Beau had chosen. It was shaping up to be another sleepless night.

Chapter 20

The first dream featured an amethyst and opal ring, which Sam was struggling to wrestle away from a dark-haired young woman who kept insisting she loved him—although she never named the man—and wouldn't give up the ring. Sam saw herself on the verge of knocking the girl's legs out from under her and sitting on her, when she woke up.

Whew—ridiculous!

She rolled to her side, trying to shake the images. After a minute, she got up and went into the bathroom. Splashing cold water on her face, she willed the stupid dream to leave, and once she'd begun to think of something else, she went back to bed.

The second dream took a bizarre twist. Sam was holding the carved box and watching the auras of everyone in a small auditorium where she was sitting in the back row, apparently waiting for some kind of concert to begin. A couple walked in and took seats three rows ahead of her. The young man's aura was a clear iridescent white while the dark-haired woman exuded vibes of muddy dark red, an evil color. When Sam got up from her seat to warn the man, everyone else in the room exhibited the same dark red auras, ganging up in a way on the one pure person. Sam looked down at her own arm and saw a halo of yellow, turning to orange, and going toward red.

She woke in a sweat, heart pounding and hands trembling.

Enough!

Obviously, staying in bed wasn't going to help matters. The clock on her phone said it was 3:32 a.m. She slipped her warm robe over her shoulders and carried her Uggs slippers and phone downstairs.

While she heated water for tea, she pondered the meanings of the two dreams. Clearly, it was herself against Lila in both cases. She was trying to save Danny in one case, and to save his grandmother's heirloom ring in the other. Subconsciously, she still believed in his innocence, even though in reality the sheriff had caught Danny in lies and the evidence was not in his favor.

Could I be so wrong about him?

He might have started out as an innocent, but maybe he snapped. It could happen.

She brewed the tea dark and carried her mug to the living room. Retrieving the carved box from her backpack, she settled into her favorite corner of the sofa. With the box on her lap and the hot tea warming her insides, she closed her eyes and hoped the answers would come to her. Although her mind settled from the jumble of the dreams, after an hour or so of quiet contemplation she couldn't exactly say she'd discovered any brilliant insights into the situation.

When she couldn't sit still any longer, she set the box aside and carried her mug toward the kitchen. It was still dark outside, and through the French doors she could see the gleam of moonlight across the pasture. From the darkened house, she watched for a few minutes. A deer picked its way across the stubble field that would soon be planted in alfalfa.

A light moved across the yard, following the pathway toward the barn. Danny was beginning his morning chores early, she realized, and she watched his figure as he entered the paddock. He must have had a sleepless night too, and no wonder. But the aura surrounding him was still clear. Unless she wanted to believe she'd lost her touch with the magic box, Sam had to trust in what she was seeing. Danny was innocent.

And she might be the one person willing to go to bat for him.

He entered the barn and she shook off her reverie. Might as well get to work—that wedding cake wasn't going to finish itself. She quietly moved upstairs where she showered and dressed in her bakery clothing—black slacks and white shirt, with her baker's jacket over it.

She left Beau a note to say she hadn't fed the dogs yet, then donned her heavy outer coat, picked up the box and stuffed it into her pack, and walked out to her car. Traffic was nearly nonexistent this time of morning, and she let herself savor the empty roads and the gray dawn.

Julio was alone at the bakery, and already the smell of cinnamon was heavy in the air. They exchanged a brief greeting and both went about their own work. By seven o'clock, when Jen arrived to open the shop, Sam already had a start on the fondant-coated tiers. She registered the normal sounds of life in the neighborhood—a garbage truck in the alley, two customers chatting with Jen, Riki's car with its squeaky brakes arriving next door.

Sam finalized a lacy border of piping and realized her shoulders were aching. Setting down her pastry bag, she stretched her arms and decided to take a short break. The scent of coffee from the front room pulled her in that direction.

"Morning, Sam," Jen said. "I peeked in on you when I got here, but wow, you were totally focused on that cake."

"Sorry. Yeah, I get that way."

"It's coming along beautifully. The customer will love it."

Sam filled her mug, automatically checking the levels in the carafes and the supplies of sugar and cream. Movement out in the parking lot caught her attention. Evan's cruiser stopped in front of Puppy Chic again. He stepped out, holding a Styrofoam food container. Ah yes, Riki was addicted to the Taoseño's breakfast burritos too. Sam watched while he carried it in, and then timed her move out the front door as he emerged from his wife's business.

"Evan, hey! Got a minute?"

He glanced at his watch. "A minute is about right. Sure, Sam. What's on your mind?"

As if he didn't know.

"Just hoping you've found some other suspects in the Contreras murder—other than Danny Flores. Evan, I just *know* he's innocent."

"Can you give him an alibi for the night she died?"

"Well, not directly."

"Okay. Well, all we can do is follow the evidence."

It was exactly what Beau would have said, and she couldn't very well argue.

"Sam, we've put a technical forensics expert on gathering the evidence from the victim's phone. I'm afraid it doesn't look good for your guy."

"I thought you said …"

"The expert found a whole bunch of texts that had been deleted. Basically everything that transpired between Flores and Contreras for the last couple of months. Yes, initially we found only one message. But people don't understand—everything that goes out electronically leaves a trail and can be found. Once it's on the internet or in an email … it's out there, and it's fair game."

"But—"

"Danny Flores had possession of that phone from the last time he admits seeing her, at Java Joe's, until he turned it over to us. So who do you suppose erased those messages?"

Sam took a different angle. "So, if you've read the communications, you must know that Lila was harassing Danny, stalking him, that she'd posted all kinds of trash about him on social media, and she'd followed him here."

"Yes … we do. We even found the part about how the angels told her she and Danny were meant to be together." He held up a hand to shush Sam. "Yes, she was nutty, and yes, probably a complete pain. Still, there are legal ways to deal with people like her. Crazy or not, murder is murder."

Sam realized that everything he'd just said would look like a pretty strong motive for Danny to have gotten rid of his crazy ex.

"I meant what I told Danny yesterday, Sam. He can't leave town. Don't you try to warn him or help him escape. We're getting our evidence lined up. I don't want you in trouble for obstructing justice."

Not to mention, Beau wouldn't like it at all and would make her feel guilty forever if she tried to circumvent the law. She started to make one more plea with Evan to at least consider other suspects, but he'd already opened his car door and was halfway inside. With a friendly wave, he backed out and drove away.

The mug in her hand had gone cold, not to mention her tootsies were frigid. She went back into the bakery, feeling edgy.

Kelly was in the kitchen, chatting with Becky, when Sam walked in.

"When did you get here? How did I miss seeing your car?"

Kelly shrugged largely. "No idea. I pulled up in back of Puppy Chic and thought I'd pop in and say hi to all of you before I start my morning there. Riki's got a full house today so I offered to do the dog baths."

She admired the partly finished wedding cake. "Mom, what's going on with Evan? Riki sounded grumpy when she called me this morning, and I got the feeling Evan's said something about you siding with Danny against him."

Sam sighed. "I'm not going there. There are no sides—I just made the point with Evan that I hoped he would carefully weigh all the evidence and not jump to the quickest conclusion." She took Kelly's hand and gave a squeeze. "I don't want anything affecting your friendship with Riki. I will not say another word to Evan, or anyone else."

She made a zipping motion across her closed lips and Kelly laughed.

"Okay. I won't either."

Sam gave Kelly two cupcakes and sent her on her way. How she would keep her mouth shut, she had no idea.

Chapter 21

As always, the creative hours passed happily, and Sam was setting the last daffodil on top of the wedding cake when her phone rang down inside her pocket. She wiped her sticky fingers on a damp towel and pulled the phone out to take a look. It was a local number she didn't recognize, but she took the call anyway.

"Mrs. Sweet?" said a shaky female voice. "This is Pauline Lopez. I'm Faustina's daughter. My mother asked me to call. She's so upset."

Sam could hear Faustina's voice in the background.

Kelly walked in the back door in time to hear Sam ask what was the matter.

"It's about Danny. We need some advice. Can you come to our house this afternoon? Do you remember where it is?"

Just a couple of blocks off the plaza. Sam confirmed

that they were still in the same house she remembered and said she would be able to get there within the hour.

"What's that all about?" Kelly asked.

Evan had told Sam to butt out of the Flores business, but surely she could visit an old friend. "Faustina's really upset. I'm going—"

"I'm finished with dog baths for the day. I'll come with you."

Sam had a bad feeling about the call. "Thanks, Kel."

"Mom … what are we getting into?"

"I'm going with the answer that Faustina placed a bakery order and called to ask me to deliver it."

"Okay … Right." But Kelly was all in, and on her way to the door.

They took Sam's car and pulled up in front of the Lopez house just a few minutes later. The small frame house had a small garden in front, and although mostly winter-brown now, Sam remembered Faustina as being quite a gardener. The yard in summer would be filled with tall hollyhocks and beds of roses, dahlias, marigolds, and delphinium. These were people with almost nothing, who made the most of what they did have.

She and Kelly walked up the cracked concrete sidewalk and knocked at the door. It opened almost immediately.

"Samantha! Come in," said Faustina. The older woman was a bit more stooped than Sam remembered, and her eyes were red and full of pain.

Pauline stepped forward from the kitchen, wiping her hands on a towel. Sam had less-clear memories of Faustina's daughter, and neither of them had met Kelly in her adult years, so there was a flurry of introductions. Sam held out the small box of cookies she'd brought for the ladies.

Faustina drew herself up straight and reverted to her inborn social self. "Come in, come in. Pauline can make coffee to go with the cookies."

"Don't go to the trouble," Sam said as they took seats in the very '80s living room, which was stifling hot. "And the cookies are yours for later. You sounded upset on the phone. Tell me what's happened."

Faustina's social veneer dropped away and her mouth quivered. "It's my Danny. He's been arrested! That doesn't happen in our family. Ever."

Well, Evan certainly hadn't wasted any time gathering more evidence, had he?

Pauline sat at the edge of her chair, wringing her hands. "Danielito didn't tell Mama what it was about, only that he needs a lawyer."

"I think I know what it's about," Sam said. "Let's deal with the important thing first. Yes, he should have a lawyer—did you call someone?"

"No," Faustina said, nearly wailing the word. "Our family doesn't have anyone like that to call."

True, Sam thought. Most law-abiding, ordinary folks didn't just keep an attorney on retainer, and she would guess Faustina had never consulted one in her life.

"Let me make a call or two," Sam suggested. "Maybe I can get a recommendation."

Kelly tried to distract the women with chit-chat but they both stared after Sam anxiously. She pulled out her phone and stepped into the kitchen to keep her questions from upsetting the women. Her first call went to Beau.

"What happened with Danny?" she asked without preamble.

"He's been charged with Lila's death. Evan came out this morning."

While Sam was happily decorating a wedding cake. "Is there anything you can do? We *know* he's innocent."

"Sam, I have no pull anymore. We just have to let due process take its course."

"But—"

"Let's see what happens before we try to jump in." His voice was calm, although she picked up an underlying irritation.

She grudgingly told him what he wanted to hear, ended the call, and immediately dialed the attorney who had handled her will a few years ago. At least maybe she could get a recommendation for a criminal defense lawyer.

She came back with a name, Delia Sanchez, and a phone number.

"It's best if you make the call yourself. Explain what's happened and be sure to tell Ms. Sanchez that cost is a factor. My attorney said she'll put in a recommendation for you, and she says Delia is very nice." She handed over the slip of paper.

Sam hoped the attorney would take the case on a pro bono basis, but there was no way she could get Faustina's hopes up at this point.

"Did Danny say anything else when he called?" Sam pictured him arriving at the sheriff's office in handcuffs, being questioned for several hours, finally being allowed one phone call. He could have called his parents in Texas, but maybe they seemed too far away and he was hoping his grandmother had local connections.

Which she did—Sam.

Pauline seemed more flustered than her elderly mother. She kept repeating that it was going to be hard to break the news to Hector and Sally. Faustina got up and went to a hutch in the L-shaped dining area. From a drawer she pulled out a small address book and a steno pad. She sat down and began copying information.

"I would like for you to talk to Sally, Danny's mother. And his father, Hector. And his sister, Patsy. Please find out what you can about this girl who came here."

"Lila."

"Yes. She came here to the house, trying to find my grandson. I did not like the looks of that girl. She had a false smile. You know what I mean?"

"Buttering you up so you would share information about Danny?"

"Yes. I am sad to say, though I think she fooled Patsy." She handed Sam the sheet she ripped from the steno pad. On it in small, neat script she had written names, phone numbers, and addresses. "Can you go there? Talk to them?"

Go there?

"Let me see what I can learn on the phone first. Maybe we can get something that would be helpful to his case."

Pauline wrung her hands; Faustina shook her head sadly. "It will be best if you can go."

Sam folded the page with the names and carefully avoided promising anything. "Talk with the lawyer first, then you'll need to inform Danny's parents about what's happened. I will also call them and ask a few questions. After that, we'll see where it leads."

She and Kelly escaped the overly warm house a few minutes later.

"Wow, Mom, you sure know how to get dragged into the midst," Kelly said before they'd reached the SUV. "What are you going to do now?"

"Just what I promised. Hopefully, the attorney will take

the reins and reassure everyone and find a miracle and get
the case thrown out before it even starts. Otherwise, I'm
open to suggestions. Got any magic fixes for something
like this?"

Chapter 22

Sam spotted Kelly at the living room window when she pulled up to the Victorian the following morning. By the time she parked under the portico and walked into the kitchen, her daughter was there, staring at a pile of bowls and utensils on the kitchen island.

"I was hoping you'd drop by. I can't find the recipe for ganache icing and I'm betting you know it by heart."

Sam laughed as she shed her coat. "I do." She surveyed the countertop. "First off, is your cake completely cooled? If not, the ganache will soak right in."

"Got it." Kelly pointed to a single layer cake sitting near the sink.

"Do you have heavy cream and some bittersweet chocolate?"

"Got 'em. What else?"

"That's it. It's also probably why I never wrote down the recipe for you. Use equal amounts of each."

Kelly was still looking a little helpless, so Sam found a saucepan and poured the cream into it, directing Kelly to chop up the chocolate and put it in a bowl. When the cream had barely reached a simmer, she poured the hot cream over the chocolate.

"Okay, we let it sit a minute or so until the chocolate softens up, then give it a stir. And you're—" Her phone startled her. "—you're done."

She reached for the phone in her pocket.

"Samantha Sweet? This is Delia Sanchez."

Since yesterday afternoon Sam had wondered if she would hear from the attorney.

"I spoke with Danny Flores briefly and he asked me to contact you."

"Yes—and it's Sam. Please. Is he all right? Have you been able to help him?"

"He's been taken to the county detention center and is facing arraignment later today."

"So, he wasn't able to convince Sheriff Richards they have the wrong person?"

"I've advised my client not to talk. Until I have a chance to review everything, I don't want him saying anything that will hurt more than help his case. That goes for his friends, too, Ms. Sweet. I'm not implying anything, but it would be best if you don't volunteer information to the sheriff either. Of course, you would have to answer any direct questions, and answer them truthfully, but …"

"I understand. But I feel certain Danny is innocent, and I'm worried that the sheriff won't go looking any further for the real killer now that he's got Danny in custody."

Delia Sanchez's voice softened. "I agree with all of that. It's part of the reason I've called you. Aside from Danny's trust and friendship with you, I've heard that you have a reputation for helping in these types of situations. Our firm is small and we don't have a private investigator as part of our staff. So … I'd like to ask your assistance."

"Whatever I can do." Sam noticed the bowl of chocolate Kelly was stirring, and gave the nod that it was ready to pour over the cake.

"Could we start with a search of his living quarters? I understand he lives on your property. As his landlord you would have the right to inspect his rooms without our having to get a warrant. I'm afraid I don't have any specific thing to tell you to look for, but you've done this before. Anything that might relate to the case, connections between my client and the victim. Keep in mind, you cannot hide evidence from the law enforcement officers. But if I were to learn of it first … get copies of any written evidence …"

"Absolutely."

Delia sighed. "I suspect Sheriff Richards has already obtained a warrant and may be along to search the premises right away. Don't get in his way. We can't have obstruction of justice charges clouding the works. But let me know if you find anything else."

"I will. What about questioning friends of Danny's who also knew Lila? He gave me names of some mutual friends back in Texas."

"That was going to be my next question for you. Sam, can you go to San Antonio and search them out? Soon?"

"Give me a day or two to make plans?"

"Of course. Keep me posted, and naturally I'll—" she

halted. "Can I put you on hold a moment? This may be relevant."

Sam turned to Kelly. "Did you get the gist?"

"Bits and pieces."

Sam started to mention the trip but Delia was on the line again right away.

"That was the medical investigator in Albuquerque. They've released the body to Sheriff Richards, and it seems Lila Contreras's parents will be coming to Taos. I don't know …"

"You wonder if I might talk with them, since they aren't very likely to be friendly toward Danny's defense attorney."

"That thought crossed my mind."

"They may not be exactly cordial toward his employer either, but I'll see what I can do," Sam promised as they ended the call.

Kelly had finished pouring the ganache over her cake and was stacking the saucepan and bowl in the sink.

"So … sounds like you've got a few jobs all of a sudden," she said, turning toward Sam.

"Sounds like."

"Are you sure you want to become this involved, Mom? Talking to the parents doesn't sound like much fun."

"Danny's family are old friends, Kel. I can't ignore how upset Faustina and Pauline were yesterday. I feel like I have to do this." She stared at her phone screen for a minute, then looked back up at Kelly. "Plus, it looks like there's a trip to San Antonio in the deal. Want to come along?"

"Seriously? It's been four years since I went anywhere without a husband and/or baby tagging along. I would *love* to go!"

Chapter 23

Sam thought about the lawyer's phone call all the way home. Kelly was right—talking to the dead girl's parents wouldn't be easy, especially since Sam had heard only Danny's side of it and was inclined to think Lila had been a nutcase. But maybe that was precisely why she *should* see them. They no doubt had a whole different perspective on the relationship.

And then there was the task of searching through the casita to see if she could find evidence that would help exonerate their ranch hand. How would she even know what that might be?

Finally, the prospect of traveling to an unfamiliar city to track down a bunch of kids thirty years her junior and quiz them about their friends ... she was beginning to feel queasy.

Well, I guess the thing is to tackle it the same way a person eats an elephant—one bite at a time.

The sight of Danny's truck parked beside the casita startled her momentarily. Of course—he would have been driven to his booking, courtesy of a department cruiser. The vehicle had a sticker pasted to the driver's side window, notification that it had been searched by law enforcement. The front door of the casita boasted a similar one—it was not a crime scene and this was not exactly a Do Not Enter notice, but Sam got the message. The law had gotten here before her.

She tried the doorknob and it opened.

Inside, the whole room had been tossed. Bedding lay on the floor, the mattress had been upended and dropped crookedly in place, all the cabinet doors in the tiny kitchenette stood open, and the small closet niche held a tumble of clothing and boots. Sam fumed—these were the local guys, the men who had worked for Beau for years. Okay, she understood their need to find and gather evidence, and housekeeping most definitely was not their strong suit, but why not show respect for the property.

She hung her jacket on the back of a chair and set to work, with little idea of what she was looking for.

Clues about Danny and Lila's relationship—from what bits she already knew, those were likely the text messages on his phone. If Lila had left anything in writing, Evan's men had probably found it. And from what Kelly had told her about the psychology of gaslighting, the tormentor's techniques were most often verbal. Tone of voice and body language were used to intimidate, giving the victim little or nothing in the way of actual evidence. Being able to laugh off their victim's allegations was what gave the abuser such power. Still—there had to be something, and

Sam was determined to find it.

She started with the kitchen area. The small fridge held a Styrofoam container with leftover restaurant enchiladas, a near-empty carton of milk, a full ketchup bottle, a packet of sliced ham lunchmeat, and a tiny jar of mayo. The freezer section had a small ice cube tray and a frozen Hungry Man dinner. No foil-wrapped packages (although the deputies would have surely taken those if there had been). The freezer could stand to be defrosted, she noted, but she would do that later.

The cupboards had been disturbed, and she began restacking mugs and straightening the foodstuffs—a box of cereal (Frosted Flakes), a jar of instant coffee, a box of white sugar, the kind with the little metal pour spout, a package of energy bars, and one of Chips Ahoy cookies with two left. Either Danny was due for a grocery trip or he was a man of very simple tastes. No wonder he stayed so slim.

As she set aside the stack of four dinner plates, she felt something odd. Between the one on the bottom and the next, was a small envelope. She pulled it out. A letter from his mother. Hmm. Very possibly of no interest to the deputies, but this was still an odd place to stash it. Sam got the feeling she may have found something they'd missed.

The single sheet was covered in neat script written in blue ink on feminine stationery with a rose printed in the upper left corner. She could imagine Sally Flores owning a whole tablet of these, probably since 1970. Sam read through a standard greeting and a lot of 'hope you're doing well and enjoy working for Mr. Cardwell' type of stuff. The one reference to Danny's new relationship came near the end:

Lila has been coming around, asking about you all the time. She misses you, son. Won't you give her a call? Patsy sends her love, as do your dad and I. Take care of yourself.

The message could be read several ways. From his mother's point of view, Lila's coming around could be seen as loving and thoughtful; as Danny saw it, the girlfriend was hunting him down. Was this a clue? Who knew? Sam refolded the letter and stuck it into her pocket to hand over to the lawyer.

The door opened behind her and she jumped.

"Sorry, didn't mean to scare you," Beau said.

She spread her arms toward the center of the room. "Do they always make this much of a mess when they search a place?"

He gave a wry grin. "Sometimes worse than others."

"Maybe you can give me a hand with the mattress and we can straighten up a little bit."

While they tugged the bed back into place Sam told him about the call from the lawyer enlisting her help.

"You want to do that?" he asked.

"Well, yeah, to help the Flores family. Absolutely. I was hoping to find an address book or something that would put me in contact with his group of friends. But I guess that makes me hopelessly old-school, doesn't it? Everyone keeps their contacts on their phones."

He gently chucked her chin. "Yeah they do. And you're not hopeless, just traditional."

Oh, god, when did I lose my savvy? Traditional?

He gave her a wink and flashed his wonderful smile. "I still love that about you."

She returned the smile. "I'm going to stay out here and get this place in order."

"When do you leave for San Antonio?"

See? He already knew I would go, even before I've made up my mind or checked into flights.

"Not sure. But you'll be the first to know, you mind reader."

He shook his head. "Uh-uh, not me. I'm going back to my horses and leaving all this detecting to you."

What a switch, Sam thought as he closed the door behind him. She put aside the comparison—Beau, then and now—and went back to rummaging through the casita's contents. But it seemed anything that might have been of value had already been found and taken during the official search.

Chapter 24

Faustina Flores called Sam just as she was locking the casita's front door.

"You will never guess who called me this morning," the older woman began.

Sam was having enough struggle to realize it was Faustina on the line, as she hadn't identified herself.

"Margaret Contreras."

"Lila's …"

"Yes, her mother. She is driving up from Albuquerque and thinks we should get together. 'We're both grieving,' she told me. I've never met the woman, and I have no idea how she got my phone number."

That's right, Sam remembered, the parents are coming to claim Lila's body. She reached the house and went inside.

"What did you say to her?" she asked Faustina. "Did

you agree to meet?"

"Not exactly. But I have a feeling she may show up at my door any minute now."

"Any minute? Are you okay with that?"

"What choice do I have? I cannot be rude. But I'm here alone for the day because Pauline is volunteering at the church."

Sam rolled her eyes upward to the ceiling. "Would you like me to come over?"

"Yes—I was hoping you would say that. Can you come now? She was calling from the Albuquerque airport, and that was nearly three hours ago."

Faustina was right—Margaret Contreras could show up any moment. Sam felt for the older woman whose social upbringing wouldn't allow her to just say no. She changed to a clean blouse and got into her car.

A white rental sedan sat at the curb when Sam arrived at the Flores home. It was eerily similar to the one Lila had been driving, same make and model. Sam ignored that and *accidentally* bumped her horn to give a quick heads-up.

Faustina met her at the door, looking overjoyed to see her. "Samantha, please come in and meet my visitor, Mrs. Contreras."

The woman who stepped forward was close to Sam's age, with dark hair and chocolate eyes behind fashionable eyeglasses. She wore a turquoise pantsuit that went out of fashion twenty years ago, but it was sharply pressed and brightly accented with a pink and turquoise scarf that draped over her shoulders.

"I'm Margaret," she said, with a smile that failed to break through the grief in her eyes.

"I was very sorry to hear of your loss," Sam said.

"Both of our families are suffering," Margaret said. "My ex-husband and I are here in town for reasons we would have never imagined. I reached out to Sally before we left, and I just thought it would be kind to come and see Faustina and Pauline as well. I pray for all of you, for all of us."

Bizarre. Reaching out to the family of the man accused of killing your daughter? Social niceties were one thing, but this seemed way off the charts. Sam felt her smile waver and sent a glance toward Faustina, who clearly didn't know what she should say next.

Luckily Sam had reached for the first little gift she could think to bring, a bag of coffee from her shop. She handed it to her hostess, who made a much bigger fuss than necessary. They had moved into the living room and taken seats, although Sam felt ready to spring from her chair on a moment's notice to escape the awkward situation.

"I've come straight from the airport," Margaret said. "I thought I would offer to stay with you, Faustina, if you'd like the company. Sally is very upset about Danny and said you were too."

Faustina's eyes grew wide and her mouth flapped open and shut again.

"That won't be at all necessary," Sam said. "Faustina and Pauline have a huge number of friends here in town for support. Pauline is, in fact, at the church today with a lot of them."

She gave Margaret a firm look. "I assume you wouldn't have flown to New Mexico and driven all the way to Taos without a hotel reservation already booked? And if not, it shouldn't be a problem to get one on short notice at this time of year. The Riverside Hotel is a nice place."

"I believe Miguel booked rooms for us there already."

Sam stood and held out a hand in Margaret's direction, a clear indicator that it was time for her to go. The obtuse woman didn't take the hint. *Okay then, this is the perfect time to ask a few questions.*

Sam walked toward the front windows and back, in her best Sherlock Holmes imitation. "You mentioned your ex-husband. He's also in town now?"

Margaret cleared her throat. "Well, yes. He went directly to speak with the police—or is it the sheriff, here in Taos?"

Sam didn't think she would reveal a whole lot to the family.

"He must have been close to your daughter."

"Oh, yes. Lila was always something of a daddy's girl." Margaret sniffled and reached into her pocket for a tissue, the most emotion Sam had yet seen from her. "When he and I separated, I chose to stay in Nuevo Laredo. Lila insisted on moving to San Antonio with Miguel. She'd finished school and thought the larger city would offer more career opportunities."

"Oh? What was her career?" Sam didn't recall anyone mentioning one. Lila worked in a mall and after hours seemed to be the party girl who'd followed Danny everywhere he went.

"Fashion. She took online courses for a certificate, and she was on her way to becoming a very successful designer."

San Antonio didn't exactly seem like a perfect match for that, but Sam only nodded.

"I suggested that she branch out, go to New York or L.A. to get a foothold in the industry," Margaret said. "I just thought … well, her talents could really shine in those places."

Her job at the mall must have been a great stepping stone.

"Miguel didn't see it that way at all. He always let Lila have her way, and she was skilled at getting it."

Not very nice words from a mother. Apparently, the bitterness toward the ex ran deep.

Sam glanced up to see movement outside the window, a car pulling into the driveway. Pauline got out, toting an armful of lilies and trailing some white ribbons along. She walked over to open the front door for her.

"Sam! Hi, and thanks." Pauline stepped inside and came to an abrupt stop when she spotted Margaret. Faustina filled the gap with a quick introduction.

Pauline offered the obligatory "sorry for your loss" and Margaret went into the same "I thought I'd offer condolences to you" that she'd gone through with Faustina, but both of the Lopez women seemed baffled by the presence of their uninvited guest.

This time, because Margaret was already standing when Sam held out an arm, the visitor picked up her purse and jammed her arm through the handles as she was escorted toward the door. People handle grief in many different ways, Sam realized. Margaret still seemed to be in denial.

Faustina practically collapsed as they watched Margaret get into her rental car.

"Oh, thank goodness you were here, Sam. She was driving me crazy and she'd only been here fifteen minutes."

"Why did you let her come, Mama?" Paulina walked to the dining table where she carefully set the flowers down.

"I don't know ... I can't be rude. I wish I could sometimes."

"Mama, it's not rude to tell someone you aren't up for company. Especially someone like her."

Sam edged toward the door. "I'll just ..."

"No, no, no, Sam. You're fine. I'm so glad you came when Mama called. I hear that you spoke with Danny's attorney."

Pauline ushered her back to the center of the room and Faustina offered to make coffee, rushing into the kitchen before Sam could decline.

"Yes, actually I talked to Delia this morning. She's asked me to go to San Antonio and see what I can learn from Danny's friends. Maybe others will corroborate what he's told us about Lila and the relationship."

Pauline pulled a large glass vase from the nearby hutch and stuck the massive bunch of lilies into it. When she came back from filling it with water in the kitchen, she said, "Be sure you talk to Patsy."

Danny's sister who'd become such great friends with Lila. Now that might have interesting results.

"If nothing else, Patsy can give you a list of their friends. She and Danny weren't exactly hanging out all the time, but she would know who did."

"Great idea. I'll do that."

Faustina came from the kitchen, promising coffee in just five more minutes. Sam gave a glance at a big clock on the dining room wall and begged off. "I need to get home and look at travel plans."

Pauline hugged her. "I'm so glad you'll be helping the attorney. We need everyone we can get on Danny's side."

"I know. I feel that way, too."

Faustina gave her a hug with arms that felt like twigs around Sam's shoulders. She rubbed the older woman's back. "I'll do my best."

If only my best is good enough.

Chapter 25

Although she'd used the excuse of getting home to make her travel plans, Sam realized her chances to catch Miguel Contreras and ask questions would be limited. Presumably the couple would identify Lila and make arrangements to go back to Texas fairly quickly. She was on Paseo del Pueblo Sur anyway, and it was easy to stop at the hotel on her way home.

She parked in the lot and walked into the lobby, stopping to ask at the front desk. The young clerk began tapping computer keys.

"Contreras … did you say Margaret?"

"No! I mean, no, it's Miguel Contreras I need to speak with."

"Ah yes. Please step to the house phone there and I'll connect you."

The phone rang six times and Sam began to itch. She should have asked Margaret for her ex-husband's cell number. He could be anywhere in town right now, most likely still at the sheriff's department. She was about ready to hang up when a male voice answered.

"Yeah." He sounded out of breath and Sam pictured him hearing the phone from out in the corridor and making a mad dash for it.

"Miguel Contreras?" She turned her back to the curious clerk and quickly introduced herself. "I wonder if I might have a few minutes of your time to talk about your daughter? I'd be happy to buy you a coffee, or a drink. The hotel has both a coffee shop and a bar, right here off the lobby. Please. I'm sure you won't be in town long."

There were shuffling sounds over the line, as if he was wrestling his way out of a coat or maybe bending to untie his shoes. But something in what she'd said must have struck a note—he agreed to come back downstairs and meet her. Sam thanked him and hung up the phone. She turned toward the coffee shop and spotted Margaret Contreras coming out.

Definitely not someone she wanted to get tied up with, especially with her bitter ex headed downstairs at this moment. She wished for a magic portal to another world, but nothing like that appeared. She settled for a tall, polished stone sculpture of an Indian corn maiden and ducked behind it.

Margaret was staring down at her phone screen with a scowl on her face. Gone was the fakey-caring woman who'd offered to stay with Faustina for comfort. This one would be little comfort for anyone. Sam stared from beneath the corn maiden's armpit and saw Margaret head for the elevator and press the button.

When the doors slid open, the man who stepped out muttered something, and Margaret glared at him. Uh-oh. It seemed the couple weren't bothering to be polite with each other even in their time of grief.

Sam edged around the opposite side of the sculpture and quick-stepped over to the coffee shop entrance. When the man walked up behind her, she turned and put on a smile.

"You must be Miguel." When she said his name, his tight-lipped mouth went into a smile, and Sam caught a glimpse of Lila's expression in the straight, white teeth and curve of the lips.

He was about two inches taller than Sam, balding, with a dark fringe of hair above the ears. His café au lait skin was smooth except for squint lines around the eyes and the beginnings of jowls that went along with the extra twenty-five pounds he carried around his midsection. He wore jeans, a leather belt with a large silver and turquoise buckle, and a button-down white shirt with narrow blue stripes. Someone must have told him vertical stripes were slimming, but it didn't quite work on him.

They were shown to a table and she went through the usual condolences and mentioned she'd met Lila's mother earlier at a friend's home.

A grimace crossed his features, one Sam read to mean: *Ugh, Margaret, what a pain.*

They ordered coffee, although it was the last thing Sam wanted.

"I should let you know; Danny Flores works for my husband at our ranch north of town," Sam said. "Beau used to be the sheriff of Taos County."

He held back whatever opinion he held about Danny.

"So, what's this, a condolence call or an interrogation?"

Sam went for a light mood, chuckling slightly. "I'm no interrogator. Beau and I befriended Danny and I met Lila once. It's sad what's happened, but I truly don't think Danny had anything to do with your daughter's death. The reason I'm here, and the reason I'm talking to people who knew them both, is because his attorney and his family have asked me to."

He stirred four packets of sugar into the mug the waitress had set in front of him.

"Okay, fair enough. I always thought Danny was a nice kid, well-mannered, polite. Not much of a go-getter, frankly. I wasn't sure what Lila saw in him, but she seemed crazy about him."

Or just plain crazy.

"She said they planned to get married," Sam ventured, "but Danny didn't seem quite so sure about that."

Miguel started to say something, thought better of it, raised his cup to his lips.

Sam went on. "There were a lot of text messages between them, and they sounded like Lila was getting very pushy on the subject. Apparently, Danny was very uncomfortable with her tone. He said he moved here to give himself some space."

"Oh yeah? Uncomfortable enough to harm her? Space enough to get rid of her?"

Uh-oh. This was taking a nasty turn.

Miguel leaned forward, hands wrapped around his mug, forearms on the table. "I know this. My daughter did nothing wrong, and if their relationship went south, it was his doing. She was devastated when he suddenly moved away without telling her. She moved heaven and earth to figure out a way just to talk to him about it."

There was another side to every story, Sam realized. Maybe Lila truly had believed she and Danny were meant to be together and by coming here she was merely trying to talk to him. But her father clearly didn't know about the many calls and texts, and Lila had obviously not told him that Danny broke it off with her.

Parents have blind spots when it comes to their kids. Everyone does. Sam knew she would never convince this man that his daughter had problems, much less that she was a deranged stalker. Nor should she. He needed his memories to be positive ones.

But Danny's family had needs too, and their need to know the truth about Lila's killer was going to outweigh Miguel's need to believe his daughter was an angel. Sam couldn't sit by and see Danny tried and convicted for something he didn't do, and right now it seemed as if she was the only one out there looking for proof of his innocence.

Sam thanked Miguel for meeting with her, placed money on the table to cover the coffee, and left. She arrived home to find an email from Kelly with their travel arrangements all done. They would be heading for the airport in the morning.

Chapter 26

Living in the northern part of New Mexico had plenty of charms, but one of them was not about the ease of air travel. The almost three-hour drive to the airport had to be factored into every trip, so Sam and Kelly were on the road shortly after five a.m. the next morning, Virtu and Manichee riding along in their carry-on bags. By eight-thirty they were in the boarding line at gate A-23.

And that's when Sam spotted the Contreras parents. Not together. Margaret wore a pink pantsuit, which might have been the other-color twin of the one she'd had on yesterday at Faustina's home. She was sitting primly upright on her seat in the waiting area, a magazine spread across her lap and a vacant look in her eyes. Miguel was already in the boarding line—of course he'd paid for a premium spot so he wouldn't have to take a less than choice seat—staring at his phone screen and giving an occasional glance toward the head of the line.

Sam pointed them out to Kelly. "I'm going to lay low since I don't especially want them to know I'm heading to their city." She diverted to the coffee kiosk on the other side of the large space.

Twenty minutes later they were aboard, Kelly having walked down the aircraft aisle ahead of Sam. They chose seats farther back than either of Lila's parents.

"I suppose this means Lila is also on board," Kelly said in a somber voice as she pulled out the inflight magazine for a quick browse.

Sam glanced at the floor. Kelly was probably right— the casket must be somewhere here beneath their feet. She wondered if the parents were having the same thought.

The flight was a short one, they didn't see either of the Contrerases in the San Antonio terminal, and everything went smoothly at the car rental desk. By noon, they had settled into their hotel at the edge of the famed Riverwalk and were walking along the lovely shaded riverside sidewalk, deciding on a place for lunch.

"So, during the flight I organized the contact info I put together for the people I want to talk to," Sam said, taking her seat at Joe's Crab Shack. She pulled out her phone. "I think we owe it to Danny's parents to talk with them first. Faustina gave me their phone number and address. I'm going to see if they're available after lunch."

Kelly pointed out the sampler platter on the menu and they opted to share it. When the server walked away, Sam dialed the Flores home and Sally answered right away.

"Oh, Sam. Yes, I was told you would be in town today. I'm almost ready to put lunch on the table if you can get here right away. It's beef tacos and beans."

"That's sweet of you, but we're good on lunch. How about if we come by around one-thirty?"

The plan was set, the seafood lunch was just what two ladies from the mountains were hungry for, and they found the Flores home without any trouble, using the rental's GPS. The brick home sat in a well-maintained middle class neighborhood, and Sally had evidently inherited Faustina's love of gardening. Brilliant red hibiscus flowers, pale yellow columbine, and purple salvia adorned the front yard.

"This is one thing I miss, living at seven thousand feet," Kelly said. "Having the flowers blooming this early in the season. Spring comes later than I'd like for us."

Sam remembered her own childhood in Texas, where one of the pleasures was always having plenty of grassy spots and filled flowerbeds in which to hunt for Easter eggs. The image reminded her that the holiday was sneaking up—she needed to plan something special for Ana this year.

"Samantha?" came a voice from the front porch. "I'm Sally."

"I remember, from your summers at the insurance agency," Sam said. They exchanged a quick hug.

"Hector's inside and he spotted you from the front windows." Sally was about forty-five, more heavyset than her mother or sister, with dark hair cut in a pixie. She wore gray slacks, a bright yellow pullover top, and a worried expression.

"If possible, let's keep the conversation light," Sally said. "Hector won't tell you this, but he began having chest pains when he heard that Danny was arrested. At work, they called an ambulance and he spent last night in the hospital. It wasn't a heart attack, thank the Lord, but the doctor wants me to keep an eye on him. He's supposed to stay home and take it easy the rest of the week."

"Oh, no," Kelly said.

"Have you told Pauline and your mother?" Sam asked.

"Not yet. They have enough to worry about." Sally turned to put her hand on the doorknob. "If it should get worse, of course I will tell them." She pushed the door open and led the way.

They walked inside a 1990s version of Faustina's 1970s home. Interesting how Sally's taste mirrored her mother's in so many ways.

Hector stood near the living room window, hands behind his back, staring out toward the street. He was the fifty-year-old version of Danny. He turned and greeted them cordially, although his eyes revealed the toll this ordeal was taking. "Faustina says you're going to help our son. She has a lot of faith in you." By his tone, it wasn't clear whether he felt the same. Sam got the idea he was reserving judgment.

"I was just making some iced tea to take out back. The sun is so nice today, we try to enjoy the spring days before summer drives us back indoors again."

"That sounds lovely," Kelly said. "I can help you carry things out."

They settled into chairs around a glass-topped outdoor dining table.

"Have you had the chance to speak to Danny yet?" Sam asked after complimenting Sally on the cookies.

Sally shook her head. "Pauline went to visit him this morning and we got a long report. She says he's doing all right and he doesn't want us to worry."

"I was all set to pack the car," Hector said, "but she talked me out of us going now. Said there wouldn't be any point."

"You were in the hospital yesterday," Sally said, laying a gentle hand on his arm. "There's no way you're making a road trip now."

"Sally's right. Danny will be limited on visitors and how much time each can spend. Your support would be better during the trial." Sam caught herself. "Of course we're hoping there won't be a trial. If we can find evidence to exonerate your son, we will, and we hope that will lead the sheriff to the real killer. We all want to see Danny freed."

"I just don't understand this," Sally said. "We met Lila. She was beautiful and charming. Who would want to hurt her? Not our Danny, that's for sure."

It was the same way Lila's own parents described her. Finding someone angry enough to murder her was going to be a challenge, Sam knew.

"Danny says she was becoming somewhat … overbearing. Pressing him to get married right away. He told me that was why he moved to Taos. Maybe it was to give himself some time and space to think about the commitment?" Sam suggested.

"If anything, I always thought she would move along before he did," Hector said. "She was a few years older than him and always seemed kind of … above us. Or she thought she was."

"Because she was beautiful?" Kelly asked. "Pretty girls can be full of themselves."

"It was that, sure. I don't know exactly. Her dad's a cop, not exactly some millionaire. Sally's a hair stylist, I work for the postal service sorting mail at night. It's not like any of us are, you know, bigwigs."

Miguel Contreras is a cop? Sam digested the news for a moment. No wonder he'd made a beeline for Evan Richards' office when he got to Taos. She had to wonder how his opinion would skew the sheriff's view of both the victim and of Danny? She set those thoughts aside for later. Right now she was out to find evidence.

She set her glass down and leaned forward. "When Danny moved to Taos, he didn't bring a lot of personal belongings with him. I wonder ... did he leave some of his things behind, here at your house?"

"Oh sure. You know how it is with kids these days. It can take years for them to completely move away from home."

Kelly and Sam exchanged a look and both laughed. "This one," Sam said, "still had things at home when she came back nearly ten years later."

Sally gave a knowing nod. "Oh! Speaking of things left behind. Danny never has changed his address for some billing and banking, so I keep his mail and send him a packet once a week or so."

"I'd be happy to take it to him, if you'd like," Sam offered.

"Yes, thanks. But what I was thinking of was something ..." She got up and went back into the house. When she returned, she held out a white envelope to Sam. "His bank statement. I have to admit, I opened it. When I heard about his arrest I wanted to see if he had some money in his account to cover his expenses. I was worried about the price of this lawyer."

Sam took the envelope hesitantly. "I don't—"

"You can look. He had several thousand dollars in

there at the beginning of the month. And now—nothing! He took out all but a few dollars."

Sam pulled out the single sheet statement. Sure enough, the balance was now $10.48, down from nearly ten thousand.

"Danny was always very careful with his money," Hector said. "Saved every week from his pay, saved all his graduation and birthday money, and he was careful with his spending."

"I can see that," Sam said, scanning the deposits and expenses. Knowing what Beau paid, it appeared Danny had kept out enough for gas and food and banked the rest. "Have you called the bank to find out more about the transaction?"

Sally shook her head. "It just came yesterday."

"Do you mind if I take a picture of this?" Kelly asked. "We could show it to Danny when we get back home."

"Please. Go ahead."

"Meanwhile, I'd like to look in his bedroom or wherever his things are, the stuff he left behind. Maybe there's something more about his relationship with Lila, something we don't know already."

Sally led the way to a back bedroom decorated in blue and red, furnished simply with a single bed, student desk, chest of drawers, and bookshelf. School mementos and baseball trophies sat on the shelves. Sam saw the same pattern of neatness in the way Danny kept this room and the casita at their place.

"Take your time," Sally told them. "I can't think what would be here that might help—it's all his old childhood and high school junk—but maybe you'll know what you need." She walked down the hall, leaving the door open.

Kelly was perusing her phone, stretching the photo of the bank statement to enlarge it. "Mom, did you notice the date on that big withdrawal? It was the day before Lila died."

Sam paused with a desk drawer half open. She hadn't paid attention to that.

"Did he say anything about needing money for something? Maybe he was buying a new truck or something. Maybe he hoped to pay Lila off, get her to go away."

"No, he didn't mention anything at all."

"It's a mobile banking transaction. We'd need access to the account to see the details."

"Or we just ask him about it when we get home."

"Oh, that's what I meant. Mom, you're watching too many cop shows where they hack into people's accounts with just a couple of clicks and instantly know everything about them."

"Ha. Ha." Sam turned her attention back to the desk. If only this were that easy.

Kelly rifled through the books on the lower shelves, and took photos of the items. Maybe something she collected would stir Danny's memory of an event, and that might lead to the name of whoever else was out there— out to get Lila.

Sally wandered back in. "I haven't looked through his papers and things. Are you coming up with anything that might help?"

Sam shook her head. "Danny told me Lila was saying untrue things, spreading rumors on social media. Did he tell you about that?"

"A little. After they had dated for a couple of months, I could tell he was getting tired of the relationship. I don't know if *tired* is the right word … maybe it was more like, I don't know. He realized she wasn't the girl for him. That's when he said she was saying things about him being a liar and breaking promises." She straightened the bedspread absentmindedly. "I told him what Mama always used to say to me: 'Sticks and stones may break my bones, but words will never hurt me.' I suggested he just ignore what Lila was saying. It's no fun to bully someone who doesn't respond, and she would just go away."

"Sounds like he was trying to do that," Kelly said. She had opened the closet and was staring at an upper shelf. "Moving to Taos was a good idea to get off her radar."

"I thought so too. His dad and I were thrilled when Mama encouraged him to come, and then when he found a job right away. By the way, Sam, he really does love working for your husband. I think it's the happiest I've ever seen him, ranching."

Sam closed the last of the desk drawers, emptyhanded. "I'd like to chat with his friends while we're in town. Would you know how to put us in touch with them?"

Sally rolled her eyes. "Kids came and went from here all the time, during his high school years, but that's been a while. I got first names, at the most. And you know how kids are now—all the contact information is on their phones. I doubt he wrote down anything. Other than Sergio Sandoval. Serg was his best friend since first grade, and we know the Sandoval family well. I'll give you his mother's number."

She left the room. Kelly was busy patting down the pockets of jackets and shirts in the closet when Sally came back with a slip of paper in her hand.

"Here's Darlene Sandoval's phone number. And I

wrote down our daughter Patsy's number and address too. Good luck catching her—she's in law school and the schedule is crazy. But she'll know most of Danny's friends. She and Lila even got so close that Lila was moving into the new apartment with Patsy."

Sam's breath caught. Now *that* was an interesting tidbit. How had no one thought to mention it already?

Chapter 27

The apartment building was typical of student housing everywhere—a nothing-special tan building, a big parking lot, no real amenities. It was a place to sleep and study. Sally had told them Patsy drove a yellow VW beetle, so when Kelly spotted a young woman about to get into that very car, she pulled up alongside. The UTSA Law sweatshirt was another giveaway.

"Patsy?" Sam called as she got out of the rental.

Patsy Flores looked up with a smile full of beautifully white teeth. Her liquid brown eyes went along with wavy long, dark hair. She wore jeans with the blue and orange school logo sweatshirt. She tossed a heavy-looking backpack into the passenger side of the little car.

"You must be Sam," she said. "Mom texted me."

"Have you got a minute?"

"A minute—that's about right. I'm graduating law school in May and it's brutal. Every spare second, I'm studying." She leaned on the open door of the car.

"I was hoping to chat briefly about Danny and Lila, how they were getting along and all that. We're trying to help find Lila's killer."

Patsy shook her head woefully. "It can't be Danny— I'm sure of that. He may be flaky and noncommittal in relationships, but he's never been violent."

"You think he moved to New Mexico to get out of the relationship?"

"Well, of course. That would be his way of handling it, rather than sitting down and properly breaking it off."

"He told me he tried talking it out with her. He says she wouldn't take no for an answer."

Patsy nibbled at her lower lip for a moment, squinting her eyes. "I don't know about that. Lila always seemed reasonable. I mean, I wouldn't take on a roommate who didn't have her act together."

"And Lila did? Have her act together?" Kelly wasn't hiding her skepticism very well.

"Eh, most of the time. I mean, she was fun and knew how to party—don't we all? Well, okay, maybe not me so much, not right now, since I'm busting my fanny to finish school. Lila had a job, but didn't seem career oriented. She always had money to buy little gifts for friends, to go out, to get new clothes. Maybe she got some extra support from her parents or something. All I know is she gave me two month's rent in advance for my second bedroom here. And, hey, every little bit helps. I'm just saying, she was a nice person. It was horrible what happened to her."

"Could we take a look at her room sometime? I know—"

"Yeah, sure. I've gotta run now … but we'll catch up."
She slid down into her seat as she said it.

"Real quick," said Kelly, stepping forward to block the
car door from closing. "Could we get the numbers of a
friend or two of Danny's? We only have a couple days here
in town and need to make the most of it."

"Um, sure." Patsy reached into a side pocket of her
backpack and pulled out her phone. With a couple of
quick swipes she brought up contacts. "Here's Sergio. He'll
be an important one to talk to."

She held up the phone screen and let Kelly add the
number to her own phone.

"And here's Devon Miller's number. She and her
brother are nearly always with whatever group is going out.
She's sweet and would probably tell you whatever you need
to know."

The moment Kelly had finished taking the numbers,
Patsy pled lateness and pulled her door shut as she stuck
her key in the ignition. With a flash of a stiff smile and a
tiny wave, she backed out.

"Marginally helpful, but I guess it was worth the trip to
get the phone numbers," Sam said.

The sun was beginning to dip in the sky, and their early
awakening had begun to tell. Kelly drove and Sam used her
phone to call the new contacts.

Sergio Sandoval answered on the first ring. "Yo."

Sam explained who she was and gave the rehearsed
version of why they were in town, hoping to help Danny.

"Yeah, bummer. It sucks that Lila died, but it sucks
worse that Danny's in trouble."

"We're hoping that by talking with some of their
friends we can figure out what went wrong. We need

some evidence that would show Danny didn't commit this crime."

"I know, man, I wish I knew what to tell you. He was kind of reaching a limit with her, you know. It's why he moved away."

"Right. That's what he's told me," Sam said. "We just ran into Patsy and she said a bunch of the friends get together regularly. Could we maybe meet up, have you introduce us to some of the others?"

There was some shuffling at the other end and the sound of a car starting. "Look, I'm on my way to work now, but yeah … Anybody who's available usually shows up at Thrashed around ten or eleven. I'll be there tonight after I get off work."

Sam wasn't about to admit she was usually dead to the world by eleven. The ranching life didn't include many late nights. "Sounds great, Sergio. Thanks."

"Oh my god, nightclubbing after eleven," Kelly said. "I haven't done that since I moved back to Taos."

"Yeah, we live a pretty sheltered life, don't we?" Sam said, setting Kelly's phone on the console.

"Well, I'll never make it, especially since I've been up since before three a.m. Texas time, unless I get a nap first."

Their hotel at the Riverwalk was ten minutes away and the room's blackout drapes helped create the perfect little nap haven. Later, over dinner—salads in the hotel restaurant—they talked about what they'd learned so far.

"Patsy didn't exactly seem to take her brother's side in this whole thing, did she?" Kelly said.

"Yeah, and I'm not sure she'd be a good witness. She's almost too truthful about Danny's shortcomings."

"Not to mention, she seemed to believe Lila's version

of things over her own brother's."

"Still, I think we can learn something useful and we need to stay in contact with her. I want the chance to go through Lila's belongings that she left behind at Patsy's apartment." Sam set down her fork and stifled a yawn.

"You sure you're up for this, Mom? I could go to the club by myself."

"No way. Sorry to pull mom rank on you at your age, but I'm not sitting back in a hotel room and sending you off to some nightclub in a strange city." Sam gave a wry grin. "I wouldn't rest anyway."

"It's not like we need to stay very long. We'll see how it goes, hopefully chum up with the friends and learn something."

Kelly grabbed the check and handed over her credit card. While she was waiting for her receipt, she looked up the address of the club Sergio had mentioned.

It was slightly after ten o'clock when the perky GPS voice directed them to the parking lot on a street just off the college campus.

"I think I'm glad we handled the wooden boxes before we left the hotel," Sam said, eyeing the façade of the cinderblock building that had a violent looking mural painted on the wall that faced the parking area.

Kelly was also giving it a hard stare. "Yeah, I wonder what kind of place this is. At least I'm not getting any warning sirens in my head yet."

Sam took a deep breath. "The cars all look like typical college kid rides, don't they? I mean, the lot isn't filled with motorcycles and I didn't see any rough types hanging outside the door."

"One can hope." Kelly checked her purse for the

pepper spray she always carried. "What's the plan? If the evening should go south, maybe we need a signal or escape word for each other?"

"You're asking me? I spent my high school years in an itty-bitty Texas town where the Dairy Queen was the social life, and I escaped that as soon as I could for a pipeline camp in Alaska. Since then it's been Taos, first with a baby to raise and then a bakery where the hours begin at o-dark-thirty. I'm not exactly an expert at this."

"Okay, let's play it by ear. I'll let you know what vibes I get."

They bumped fists and got out of the car.

Chapter 28

Sam felt old the moment she stepped inside. Everything from the bouncer to the floor-vibrating music set her nerves on edge. Maybe handling the box ahead of time was a bad idea—every sensation was magnified. Kelly handled it better and took the lead. Her outfit, cobbled together from what she'd packed, was in line with what most of the kids were wearing—tight jeans or short skirts, fitted tops, big earrings. The guys were also in jeans, T-shirts on the ratty side.

They stared through the crowd. A couple dozen people were gyrating under the flashing lights on the dance floor. Tables ringed the room, including an upper level accessed by cement steps and separated by a pipe railing.

A blonde girl, wearing ripped jeans, a lowcut tank top, and a short denim jacket, approached them. "Are you Sam and Kelly? I'm Devon. Serg called earlier and said friends of Danny's from Taos were coming tonight, and you looked ... um, sort of ... lost."

Kelly laughed, the curls she'd pulled up on top of her head bouncing. "Hey, Devon, yeah I guess we kind of are."

"Serg said you're trying to help Danny, and that makes you a friend of ours. He'll be along soon. There's our group up there," she said, waving vaguely up the steps. "Come join, if you want, and I'll introduce you around."

They followed Devon up four steps and wound their way to a table in a corner. The music volume dropped when the DJ took a break and put on some canned recording, and at least half the dancers wandered off the dance floor. Devon turned as soon as they reached the table.

"Hey, everyone, this is Kelly and Sam. Ladies—this is the gang. Chad, Josh, Michael and Emily, Abby."

The names went by fast and Devon's vague finger pointing left Sam unsure who was who, but they all smiled politely enough.

"Oh, and here's Sergio now," Devon said, turning to look behind Sam.

The young man reached out a hand to shake when she turned to face him. "Sam and Kelly—good to meet you."

Manners. Refreshing. He reminded her of Danny in a lot of ways, although shorter and stockier, with a wrestler's build. Sam thought she remembered Danny saying his buddy worked at a lumber yard, and he looked as if he was built for hefting sheets of plywood. His open face exuded honesty—or that might be an observation from handling the box first—and his wide smile was genuine.

"Grab a seat," Devon invited. "We'll pull up more chairs if anyone else comes."

Sam took the empty spot next to Devon, who introduced Josh across the table as her brother. That's right, she thought, Danny had said they were twins. Their similar coloring and the way they smiled would have given it away. Kelly ended up at the other end of the table, seated between Sergio and a clean-cut preppie type.

"Chad Smith," Devon whispered to Sam when she noticed her looking. "He and Patsy are our two college geeks. She's going into law, and I think he's studying business, planning to go into something with his dad. I'm not sure exactly what."

Josh leaned across the table toward Sam. "So, somebody said Danny works at your ranch in New Mexico?"

"Yeah, he does. He seems to love it, especially working with the horses."

"Would you have ever believed that?" Josh said to Sergio. "Danny the brain in high school, and now he's turning into a rancher."

Sam ignored the edgy tone.

Devon shot her brother a look. "Two beers and he turns into a *jerk*!" But her tone was teasing. She turned back to Sam.

"I heard from Danny's mom yesterday and she told me what happened. I can't believe it—I mean, Danny would *never* hurt someone." Devon's eyes grew soft when she said Danny's name.

"I agree. We've only known him a few months, but I don't see him doing something like that, especially to someone he was close to." Sam watched Devon's face. "I'm guessing he and Lila were close, at some point?"

"Lila was … interesting."

Sam looked around the group. Other conversations

had picked up where they left off. Michael, Emily, and Josh were laughing loudly at something. She turned to Devon and lowered her voice.

"What can you tell me about them as a couple?"

Devon raised a slender shoulder. "I don't know ... It's weird when you know someone a long time and they hook up with somebody who's kind of a stranger."

Sam sipped the rum and Coke she'd ordered and let Devon put her thoughts together.

"Lila just came on the scene kind of all at once. I mean, I heard that her parents split, and that's hard on anyone. And being out of school, well that's another thing. When you move and start at a new school at least you meet a bunch of potential friends at once. So, Lila was, like, twenty-four I think when she came here. So we all kind of met here at Thrashed. She was dating somebody, but that ended about five minutes after she met Danny."

"A love at first sight kind of thing?"

"Love, lust—who knows? He was attracted. *Every* guy was attracted to Lila."

"And she was ..."

"Was she attracted to every guy?" Devon's mouth pinched tight for a moment. "She flirted with them all, especially at first. But it seemed like once she settled on Danny, she stuck with him. Maybe didn't want to mess it up. He's pretty straightlaced, as you probably know. Not the kind of guy who would like his girlfriend playing around."

She stopped short. "No—not that she was, or he would be so jealous that he'd—No! Not at all."

Sam patted her shoulder. "That's not the way I took it. Danny told us he wanted to break it off with Lila and that's why he moved out of state."

Devon seemed relieved. "I'm glad. That's kind of the

feeling I got, but I wasn't sure."

The girl on the other side of Devon, Emily, tapped her shoulder and whispered something. Sam turned her attention toward Sergio.

"Danny told me your husband used to be the sheriff or something like that," he said.

Sam nodded.

"So, that, plus what Patsy told me about you coming here and talking to people who know Danny ... Are you asking questions officially or something like that?"

"No, nothing official. I'm just scared for Danny and wanting to get any information I can that might take the heat off him."

"I get that, man. I can't believe it about him getting arrested."

"Tell me what you thought about them as a couple. Was Lila good to him?"

"Lila was ... hot ..." He stopped. "Okay, yeah, you got me. She was one hot girl, and I don't think there's a real guy on the earth who wouldn't say that."

Sam remembered the flowing dark curls, the mysterious eyes, and the figure to die for. She smiled at Sergio's description and nodded an acknowledgement.

He turned slightly sideways, eyeing the conversations around the table, and then spoke softly to Sam. "Yeah, and she was a bitch, a devious one."

"What do you mean?"

"Danny showed me the texts. 'Sweet dreams, my love.' Gag me. She'd say stuff like that one minute and make a threat the next."

"Threats. Like?"

"Like, 'Don't ever leave me or I'll track you down.' Once, he questioned her on that—'you'd track me down?'

he asked. And then she laughed it off. I'm telling you, the girl ran hot and cold, and you could never tell what she'd say next." He toyed with the paper coaster under his beer bottle, peeling little shreds from the wet edges. "That comment about tracking him down, I confronted her on that, asked her what she meant. She gave me this big wide-eyed look and said 'I don't know what you mean.' Sam, I had his phone in my hand with the text message right there, and she denied that she'd sent it. Nut case."

This was sounding a lot like what Sam had heard from Danny. She wondered if Sergio would be willing to testify about it. She was about to ask, but another couple walked in and the guy punched Sergio playfully on the arm.

"Hey, Matt." Sergio stood and gave the guy and his girlfriend hugs. "Sam, this is Matt and Taylor."

Quick hellos and they edged down to the other end of the table where two empty chairs sat. Sam made eye contact with Kelly, guessed everything was going okay there, and knew they would catch up and compare notes at the end of the evening. The DJ was back and the music ramped up again.

She turned back to Devon. "Doesn't look like I'll get to talk to everyone tonight. Do you think they'd mind if you gave me their numbers so I can reach out later?"

Devon, sweetheart that she was, pulled out her phone and sent Sam the contact info for everyone at the table.

Michael and Emily jumped up and headed for the dance floor. At the other end of the table Chad grabbed Abby's hand and pulled her in that direction too. Kelly was suddenly sitting relatively alone and she caught Sam's eye. Time to go.

Chapter 29

I was about to beg you to shoot me," Kelly said as they got into the car. "If I'd had five more minutes of Chad Smith's bragging about his grade point averages and how he's going to take over his dad's mega-big business after he graduates this spring ... ugh, I'd have shot *myself.* Especially when it came out that this *fantastic* job means running a car dealership. I suppose there's a lot of money in it, but seriously? You'd think he was about to become CEO of Google or something."

Kelly suddenly burst out with the giggles. "I can't believe how strange that was." She settled into the passenger seat and let Sam take the wheel.

"What? You mean, the club ... Kel, how many drinks did you have?"

"Two! That's what I mean. Two drinks, an hour of

conversation with, oh my gosh, the very people I used to *be* … I'm so out of it now." Her voice descended into a whine. "I'm not thirty anymore."

"And I'm not fifty anymore. It's called real life, hon."

Sam steered out of the parking lot, happy to be away from the crowded place, although handling the box had left her energetically charged. By all logic, she should have been out there on the dance floor, raving it up with the twenty-somethings.

"Oh, I'm not complaining. I am *so* thankful!" Kelly said, melting back into her seat.

"Me too. And I am completely not sleepy now. We need to work off this energy from the boxes. At home I always went to the bakery and pulled an all-nighter." Which wasn't always easy to explain to the help when they came in and found racks of finished pastries and shelves filled with complicated cakes. "Let's park the car and just walk. Like, miles if we have to."

"Yes!" Kelly leaned her head back and smiled. "On the other hand, Matt and Taylor seemed nice, and Abby was a real sweetheart."

Sam gave a little head-shake at the abrupt switch in topics, but she let the GPS guide her back to the hotel. There, they left the car in the parking garage and pulled out shawls they'd left in the back seat.

The evening was cool and the Riverwalk foot traffic had subsided quite a lot from earlier in the day. Most of the retail shops were closed, but the bars and restaurants were hopping. Strings of fairy lights sparkled in the tree branches, and tour boats cruised quietly along, filled mainly with couples who cuddled together on the bench seats.

Sam set a fairly strong pace and they walked along

briskly. "So, you told me about the self-centered Chad. Who else did you talk to?"

"Matt and Taylor said they've known Danny since grade school. I guess they all grew up in the same neighborhood. They both like him a lot. About Lila, they didn't say a whole lot. Matt said she was gorgeous, but when Taylor gave him the eye he backtracked and added that she completely wasn't his type."

"I kind of got the same from Josh. Guys are funny— what they notice and then how they interpret."

"Abby, the girl across from me ... she seemed super genuine. A bit of a hippie, maybe. Anyway, I got the vibes from her expression and, you know, just what I was noticing in my own heightened state, that she didn't care much for Lila at all. Different personalities, yeah. But there was more. She exuded distrust." Kelly turned toward Sam. "Is it always this way, after handling the boxes? This ... being able to notice how people are feeling, what they're thinking?"

"I suppose so. I've had that experience."

"Okay, whew! I was afraid it was the drinks and the nightclub, in which case I'm not sure I'd trust my perceptions."

"No, I think you're on track. I was getting some of the same feelings from the others."

"When I asked Abby outright for her impressions of Lila, she listed two words: slick and conceited."

"Devon added bitchy and devious. And from reading those texts she sent to Danny, I think that can be summed up as self-centered," Sam said. "I also got the impression, a strong one, that Devon has a major crush on Danny."

"But you know what was kind of weird, too? Matt and

Chad both kind of hinted that Danny has some of those traits—a little bit devious, a little self-centered. Of course, if I were back in psychology 101, I'd probably be learning that we all have some of that."

Sam chuckled. "Well, I have felt somewhat devious at times since the box came into my life and I haven't shared everything I know with Beau."

Kelly gave her a look. "No one tells their spouse *everything*. Besides, if you did, then where would be the mystery or the romance?"

"I think we're getting off the subject we came here for. What have we learned that could point to someone else as Lila's killer?"

They had reached a point where the activity along the river was waning and the sidewalk was dark in places. It seemed like the right spot to turn around. Kelly flipped the end of her shawl over her left shoulder and looked up. A man was standing in the doorway of a closed souvenir shop, watching them.

"Mom ..."

"Yeah," Sam whispered. "Just keep going."

They edged toward the river but before they'd cleared the doorway of the darkened shop the man stepped out, blocking their path. Of medium build, with wide shoulders, dressed in dark colors, he kept his hands in the pockets of his jacket, his feet spread apart.

"You're asking questions where you shouldn't be."

Sam had expected something like "hand over your purses" and she had to ask him to repeat.

"Stop asking about the Contreras girl. It's none of your business." His voice was low, barely above a whisper, but the threat was obvious.

"What are you *talking* about?" Kelly raised her voice to draw attention. "Who *are* you?"

The stranger made that odd little gesture with two fingers pointing toward his own eyes, then at them. *I'm watching you.*

Then he pushed past them, bumping Sam hard with his shoulder, and dashing off into the darkness behind them.

Sam stumbled toward the river and teetered on the edge of the concrete embankment before Kelly grabbed her arm and pulled her back. The two of them stared into the dark space, lit in the distance by a few stray lights, but there was no sign of the man.

"What the *hell*." Sam sputtered.

Kelly's earlier bubbly giggles had completely vanished. "Let's get back where it's more crowded." She took Sam's arm and began speed walking toward the nearest restaurant with outdoor tables.

"He must have overheard our conversation and followed us. But how—?"

"How did he know which Lila we were talking about?"

"And that warning—it's none of our business—what prompted that?" Sam's mind was reeling with possibilities. Had he been following them since they left the club? Or even before that?

Music from a mariachi band came wafting out of a Mexican restaurant where sidewalk tables held pitchers of margaritas and were occupied by people laughing and talking without a care. Sam pulled Kelly inside and asked the hostess for an indoor table near the windows.

"I need to see if that guy comes back," she said as they took seats and ordered guacamole and chips.

"Would you recognize him again?"

"Right now, probably. By tomorrow, in the light of day and in a different place … I'm not sure."

Most of the foot traffic was coming from the other direction, and although they watched for the next half hour, there was no sign of the man who'd threatened them. When a boisterous group from another table got up to leave, Sam pulled money from her pocket and left it on the table; they blended with the others to walk the distance back to their hotel.

The man obviously knew the area well enough to know another way out. He might also be familiar with the hotels, and could have followed them since they parked.

Sam didn't relax until they were safely behind the locked door of their room.

Chapter 30

Late-morning sun was streaming in around the dark curtains when Sam stretched and came awake. She and Kelly had been up half the night, energized still by the boxes, thoughts flying about all they had learned from Danny's friends. Not to mention the warning from the stranger who now seemed somewhat phantomlike. In the bright light of morning, Sam wondered if she could have imagined his voice and the threatening tone.

Kelly was up, cuddled into a corner of the small sofa in the room, paging through the little notebook where the two of them had put together notes on their thoughts while the interviews were fresh.

"I thought I smelled coffee," Sam said as she cast aside the covers.

"Help yourself. That tiny pot actually made two cups." Kelly set the notebook down and picked up her phone. "I'm going to call Patsy Flores and see if we can set something up to meet with her today."

"Anytime is fine. I'll be quick in the shower." Sam grabbed clean clothes from her bag and headed toward the bathroom.

Five minutes later Kelly poked her head around the door. "Patsy says she's studying at her apartment until two, then she's going to Lila's funeral. We're free to come by now."

Sam shut off the shower and reached from behind the curtain to grab a towel. "Excellent. Give me five minutes."

She caught herself watching the traffic around them as they drove to Patsy's apartment. Twice, there was a car behind them that might have been following, but it would turn or they would turn. No one stayed with them the whole way.

The cinderblock building seemed more depressing on their second visit. The shrubs hadn't been pruned in a long time, and drifts of discarded food wrappers had collected around them. An old tire leaned against a wall. The tan paint had a yellowish cast, and there were rust-colored stains where water had run off the roof for years.

Patsy answered the door of unit 218 and stood back for them to enter.

Kelly eyed the stack of books sitting beside an older laptop on a desk in the tiny living room. A two-person dining table was pushed up against the kitchen counter, and they could see the sort of outcast appliances students everywhere seemed to inherit with the cheap rentals that went along with the lifestyle.

"Looks like your classes are keeping you plenty busy," she said.

Patsy raised her eyes to the ceiling. "I had no idea. But I'm almost at the finish line. Six weeks until finals. Praying that goes well. Then studying for the bar, which should be another real joy."

"What field of law do you plan to go into?" Sam asked.

"Oh, definitely it's family law. I've interned at a small local firm owned by a woman who's a strong advocate for the rights of women and children, especially those with abuse in their backgrounds. We advocate for them during a sticky divorce or child custody situation, help them get their legal paperwork in order, such as making a will after they suddenly find themselves on their own. Sometimes we help them get into a safe living space if there's been abuse in the household. With my degree I've got a fairly sure position there."

"Sounds like really worthy work," Kelly said with a smile.

"Well, your time is precious," said Sam, "so we should get to our questions."

"Please. Can I offer you something to drink? Afraid it's limited to water or Cokes right now. Even the coffee ran out this morning."

They declined. "If you can tell us anything that might point us toward Lila's killer, someone who had a grudge or a recent fight with her?" Sam asked. "I just don't see Danny for this at all, but we need another direction to go."

Patsy thought for a moment, shaking her head slightly. "I love my brother, but Lila was such a sweetheart. I can't imagine what happened to make him take off like that, especially not telling her where he was going. And Lila, well from everything I could see she was a hundred percent true to him. I knew her well enough that I think I would have spotted signs if she was cheating."

While studying ungodly hours, backing away from her social life, and not particularly paying attention to her new roommate's activities—Sam doubted Patsy's observations would have been quite as keen as she was saying.

"I saw messages on Danny's phone," she said. "Lila was subtle about it, but she was definitely playing head games with him."

Patsy shook her head more vigorously. "Are you sure he didn't just misinterpret? He's a guy, and sometimes an oblivious one."

"She told him he'd proposed and given her your grandmother's ring. Then we learned it wasn't true at all. Your aunt Pauline has it at their home."

"I don't know ..."

Sam wasn't about to get into an argument. She still needed information Patsy could provide. "You said Lila was in the process of moving in here. Could we take a look at her room? Just see if she left anything that might give us some clues?"

"Sure, go for it, the room to the left of the bathroom. I really need to get back to the books—"

"Absolutely." *In fact, it's better if you're not watching over our shoulders.*

Lila's room was pretty much what Sam had expected—occupied but not truly lived-in. The bed was made, topped with a white duvet and a couple of knitted afghans tossed on top, and the closet was filled with high-end clothing, designer bags and shoes that were probably knock-offs. But there were no pictures on the walls and no personal mementos on the shelves or dresser. A large purple suitcase and three cardboard boxes had been shoved out of the way against one wall.

"Looks like maybe she wasn't quite done unpacking," Kelly said. "So, what are we looking for?"

Sam had thought about this. "Banking information that might show she's the one who took Danny's money." Although that might provide more motive for him than for someone else. "Personal notes or letters, especially if they're from another man. Photos could be interesting, jewelry."

"I'll go through the purses and clothes, if you want to take the drawers or the boxes." Kelly pulled the bags from the closet shelf and tossed them on the bed, where she plopped down and began opening them, one by one.

Sam pulled open the dresser drawers, which were filled with lacy, skimpy things but not much else. One drawer held sweaters and tops, all neatly folded. No stash of secret letters bound in a scarlet ribbon or photos of an ex-boyfriend.

It made sense that the girl would have first unpacked the items she used daily. Older things were probably in the boxes that were still sealed with packing tape. She ripped the clear tape off the first one. It contained a set of dishes.

The second box yielded a few more kitchen utensils—apparently Lila had her own place before coming here. Either that or her mother had put together a collection of the basics for when her daughter set up house.

The third box held the types of things young girls collect in their dresser drawers during high school—a yearbook from Nuevo Laredo High, photos of the sort probably taken by grandparents who still thought prints were the way to go, a few CDs of the Britney Spears ilk, birthday and graduation cards (those could prove informative), and oh—what's this?—a diary.

Sam flipped quickly through it. The handwriting

started out as that of a twelve-year-old, but in the latter pages the writing became more mature. There could be something here. She slipped the diary into her pack and turned to the cards. Most were obviously from Mom, Dad, Grandma, and an assortment of aunts and uncles, and contained congratulatory notes and references to gift money that had been enclosed. A few seemed to be from friends—signed with nicknames, embellished with hearts and flowers drawn in gel pen ink.

On the surface it didn't seem that any would relate to the current situation but, just in case, Sam snapped quick pictures of the interiors and signatures. Maybe a name they didn't know now would end up being helpful.

"Well, the purses seem like a bust," Kelly said, "unless you think lip glosses, used tissues, and ballpoint pens are useful. The girl seems to own a lot of that junk."

"Do the ballpoint pens have logos on them? Those could provide connections to ... something."

"Most of them are the girly type she probably picked up at a card shop or someplace—lots of glitter and cutesy designs. But I'll snag the printed ones."

Sam browsed the yearbook, finding the usual signatures. Lila had been voted prettiest senior and prom queen. Interesting that seven years later she was working at The Gap, living in a fairly crummy student apartment, and chasing after a rancher. Not that there was anything wrong with those things ... it just showed that popularity was a fleeting thing and high school was little indicator of success in life. Inside the book, she snapped photos of the signatures and all the 'love you, beautiful girl' types of messages her fellow students had written. Again, who knew where an important clue would come from?

Kelly re-stashed the purses, systematically went through the shoes, tapping them and turning them upside down to see if any valuable jewelry or wads of money would fall out. All she got was a dead cockroach from a black Manolo Blahnik high heel and a lint ball from one of the Nike running shoes.

She sidestepped those and went on to pat down the pockets of the clothing on hangers. "Any luck, Mom?"

Sam described the few things she'd photographed. "We can take them back to the room and see if we can put together anything useful. What do you think about this stack of photos? Maybe we should take a look. I can always mail them anonymously back to her mother after we're finished with them."

"Do it. I have a feeling we're going to strike out on the banking info. Everyone does that online anymore, most likely from her phone. And since we don't have that …"

"Yeah, too bad one of us isn't a whiz with hacking and able to get into the phone databases so we could pull up all her stuff on a big screen monitor."

"You're watching too much *NCIS*, Mom. I think we'll have to come up with other means." Kelly turned from the closet, empty handed. "What about that humongous suitcase?"

Sam unzipped it, but it was empty. Most likely it had been the means of bringing in the clothing, and it was now sitting in the corner because there wasn't a better place to store it.

"I'm starving, Mom. We never had breakfast." With a final look around the room, they decided it was time to call it a morning.

Chapter 31

A diner around the corner from Patsy's place provided substantial breakfast fare, cheaply, and both women felt reinvigorated afterward.

"Patsy mentioned Lila's funeral at two o'clock. What do you think? Should we spy, see if we learn anything new?"

Sam pondered the question. Who would be there? Both of Lila's parents. She'd probably already learned what she could from them. There would be tension between them, and she might catch a peek at Margaret's new man, but a funeral wasn't the time or place to step up and ask questions anyway. Still, it might be interesting to see which of the friends showed up. Someone's appearance, or lack of appearance, at the event might give weight to the information each had provided. A friend claiming to love the girl, but not showing up for the funeral ... that could be very telling.

She glanced at the time. "It's one-fifteen now and we have no idea where the service is."

"We're only two blocks from Patsy's. We could follow her."

They paid, left, and found a curbside spot within view of her apartment's parking lot. The yellow VW stood out and would be easy to track. Twenty minutes later, Patsy emerged, wearing a black dress and heels, her hair pulled away from her face in a half-up with a clip. She didn't glance in their direction at all, but went straight to her car.

"Either the place is fairly nearby or she's running late," Kelly said, starting the rental.

Judging by the way Patsy threw her car in gear and ripped out of the parking lot with barely a glance at the traffic, it was the latter. She got decent speed out of the little Beetle and wove her way knowledgeably through the streets. Kelly kept pace, but trying to do it clandestinely was impossible.

"Don't worry about staying back," Sam advised. "She's not suspicious and she wouldn't know this car anyway. Just get us to wherever she's going."

They zoomed through a couple of the traffic lights at the last possible second, but managed to stick with their quarry. Ten minutes later, Patsy slowed and made a right turn into the parking lot of an elaborate looking Catholic church.

Kelly slowed down enough to watch the little yellow car pull into a parking slot then she turned left, bringing their car to a stop in front of a pawn shop across from the church. The little strip center held a Laundromat, the pawn shop, a butcher shop, and a tiny café whose big claim to fame—on Day-Glo yellow window signs—was menudo.

"This isn't ideal," Kelly said. "Shall I move the car

somewhere else?"

"That's okay," Sam said, unbuckling her seatbelt and turning around. "I can see the front door, and we have a pretty clear view of who's coming and going."

"At least we're unobtrusive."

Patsy walked in, pausing a moment at the top of the steps to say hello to a priest in a black cassock. Several men in suits stood around, a couple of them smoking, apparently not wanting to be cooped up inside until they absolutely had to.

"They seem older than Lila and her friends," Kelly said. "Maybe friends of the parents?"

Sam nodded. Josh and Devon Miller arrived. From their body language, Sam guessed that Devon had somewhat forced her brother to come. He wore sneakers with his jeans and a black jacket; she had on a knee-length navy blue skirt and a navy T-top.

The men with cigarettes stubbed them out in a large planter near the door, straightened their jackets, and walked inside. They were no sooner through the doorway than the priest turned and closed the heavy carved doors.

"How long do you suppose this will go on?" Sam asked.

"I've never been to a Catholic funeral before, but if it's anything like a Catholic wedding … a long time."

"Maybe it won't be a religious service, just a short memorial." Sam knew her voice sounded hopeful.

"We could go in and find out," Kelly said, giving a glance at their clothing. "Yeah, no. Dusty jeans and sandals probably don't cut it in church."

"Especially since our whole point is to be unnoticed."

"One of those men, just now …" Kelly said. "I may be imagining things, but the guy who wasn't smoking … he seemed familiar, the same size and build as the man who confronted us last night and told us to back off."

"I wish I'd taken a better look."

"I know—I should have pointed him out, but it just kind of came to me now."

"So, what do you think? Can you be sure?"

Kelly sighed. "Not really. It was too dark to see his face much last night, and all I could tell was that he was husky and had dark hair. A hundred guys who just happen to work out at the gym could fit that description."

Sam turned to face forward in her seat again. "True. Not much we could do, even with proof. Nothing actually happened."

In their mirrors they stared at the closed church doors for another ten minutes.

"I'm not sure how Beau and his guys ever did surveillance—it's the most boring thing *ever*," Kelly said.

"We could make the most of our time by going through the things I swiped from Lila's boxes at the apartment." Sam reached for her jacket, which she'd tossed into the back seat of the car.

She pulled out the diary and the packet of photos, which Kelly picked up. Keeping an eye toward the church, she began flipping through them.

"Looks like the same group of kids, pretty much. They must have been on some kind of an outing together. The buildings in the background look like old places. There are some ruins in this one."

Sam glanced at them but didn't recognize the setting.

"Here are the guys—Josh, Chad, Sergio, Matt, Danny. And this one has the girls. There's Devon, Lila, Emily, Taylor. I don't see Abby, but I've kind of wondered how much she's a part of their crowd. A few of them as a whole group ..." At the back of the packet were some older shots. "Hm. Looks like this could be back in Nuevo Laredo. There's one with Lila and both of her parents. And here's a guy I don't recognize."

She held up the photo for Sam. Lila and the young man were embracing, her arms around his waist, his over her shoulder, both facing the camera. Lila's hair was a bit shorter then, falling to her shoulders. "I don't know him either," Sam said. "He isn't one of the current group we've met. He's got great posture, almost a military look about him, don't you think?"

Kelly took another look and nodded.

"We could ask her mother about him. They look like more than school chums or drinking buddies."

Movement at the church caught Kelly's attention and she nudged Sam. But the open door only discharged one person before it closed again, one of the smokers from earlier.

"Thirty minutes. He's got it bad," Kelly observed.

Sam, meanwhile, had paged through the diary from the back, coming to Lila's most recent entries. The girl apparently hadn't thought to date the entries, so it was anyone's guess how long ago she'd written them. Sam began reading, looking for any references to Taos.

There were none, but one entry caught her eye.

Maybe if I tell D he gave me that ring from his grandmother, he'll think he actually proposed. He was pretty wasted Saturday night.

It went along with Danny's version of things, but what was Lila going to do when he said okay, we're engaged, start wearing the ring. She'd obviously seen it somewhere but she didn't actually have it. Pauline had confirmed that much.

The diary entry went on: *I can always get a guy to do what I want, just like R.*

"Which of the friends has the initial R?" Sam asked.

Kelly ticked them off on her fingers silently as she pondered the list. "I can't think of any. Is it a first name or last?"

"I'm assuming first name by the way she wrote this. But she could be referring to a last name or a nickname, for that matter."

"Or to that unknown guy in the photo?"

"Maybe … this is one of her last diary entries and she's mostly talking about Danny at this point."

"So she was stringing along two men at once?"

"That's another possibility." Sam leaned back in her seat. "This is getting complicated."

"Mom, I doubt any mystery gets solved because something was spelled out verbatim in a diary."

Sam laughed. "Okay, you're right. I need to keep reading."

She turned back to the book and was partway through the next page when Kelly elbowed her arm. "They're coming out. What do we do now?"

A white casket topped with pink flowers was being wheeled to a hearse at the curb in front of the church. "Follow to the cemetery?"

"I'm game if you are."

Sam counted twenty-five people, including the friends they knew and the parents, trailing behind the hearse and dispersing toward other vehicles. Margaret leaned heavily on the arm of a man, one of the smokers, who handed her into a black limousine parked at the curb. Miguel's entourage consisted of four men, two in dark suits, like his own, and two in uniform. The uniforms chatted and interacted with the others as friends. This was no official duty today. Someone had mentioned that Lila's father was a cop—Sally Flores. A few other key answers slotted into place.

Kelly started the car and watched as the hearse and two limos drove slowly southbound. Cars from the parking lot fell in line, although a fair number turned in the opposite direction. During a break in the traffic, Kelly joined the cemetery-bound contingent.

In less than ten minutes, the vehicles began pulling over. A three-foot-high rock wall enclosed the cemetery, a dirt patch filled with white crosses, with a few scraggly trees around the bordering edges. A green awning tent stood over an open grave fifty yards into the enclosed acreage.

"What do you think, Mom? Looks like there is no way at all to keep out of sight if we walk in there."

"No, that won't work. Let's just observe and take note of who's here. I can't see any point in trying to talk with them here anyway. They'll stay a short while and then go somewhere for a meal."

"Well, there are the two limos with the parents. Those two are definitely in his and hers camps today, aren't they?"

"The men hanging around with Miguel must be co-workers. They have that look, more than relatives. And I'm guessing the man Margaret is leaning on is her new husband, significant other, or whatever."

A few younger people had come along, but neither Sam nor Kelly recognized any of them. School friends, probably. Even Patsy hadn't opted for this portion of the ceremony, most likely due to her study schedule. The other few who trailed along the dusty pathway were presumably the parents' friends who'd known Lila from childhood.

Sam felt a sudden wash of sadness. Twenty-five years old, at the prime of her beauty, just beginning her young adult life, and Lila had left this world with so few true friends. Had she really been so abrasive as to deserve this? She and Kelly exchanged a regretful look then drove away.

Chapter 32

O kay, what evidence do we have and where can we go from here?" Kelly asked. They'd arrived back in their comfy hotel room and kicked off their shoes. "Since neither of us can stay here in San Antonio indefinitely, we need to make the most of our time."

She was missing Ana and Scott desperately, Sam knew. As for herself, home life at the ranch beckoned. On the other hand, she wanted to stay until she could go back with something that could be of real help to Danny.

"Let's spread out everything where we can look it over, and we'll make notes," Sam said.

Kelly grabbed her little notebook. Sam covered the surface of the coffee table with photos and set the diary beside them. From her jacket pockets, Kelly brought out two ballpoint pens and a matchbook she had retrieved from Lila's purses and pockets at the apartment.

"Wow, I haven't seen one of these in ages," Sam said, picking up the matchbook. "When I was a kid, every restaurant had them printed up and there would be a big bowl of them near the door."

"That one's from Thrashed," Kelly pointed out. "I certainly didn't see a bowl of them, but Lila must have picked it up there."

One of the pens was imprinted with The Gap logo, obviously brought home from her work. The other said Manny's Bar & Grill: San Antonio's Finest Steaks. Sam dialed the phone number on it and got a recording informing her that they opened for dinner at four o'clock.

"Maybe if we go early it won't be too busy and we can find someone to talk to," Kelly suggested.

"Hungry again already?"

"Well ... maybe a little."

Manny's Bar & Grill proved to be a hometown version of some of those big-name chains, but Manny gave it the personal touch. By the number of vehicles in the parking lot at four-thirty on a weeknight, it was a success. The women walked into a large room, decorated in hardwoods, plush fabric booths, and historic photos of the Alamo on the walls. They'd agreed in advance that the most likely place Danny's group of friends would have hung out was the bar, so they requested seats there.

The bartender, it turned out, was Manny himself, a fifty-something man with touches of gray in his dark hair, who performed his tasks behind the bar with quick, efficient movements. The women ordered drinks and food, then Sam pulled out the group photos of Danny's friends.

"Yeah, I know this bunch," Manny said, taking a look. "Some are regulars. I think this one has been coming in here since he was a kid with his parents. A couple of these, actually."

Sergio and Danny.

"The others kind of float in and out, you know."

Sam found one group shot with Lila in it and pointed to her. "This young woman—was she with them a lot?"

Manny shook his head. "Not until, I'd say, maybe four or five months ago."

"With the whole group or just one of the guys?"

His hand waggled back and forth. "Sometimes one, sometimes all of them." He picked up the group photo again and stared intently. "For awhile she was dating one dude. I'm not sure if he's in this picture."

Sam held out the one with Lila and straight-posture guy.

"Yeah, she was with him a time or two. They'd come in without the rest of the group, but that's not the one I'm thinking of either. Sorry, sometimes the customers become sort of a blur when you've been doing this twenty years."

Their burgers and fries arrived, and Manny turned his attention to another patron at the far end of the bar. He came back about five minutes later.

"You know … one thing that stands out in my mind was an evening when some of this group was in here. They were usually pretty well-mannered kids, liked to drink and laugh, but things never got ugly, you know. But one night there was some kind of a blowup."

Sam's eyes widened. "Fistfight?"

"No, no. More like a girlfriend/boyfriend thing, and it was that girl you asked about, the one with the long dark hair. The group was at that table over there, and I remember her standing up real sudden. Bumped the table and tipped over a drink, and one of the other girls shrieked when it spilled on her. That's what got my attention. So the girl who was standing was shaking her finger at a guy and yelling. Something like 'How can you do this to me?' and then she went flouncing out the door."

"Did the guy follow her? Like, was he apologizing or was he yelling back at her ..." Kelly asked.

"You know, I just don't remember. I must have gotten busy with someone else about then. As long as they weren't busting up the place, I minded my own business."

"And the guy she was mad at—can you remember which one he was, from this group?"

Manny shook his head. "Like I said, she was shaking her finger, they were all staring at her. Hard to tell which one she was yelling at."

He moved away again, and Sam looked back at the picture. It was pretty much the same group they'd met at Thrashed, plus a guy she didn't recognize, minus Abby who must not have joined them that particular night. Or maybe Abby was the one with the camera.

"This photo kind of stands out, doesn't it?" Kelly said, wiping her fingers on her napkin and pointing at the one of Lila and the man with the straight posture. "He doesn't seem to be part of the regular gang."

"I was just thinking the same thing." Sam had finished her burger and pushed the plate aside. "And I'm wondering who we might contact to find out who he is."

"Maybe there was a romance and a breakup, and this guy got furious over Lila's moving on with Danny? Furious enough to track her down and confront her."

The man in the photo had an edge about him, tougher, more mature than the high school chums. Sam considered Kelly's idea.

"If he wasn't part of their high school crowd, maybe

Lila's mother would be the one to ask." Sam pulled out her phone and dialed Margaret's number. It was answered on the first ring.

"I'm back home now, and if you want to come down here, I'll take a look at the picture."

"Could I send it over the phone?"

"Sorry, I don't have a cell phone that works that way."

Kelly tapped Sam on the arm. "It's only a couple hours away. Unless you want to stay over another night."

Their flight was scheduled for the following morning, and Sam didn't want to stay over, any more than Kelly did.

"We can be there by eight. Is that okay?"

Margaret hesitated. It had been a long day with the funeral and everything, but she agreed and gave them her address.

Chapter 33

It was slightly after eight when Kelly pulled up in front of the large, two-story brick and white-trimmed home in Nuevo Laredo. A tired-looking Margaret opened the door. She wore a plush robe and slippers, and although her hair was still sprayed into place, her face bore the ravages of tears. Her almost-perky demeanor from the other day in Taos had completely disappeared.

"Sorry it's getting late," Sam began. "I know it's been a rough day for you."

"Anytime Miguel and Howard are in the same place, it's a rough day for me." Margaret glanced toward the top of the staircase, then showed them into a living room that looked like something out of *House Beautiful*. Her new husband seemed more prosperous than a cop. Maybe money was part of the reason behind the split.

Sam pulled out the photo of Lila with her arms around the other man. "Do you know who he is?"

"Of course. That's Richard Potter. They dated for quite a while." Margaret gazed at the couple fondly. "I always thought he would be the one to marry my daughter."

"What happened?" Kelly blurted. "Sorry, that's probably none of my business."

Margaret shrugged. "Lila. I guess she just changed her mind. She got so set on moving to San Antonio with her dad, but Richie couldn't move there because of his work. And even though it wasn't that far away, they just drifted apart."

"Was there someone else in her life at that time? Maybe she officially broke it off with Richard?" Sam remembered Lila's diary comment about getting a guy to do anything she wanted, 'just like R.' Maybe he was too compliant, too much of a pushover for her?

Margaret handed the photo back and shook her head sadly. "I don't know. Lila could be secretive. Only this week I found out how many times her father fixed her traffic tickets and that he got her off of a DUI charge. She didn't share things with me very much. Richard stayed in touch with me. He's in the Marines and comes by anytime he's home on leave."

"Did he know Lila was dating Danny?"

"He did. Apparently, she told him."

To rub his face in the fact that she didn't need him anymore?

"He'd heard that Danny moved to Taos, again most likely through Lila. He told me this when he last came here to the house."

Maybe Lila's chasing off after someone who didn't want her was the final straw for Richard and he'd come to

New Mexico for a showdown? Sam tried to come up with a way to phrase the question gently.

"No," Margaret said quietly. "Richard deployed to Afghanistan the day before she died. I've written to him. It didn't seem like the kind of news to send by text message, if you know what I mean."

Sam and Kelly offered their sympathies and left.

"Well, that rules out Richard as a suspect for the murder," Sam said as they got into the car.

"I hate to say it, but I was kind of hoping it would be him." Kelly was yawning as she took her seat.

Sam reached into the back seat and pulled the carved box from Kelly's pack. "Wake yourself up before we start the drive back."

She did the same with the box from her own pack. "Yes, the pieces certainly could have fit for this Richard being the killer. Jealousy, holding out hope of getting Lila back, knowing that she had followed Danny to Taos. But I suppose the US military is a pretty infallible alibi."

They arrived at the outskirts of San Antonio shortly before eleven.

"Are you sleepy, Mom?"

Sam glanced over and saw that Kelly seemed wired for action. She felt the same.

"I'm fine. In fact I was thinking we might get one more chance to talk to Sergio. He works late, remember, so maybe we could meet up, show him the pictures, remind him of the incident at Manny's and see what he remembers about that."

"Call him."

Sergio told Sam he'd worked until ten and was settling in at home, but they were welcome to come by.

"He sounded tired from taking inventory so late, but at least he's willing," Sam said. She told the GPS the address he'd given her.

His apartment was half of a duplex in a neighborhood that had seen better days. Most of the flat-roofed houses on small lots were probably rentals now, based on the condition of the yards and the number of motorcycles parked where grass used to grow. Sergio must have been watching from the front window; he opened the door when they set foot on the tiny porch.

He wore loose sweats and his damp hair looked as if he'd recently showered.

"I was just having a beer before bedtime," he said. "You want one?"

"No thanks, we'll be quick." Sam pulled out the packet of photos. "We found these at Lila's and wondered if you recognize any of the people we don't know."

He reached out and took the prints. His expression softened when he looked at the group photos. "Wow, this has been awhile. These two have to be from our high school days. Danny must have given them to Lila. She wasn't part of the gang back then."

Sam stood beside him and pointed to the faces, naming the ones she thought she recognized. He nodded. "Yeah, you got most of them. This guy is Jacob Brown—he wasn't at Thrashed the other night, but he's around town still. This is Javier Montoya—he's away at college in Dallas, doesn't get back here a whole lot these days."

Sam showed the photo of Lila with her arms around Richard Potter. "We heard that she dated him before she moved to town."

"Yeah. He came around a few times, went out with

all of us at least once, but I guess it was pretty much over between them."

Kelly spoke up. "The owner at Manny's Bar & Grill said there was an incident once, Lila yelling at a guy in the group, then getting up and storming out. Do you remember that time?"

Sergio shook his head. "No, not at all. I must not have been there."

"Do you think it could have been Richard she was breaking up with?"

He shrugged. "It even could have been Danny. I tell you, the girl's moods were all over the place. People say hormonal—well, if that's the case Lila was off the charts. Sweet, bitchy, hot and cold. It didn't take me very long not to trust anything she said."

Even her own mother had described her as devious.

"And Danny—did he play into that drama?"

"Danny's a peacemaker. He doesn't like conflict. His whole family is like that. Everyone keeps their cool and there's no shouting or fighting at his parents' place. Lila— kind of the opposite. I never knew her parents, but I heard stuff. They get off on yelling and screaming, it seems like."

"And yet Patsy seems to really like Lila."

"Patsy's a sweetheart and she doesn't want to believe the worst about anyone. Look at her, going to law school so she can help out needy women and their kids. That's just Patsy. You gotta love her, but don't go by her impressions of somebody like Lila. She'll give *everybody* the benefit of the doubt."

He handed the photos back to Sam, picked up his beer bottle, and took a swig.

"Is there anything else you can think of, anything that

would help us figure out how to get Danny out of this mess? Maybe another man she dated besides Danny or Richard, someone who might have held a grudge?" Sam asked.

He started to shake his head, but paused. "I don't know if this relates at all, but there was something …" He set the bottle on the kitchen counter and paced the length of the room. "Something's coming back to me. It happened at work. I was on the forklift in the back lot of the lumberyard, and I had just stopped. You know, noisy equipment and when it quits there's this sudden silence. Well, I heard two men's voices. I couldn't see them behind a big stack of pallets, but one was my boss and I think the other man was a customer. I caught something like 'track that no-good scum to New Mexico.' When I walked toward the building, I saw that my boss was talking to a cop. It was the cop who'd said that."

"A cop. Could it have been Miguel Contreras? You know what he looks like, right?"

"Yeah … you know, yeah, it could have been."

Sam and Kelly exchanged a look.

"You asked about whether Lila was dating anybody else … you mean after Danny left?"

"Anytime. Before, during, or after."

"I think so. I can't be sure. Whoever it was either wasn't part of our group or he was keeping real quiet about it."

"And you think this because …?"

"Lila. It's how she was. She had to have a guy in her life, and it makes sense that once Danny was gone a couple months, she would find someone else. Richard wasn't coming around. Just saying."

"One last question, and then we'll let you get to bed,"

Sam said, remembering one other piece of the puzzle. "Is there anyone in your group who seems to have come into a lot of money in the last few days?"

"Money—wow, no." She carefully watched Sergio's face but his immediate chuckle made her believe him.

Chapter 34

"What was I thinking, booking us on a seven a.m. flight out?" Kelly said, stuffing clothes into her airline duffle bag.

"You were thinking you can't wait to be home, and this way we'll be there by noon. And neither of us was quite planning such a late night tonight, although I'm still not sleepy."

Sam had emptied the closet and neatly folded most of her things. In the morning she would simply need to grab her toiletry bag and make sure the case evidence—diary and photos—were safely in her backpack purse.

"I'm still thinking about what Sergio said and it's making sense," she told Kelly. "If Lila's father, the cop, had ways of tracking Danny through his and Lila's phone and text messages or maybe even his spending, it would have made it easy for Lila to know exactly where he went."

It made sense *and* might be a clue worth considering, but they were both exhausted now, so they crawled into their beds and turned out the lights.

They had a little sleep, an early awakening, and a mood of discouragement during the flight. They retrieved Sam's car from the airport parking lot and hit the road northbound.

"I feel like we have the answer somewhere," Sam said, once they had cleared the Albuquerque traffic and were on the open road. "We talked to so many people. What are we missing in the clues?"

"Could we be on the wrong track in thinking the killer is one of Lila's romantic conquests? What if it's a woman?"

"We can't rule out anyone, but strangulation ... that takes a lot of strength and being able to overpower the victim. It's not typically a woman's method—at least not according to things Beau told me over the years."

"So we concentrate on the male suspects but keep ourselves open to the idea it could be anyone."

"I think so."

Kelly was paging through the diary while Sam drove. "So, which of the men that we know about could have done it—Mom, what if it's none of them? What if a random stranger got into Lila's hotel room and killed her?"

"That's more rare than you think. Of course, every investigation starts out with the possibility that the killer could be anyone in the world, but motive, means and opportunity rule out many and narrow it down from *anyone*. Unfortunately, our Danny fits all three criteria, while most of those we just talked to are, at the very least, lacking opportunity. Strangling can't very well happen long-distance."

"But any of them could have made the trip. We're covering the distance in less than half a day. By driving the whole way …" Kelly tapped a query into her phone. "It's a little over ten hours for a person following the speed limit. It's doable for any of them."

"You're not exactly narrowing the field," Sam said with a chuckle. "But we'll figure it out. We know it's not Richard Potter, and we're confident it's not Danny. Once I'm home again I'll comb through the diary for clues and see if I can narrow it down some more."

When she pulled into the driveway at the Victorian, the front door flew open and Scott and Ana came rushing out, all smiles and shrieks. Even Eliza stepped out and jumped up to the porch railing.

Sam came inside long enough to pull out the little gift she'd brought—a book with the pictorial history of the Alamo. "Your daddy will tell you all about this place in your history lesson," she said.

"How did you ladies enjoy seeing the Alamo close up?" Scott asked.

"Well … didn't actually get there. Things stayed fairly busy. For now, I'll leave you three to catch up and I'd better go find out what Beau is up to."

Whether he'd somehow managed to obtain bail for Danny, that was the bigger question.

The ranch looked peaceful under the midday sun. The two horses grazed in the far pasture, while the dozen or so head of cattle meandered toward the small pond near the northern fence. Beau's truck sat beside the barn, where he was unloading bales of hay. He turned and smiled when he saw her vehicle.

"Hey, darlin'—missed you." He dropped the bale hooks

and came over to help Sam with her bag. "Nice trip?"

"It was. Fun to spend time with Kelly, but I'm not sure if we found much to help Danny's case. I still have some materials to go through." She held the door open while he carried the bag inside. "How about you? Are you managing okay?"

"Yeah, pretty well. I guess you figured out Danny isn't here. The judge didn't grant bail. I can get along for a while without a hand, but if we don't get him out soon, I'll need to look at hiring someone else."

Sam met his eyes, her face sad. "I've got questions for him—do you suppose he'll be allowed a visitor?"

"I'll make a call, see if I can get you in," he promised.

* * *

The new county courthouse and jail facility was pristine and secure. Sam presented her ID and the front reception officer checked to be sure she was on the preapproved list. Beau had told her she would be allowed a thirty-minute visit, Danny's sole visitor for the week. Apparently, her clothing also passed inspection, and she was allowed into the visitation room.

Danny looked smaller and less confident in these surroundings, not the straight-shouldered young man astride a horse or tossing hay bales as if they were nothing.

"Hey," Sam said.

"Hey."

She asked if he was being treated all right and whether he needed anything she might be allowed to bring. He shook his head and gave a crooked smile. "A release order would be nice."

"I've got just a half hour, and a lot of questions." She briefly wondered whether she should have contacted Delia Sanchez before coming down here.

But the attorney would have surely set the schedule and monitored every question and answer. Sam wanted to get to the heart of it now. She briefly filled him in on her visits with his friends and family, including his parents' well wishes and the fact that Patsy had been cooperative in sharing information.

"First off, I need to ask about that big withdrawal from your bank account. You knew about that?"

He nodded.

"When did you learn about it?"

"The day it happened. My bank sends me text alerts to be sure everything is okay. Unfortunately, I didn't check my messages until later in the evening, so the money had been gone from the account for several hours."

"It was an online transaction, right? Danny, I have to ask—who do you think took the money?"

"My first thought was—Lila. Unless some hacker from Ukraine or someplace targeted my account. Nobody in my family is very sharp with stuff like that."

"Did she know your password?"

"I've thought about that. I never gave it to her, but she was pretty good at figuring things out. She could have guessed it."

"Why would she take the money?"

He ran both hands through his hair, leaving tufts sticking out on top. "Guessing—I would think maybe as leverage to get me back to San Antonio and to go ahead with the wedding. She kept talking about that, once she found me here. About how we had all these wedding plans—which I knew nothing about."

Sam could see he was getting agitated so she changed focus.

"I found some photos among her things," she said, pulling the pictures from the envelope she'd carried in.

He glanced at the group photos of his friends, a smile curving his mouth.

"What about this one?" Sam handed over the one of Lila and Richard Potter. "Do you know who he is?"

Danny shook his head, looking puzzled.

"His name is Richard Potter. Lila's mother identified him and said he and Lila were pretty serious right before she moved to San Antonio."

He shrugged. "Don't know anything about that."

Okay. Sam believed him. "Could there have been any other men in her life around the same time? I found a diary and she refers to people sometimes by just an initial or a nickname. Did you pick up any hints about there being someone else?"

"She talked like I was the moon and the stars to her. Never a hint of fooling around."

A five-minute warning came over the speaker system, advising visitors that time was almost up. Sam gathered up the photos and ended the visit by passing along the greetings and well-wishes from Sergio, Abby, and Patsy.

"Is my mom doing okay?" Danny asked. "I've only talked to her once. She says they'll come for my trial."

Sally had apparently not mentioned his father's health scare. "She told me the same thing. But hang in there. We're still looking. And the minute we find evidence that could get you released, I'm all over it."

He wasn't allowed to reach across the table to touch

her hand, but he did a prayer gesture and thanked Sam over and over. The sadness in his eyes, when the guard came to take him away, just about cut through her heart.

Outside in her SUV, Sam placed a call to Delia Sanchez. On the theory that it was better to beg forgiveness than ask permission, she told the attorney about her visit to Danny. Delia quizzed her about what he'd said, seemed satisfied but grumpy at Sam's answers. When Sam mentioned the bank withdrawal, Delia spoke up.

"Yeah, well, the sheriff has also discovered it. The money disappeared the day before Lila died, and in their minds, it's an even greater motive for Danny to have killed her."

"Crap. Sorry, I—"

"I know. I'm going to make the argument that if Danny didn't attempt to get the money back, he didn't have a strong motive to kill her. But I have no idea if that's going to fly."

Sam ended the call feeling more down than ever. Then a plan began to form.

Chapter 35

Sam drove to the copy shop on Paseo del Pueblo Sur and carried all her hard-won evidence inside. She hated to let go of what she had gathered, but all of this was needed for Danny's case. At the self-serve copier, she laid the diary open and photocopied all the pages. Then she set the photos on the glass and made copies of them too.

Purchasing a large brown envelope, she tucked the originals into it and enclosed a note. She had debated with herself during this whole process—to whom should she give the evidence? And while she would have trusted Beau in a nano-second to fairly apply everything he knew to solving the case, she still felt she didn't know Evan very well. What if he, as had been known to happen in other places, buried or 'lost' this evidence in his zeal to close the case and strike a Win on his record?

She didn't dare take that chance.

She sealed the envelope and drove to Delia Sanchez's office, where she asked the receptionist to deliver it directly to the attorney herself.

With that weight off her shoulders, Sam decided to run by Sweet's Sweets and see how things were going. Despite her having been less active in the business these past couple of years, the bakery was still her baby.

She parked out front this time and paused on the sidewalk to admire the window displays. She and Becky had planned how it would look for the upcoming Easter week, and she was pleased to see how well her decorator had implemented the designs and how the staff had set up the cute eggs, chicks, and bunnies in appealing poses. The window on the opposite side of the front door went with the religious theme, a cake in the shape of the historic San Francisco de Asis church, sprays of lilies spread over the flooring, and an elaborate cross of white. Since real chocolate couldn't withstand the temperatures in the window, everything on display was created from foam and paper. But the royal icing was real and any of the pieces could be made to a customer's specifications.

Jen greeted her at the door with a mug of coffee and a creampuff. "You look in need of a pick-me-up," she said with a warm smile.

"Thanks." Sam bit into the creampuff and moaned. "Julio did something different with these. Amaretto in the filling? Or is it Frangelico? Anyway, I have to go pay my compliments to the baker."

Movement outside the window caught her attention, and she turned to see Sheriff Richards' cruiser pull up next door. Evan got out and sent a look toward Sam's car. Did she imagine a smug look on his face? But no—he spotted her inside the bakery and walked over.

"Tell Beau that congrats are in order," Evan said, opening the door and leaning in. "Looks like I've got my first murder case wrapped up."

"Evan, with all due respect …" which was none at this moment, "… there are other viable suspects, and I don't think you've taken a close enough look at any of them."

"Sam, you need to remember you're not in the middle of department business any more."

When had things turned into a contest between them?

"In the middle or not, a friend is under arrest for something he didn't do. Have you actually looked into the character of the victim?"

"You're going to tell me about the gaslighting, that she treated him so badly it was okay for him to kill her?" He stepped inside now and drew himself up tall.

Sam was glad no customers happened to be there. She could feel Jen shrinking away and hoping to become invisible.

"Of course not. Killing someone is not okay. But neither is ignoring evidence that doesn't point directly at your suspect."

"What evidence?"

Oops. Sam wasn't about to get into explaining what she'd found. "You need to talk to Danny's attorney. Danny Flores did his best to get away from this girl who was making his life miserable, and I think she used her father's connections as a San Antonio police officer to track Danny here. She tried extortion, and when that didn't work, she stole money directly from his account."

Evan got a smirk on his face. "You're making my case for me, Sam."

"You didn't let me finish. I believe there's evidence that

she tried the same things with other men—other *suspects*. Evan, be open-minded about this. Check with Delia Sanchez and check with those who know Miguel Contreras in the SAPD. At least consider the possibility that another man came into the picture. That's all I'm asking."

He puffed out his chest and stared her straight in the eye. "You need to mind your own business and stop butting in, unless you want to be facing obstruction of justice charges." Then he walked out the door.

Sam felt her mouth drop open. *Really, Evan? You were a good cop with a sterling reputation when you came here. What's going on?*

"Plus—what obstruction? I'm finding better clues than you've got!" She shouted at his retreating back.

Jen's eyes were wide.

"Sorry. I should not have let him get to me like that," Sam said. She picked up her coffee mug and brought it shakily to her mouth. Set it down again. Took a long breath and shook her hands to dissipate the tension.

Just when she was deciding whether to follow Evan and try to talk logically or to just blow off the argument, her cell phone rang.

Chapter 36

It was Patsy Flores, and she sounded as rushed as ever. "I've got about five minutes before I need to leave for class, but I found something I think you should know about. It could help Danny's defense."

Sam watched Evan get into his cruiser and drive away. She walked out to her car. "Tell me."

"I found two cell phones. They were in a kitchen drawer, toward the back. They must be Lila's—no one else has been around, and they sure aren't mine. They're cheap things, the kind you can buy at Walmart or someplace and then add minutes with a phone card."

What the cop shows on TV called a burner.

"Do they contain anything?" She sat in the driver's seat, out of the chilly breeze.

Patsy put Sam on speaker and she could hear busy little

sounds in the background. "Let me see ... this one's got a charge—it lights up."

"Can you look at the contacts list?"

"There's no password, apparently. Yeah, here's a button ... Hm. One person on the contacts list."

"Who is it?" Sam caught herself holding her breath.

"It says S. Just an initial. Let me look at the recent calls." Patsy paused a second. "None. She must have erased them."

"What about the other phone?" Sam was thinking hard to figure out the purpose for two of these throwaways. She knew Lila had another phone with her when she'd come to Taos; presumably that was her main one.

"Okay, this one comes on too, but it's got very little battery left. Contacts—same. One person, shown as R."

Richard Potter? But who the heck was S?

"Oops, that one died," Patsy said. "When I get back later, I'll see if I have a charger that will fit it."

"Thanks. Now, the working one—no recent calls, but are there text messages?" It had been Lila's preferred means of contact with Danny, after all.

"Oh yeah, *lots* of texts."

Sam grabbed paper and pen from her bag. "Read them to me."

Patsy hedged. "I gotta be quick. Need to leave here in one minute."

"Read fast."

"Okay. Most recent one ... um, well, that's unrepeatable. Basically this S person telling Lila to get lost."

Sam assured Patsy she was familiar with the F-word and its many uses.

"Yeah, that's what it says. Anyway, before that Lila says:

I'm keeping it. Need $20K for expenses."

"And before that?"

"Hm. Several back and forth with 'yes you did' and 'no I didn't' types of things. Wait ... oh boy. Lila's telling S that she's pregnant. She attached a picture of the test stick with the little plus-sign on it."

"What are the dates on these messages?"

"Four weeks ago is when she made the big announcement. The bickering was at that time, the demand for money about two weeks ago."

"Right before she came here looking for Danny."

"I guess. Look, sorry, I need to get going or I'll be late."

"Okay, one thing real quick. First, guard those phones—somebody knows about these communications and could come around, trying to destroy the evidence."

"I can stick them in my computer bag so they're with me all day."

"We need to get this evidence to someone who can make a difference." Sam thought about Evan, but the argument with him still hung over her. More than ever she wondered if he would let the phones and the messages get lost in the shuffle of evidence so he and the prosecutor could get a swift trial for Danny? "Can you get to a FedEx or UPS office?"

"Sure, after today's classes."

"This is important, Patsy. I want you to send the phones to Danny's attorney. She'll know what to do with them. Package them up, and send them to ..." She rummaged for the lawyer's card and read off Delia Sanchez's address. "Include a note saying you were Lila's roommate and you found these in the apartment. I'll reimburse you for the shipping cost."

"He's my brother, Sam. I'll do whatever I can to help him." Clearly, Patsy's belief in Lila's innocence and goodness had flown straight out the window.

"Thanks. If you'll send me a quick message with the tracking number, I'll get with Delia and let her know what's coming. I'm excited. This definitely proves there was someone else out there with a motive."

If only she had a clue who it was.

She looked up to see Riki standing in the doorway at Puppy Chic, a forlorn look on her face, eyes a bit red. Sam got out of her car and walked over.

"I'm sorry if I upset Evan," she said. "I shouldn't—"

"Forgive him for his tone," Riki said, seemingly unaware of the argument her husband had with Sam. "It's this whole … pregnancy thing, and the fact we can't seem to do this, and now we're talking IVF, but that's horrifically expensive, and every time we talk about it, we both get upset, and—"

"Riki—it's okay. I'm so sorry about your struggles, really I am. It's going to be okay, no matter how it goes."

Each woman had her own journey in the baby game, Sam realized. She'd gotten pregnant when she least wanted to, thirty-odd years ago, but everything had turned out fine and she couldn't ask for her life to be on a better track. Now, here was a friend who desperately wanted this and it wasn't happening for them. And then there was Lila—what was her story?

She shook off the thoughts, gave Riki an extra-long hug, and wished her well. As far as her own words with Evan, that was another subject for another time. Riki dabbed her eyes with the cuff of her shirt and thanked Sam, ready to get back to her day.

Sam looked around. Jen had said everything was under control at the bakery, Riki seemed back on firm ground, and the only one in the neighborhood she hadn't checked in with was Ivan at Mysterious Happenings. She walked down to the bookshop.

"Miss Samantha, happy to be seeing you again. Rumor say you were in Texas."

"Rumor?" Oh, right. Becky would have brought the treats for Ivan's Chocoholics Anonymous book club while she was away. "You are right, Ivan. And I must say it feels good to be home again. I need a book for Ana."

"She is ready for *War and Peace* now?" Ivan laughed.

"Not quite. I'm thinking along the lines of *The Boxcar Kids*. She has discovered a love of mysteries."

He waved her toward the children's section, although Sam knew exactly where to find everything in the inventory she had nearly memorized.

She was staring at the lower shelf when the bell at the front door chimed and she heard a familiar voice. Rising, she peered over the top of the shelving units. "Hey, Rupert, how's it going?"

He ambled down the aisle between the stacks and stopped to see which book she'd chosen for Ana.

"By the way," he murmured, "the love potion ..." He gave a thumbs-up. "Tres magnifique! Jimmy and I are ... an item."

"Very good. I'm happy for you." Sam wondered if the potion itself was still causing this effect or if it had provided the needed spark and the two lovers had started their own fire. She would probably never know.

They chatted for a few more minutes before Rupert headed toward the section of blank journals and Sam for the register where she paid for her book. She arrived at Kelly's as her daughter was making sandwiches for lunch.

"Can you stay? It's easy to put two more slices of bread on the production line. You only have to say peanut butter or ham."

"Absolutely. Ham, please."

"Did someone say peanut butter?" came Scott's voice as he walked in through the dining room door.

"Yay, peanut butter!" Ana shouted, zipping past him to be first in the kitchen. "I want strawberry jam on mine."

"You got it." Kelly reached for the jar that was standing at the ready.

Ana had already turned to Sam, noticing the bookshop bag in her hand. "A new book—yay!"

"After lunch. Peanut butter and pages don't go together too well."

"Jam and paper, even less so," said Scott, taking the bag and stashing it on top of the fridge.

"Are you happy I brought your mommy back home?" Sam asked.

Ana responded by grabbing Kelly around the legs.

"I take that as a 'yes' and now we'd better let her finish the sandwiches." Sam found napkins and two bags of chips in the pantry and told Ana to put them on the kitchen table.

Scott poured iced tea for the adults and fruit juice for his daughter. "So, Kel says there were some interesting interviews in your case?"

Sam waved off the question. "Yes, but enough about that. How's the new book coming along?"

Set an author onto the topic of his own writing and an entire day can be filled with details. Scott said he had turned in the manuscript and his editor was thrilled. "She's already got the illustrator working on the key moments, you know the little drawings at the beginning of each chapter. Maddie Plimpton is at Taos Pueblo in this one, and she's learning some valuable Native American beliefs at the same time she solves a mystery."

"Your fans will love it."

"Let's hope so. Ten-year-olds can be amazingly worshipful or amazingly cruel in their comments." But Scott seemed to have them hooked. "And now I've started outlining the next one in the series," he said as he picked up his sandwich.

Ana chewed through half her sandwich, nonstop, her eyes darting to the top of the fridge every few moments. By the time she finished her lunch, she was nudging her father to talk less and eat more. Sam had to laugh. Her granddaughter's words sounded so much like her own to Kelly at age four.

Five minutes later, Scott carried his plate to the sink and retrieved the book bag. "Okay, little miss, we are off to have a story and then a little nap."

Ana's look said *Good luck with that.*

Kelly and Sam watched them leave. Eliza remained near the table, staring up at Sam with her wise green eyes. "What he really meant was, 'We'll read a story and then daddy wants a nap.' But I'll go in the living room later and find them both cuddled up asleep on the big sofa."

Sam nibbled at the last of her potato chips.

"Okay, Mom, I have a feeling there's more you want to say." It wasn't a question.

Sam filled her in on the visit to Danny, the call from Patsy, and finally the argument with Evan.

"Wow. Busy morning." Kelly stacked their plates. "You

know you need to make up with him, right?"

"Evan? Yeah … I suppose I do."

"Well, it's not likely he'll come to you. Reach out, Mom. You'll feel better about it."

Not to mention that she'd never learn any more inside info on this case or any future one if she wasn't in the good graces of the sheriff. And there was one crucial fact she needed to know right now. Was Lila actually pregnant at the time of her death?

"I'll stop by the station on my way home."

Chapter 37

The make-up talk with Evan went well. She apologized for her sharp tone; he apologized for letting a personal mood sneak into his policing work. They shook hands, turned it into a hug, and left as friends. And, most importantly, Sam was able to ask the question on her mind. According to the autopsy, Lila Contreras was not pregnant at the time of her death.

Sam pondered the answer. It seemed Danny and whoever else Lila had been texting were both off the hook. Unless she had terminated the pregnancy and hoped to keep bluffing the men. But, no, Sam decided. The medical investigator's report would have surely picked up the fact of a recent pregnancy. She arrived home, still thinking about it.

She was checking the supply of eggs in the fridge,

thinking about making an omelet for dinner, when the phone chirped with an incoming message. Patsy had shipped the two cell phones to the lawyer, and her message contained the tracking information. Sam phoned the attorney and they set an appointment to go over this new evidence together the next afternoon.

* * *

The small firm of Sanchez, Miller, and Sanchez occupied a suite of offices in an unimposing one-story adobe on a side street near the courthouse. Sam carried a small box of chocolate chip, sugar, and peanut butter cookies and walked into her meeting with Delia. The receptionist was eyeing the box and promised to put them in the break room.

"Have you gone through the messages on the phones yet?" Sam asked, once she and Delia were alone.

"Beyond plugging each of them into a charger, I haven't had a spare moment. They'll be new to both of us." The lawyer handed Sam a pair of latex gloves and one of the phones. "I don't want our prints muddying up the picture when the prosecutor talks about these. Jurors can get easily confused."

"Patsy said each phone has only one person listed in the contacts. I'm hoping once we get into the text messages themselves, it becomes apparent who they are. What do you think? Take them in chronological order or start with the most recent?"

"My brain works better in sequence," Delia said, "I'm going to scroll to the beginning."

"Okay, me too." Sam opened the inexpensive flip

phone and found the contact list. She found 'S' and a phone number. "What would happen if I called the number?"

"Give it a try."

The phone rang several times before going to a generic voicemail message. Sam hung up. No point in alerting him that someone in Taos was looking for him. When Delia did the same with the other phone, she got a recorded message: "You got Rich—speak."

"Cute. I assume this is Richard Potter?"

"Maybe the number can be traced to him. Just because Lila bought these disposable phones, it doesn't mean the men at the other end of the call weren't using their regular ones, something with an account registered to their name."

"That's a good point, Sam." Delia drummed her fingers on her desk for a moment. "It's going to take a warrant or subpoena to get the cell provider to let go of that info. If we can't get it, though, most certainly the sheriff can. I'm adding that to my list of official items we're asking for."

"Um, wait a second. My son-in-law said something a while back … I think there's a way." Sam pulled out her own phone and called Scott.

He started to go into a spiel about how to do a reverse number lookup, but must have sensed her confusion. "I'll do it for you. Give me the number."

She read the two numbers off to him and he said he'd get back to her.

"It might not be admissible in court," Sam said, "but it could be a lead for our own peace of mind."

"Right. Okay, on to the text messages," Delia said.

"I'm going to write these down. Once these phones are out of our hands, it would be smart to have a record."

"Better yet, let's get them on my computer." Delia

handed the second phone over to Sam and reached for her keyboard. "Okay, start with R and read each message aloud to me."

Sam wondered briefly if Delia was billing at her regular rates while she typed. This could get costly. But she decided to go with the moment. They needed to get the evidence compiled quickly so the attorney could turn the phones over to Evan on the same day she received them. Receiving something unexpectedly in the mail was one thing—holding it was another.

"Okay, here goes. 'Lila: Hey R. New phone. Use this one for me now.' He responds back, 'ok.' Are you sure we want all this?"

"Yes. There's a chain of evidence. We can't skip around. Give me the dates, too."

Texts and calls between Richard and Lila had started more than six months ago. It appeared she erased her recent calls now and then, but the text thread kept going. It took a few minutes to hit a rhythm, but soon Sam was reading the messages and Delia transcribing them at a fast clip.

The pattern began to feel familiar. Lila was feeding this R guy a lot of the same talk she'd used with Danny. Last October she'd been madly in love with him, wanted to take things to the next level, and at the end of most messages she would wish him sweet dreams. Sam nearly choked at the first one, pausing to tell Delia about Danny's having received the same message.

Through the holiday season, things between Lila and R had warmed up considerably, on his part as well as hers. It must have been about the time the photo was taken, the one Sam had seen with the two of them embracing.

And then, in January, she dropped the bombshell. She was pregnant—a photo of a test stick with a plus-sign was attached, and the words "congratulations, daddy!!!"

The man: Whoa, what? Thought you were on the pill.

Lila: They don't always work.

Him: We gotta talk about this. I'm shipping out overseas.

Lila: I need money for expenses.

Him: Need to see you.

"I wonder if they got together and he gave her money?" Sam said. She scrolled through the next few messages, all from Lila, without responses from the man.

"Almost sounds as though he got out of there as fast as he could."

Sam looked over at the other phone, sitting on the desk. "So, if she was trying to convince this R that he's about to be a daddy … what was she saying to the other guy?"

"Check it out. I'm going to create a separate document for each of these." Delia tapped a few more keys while Sam picked up the phone they had identified for someone called S.

Sam scanned the messages as she scrolled. "Okay, a lot more of the same … But, oh, wait—here's the pregnancy announcement again. My god, this Lila is a piece of work."

The wording was nearly the same—congratulations, daddy, followed by I need money—until it came to the man's response. S was a lot less accommodating than R. He came right out and asked if she was sure the kid was his.

Delia had pushed her keyboard aside. "Piece of work doesn't begin to describe this girl. What a scam. We already know she wasn't actually pregnant, so what did she think she was pulling here?"

Sam gave a shrug. "Maybe both men are military and

she knew they'd be deployed. With them gone for months at a time she could pull nearly anything—say she lost the baby, or just vanish from their lives? Maybe her move from Nuevo Laredo to San Antonio was part of that? Get a hundred-fifty miles away and hope he never came to check up on her?"

"And then what? I wonder if she was planning to pull the same thing on Danny. From what he says, she was angling for marriage with him. Neither of the others mention that. But ..." Sam's thoughts trailed off. The whole thing was becoming mind-boggling.

Sam's phone rang and she saw Scott's name on the screen. Delia reached for the S burner phone while Sam answered.

"Hey, Sam. I got a name. The first number you gave me—it's listed to a Richard Potter in Nuevo Laredo, Texas. The carrier is Verizon. The other number didn't give any result. Could be one of those prepaid types. Not sure."

She thanked him for the effort, although his call hadn't yielded anything new, and passed the information along to Delia.

The women spent another hour transcribing the full list of texts from the second phone, but it felt like duplicated effort, and the fact they couldn't tie the phone to anyone made it all the more discouraging. Finally, Delia dropped both phones into the FedEx box in which they'd arrived, shed her latex gloves, and stood up.

"Time to get this to the sheriff," she said, "while I can still claim 'oh, look what was mailed to me.' He may give me the stink eye but hey, that's life. Sometimes one side gets first look at new evidence, sometimes it's the other side."

"Do you want me to work on comparing everything?"

"Absolutely. You've got a good eye for this kind of thing, Sam." Delia leaned over her keyboard and hit a few keys. Within a few seconds pages began whirring off a printer in the corner of the room. She handed the sheaf to Sam. "Have fun."

Chapter 38

The dining table had become covered with a mass of papers and notes right after Sam cleared the dinner dishes. Beau had settled in front of the TV with a basketball game on, and Sam couldn't find the interest to join him; this was far more intriguing. After more than thirty minutes of flicking between the R messages and the S messages and trying to tie them to what she'd written in her notebook from Danny's phone, she decided to create a timeline. It was the only logical way her mind could grasp it.

She started with a sheet of paper turned sideways and wrote the date of the oldest message, which had begun with R—Richard Potter. The series of messages had begun in October of last year. In January she had informed him she was pregnant. And by then she had begun dating Danny, shortly after she moved to San Antonio. Within two months, she was pressing for marriage to Danny, while she was stringing Richard along with notes about their baby.

And she'd told Danny *he* was imagining things—seriously?

Sam turned to the messages for S. That little romance began about five minutes after Danny left Texas and moved to Taos. One thing about it—the tone of the lovey-dovey talk was so similar among all three of the lovers that Lila could just dash off a message without a lot of worry about who was receiving it.

To her timeline Sam added the major points: Lila told Richard she was pregnant in January, and she'd said the same thing to this S guy in early March. Had she pulled the same trick on Danny? He hadn't said so. Sam made a note to ask him about that.

Then there was the money—Richard had shipped out to the west coast for a training camp in late January, and she had asked for the money before he went. A month or so later was when she first asked Danny for cash, but he had refused. A month later, she'd found a way to take it from his account. That was shortly after Richard had deployed for a year's tour in Afghanistan. And what about S? A couple of the texts within the past month were discussing a large amount of cash with him, too, but Sam didn't find a reply where the man had agreed or refused. What had come of that?

Lila had told each man she needed to cover the expenses of having his baby—but there was no baby. So, what *did* she want the money for?

Sam stared at her timeline. She had to give Lila credit for managing an intricate balancing act; stringing along three guys couldn't have been easy. She remembered things Danny had told her, about Lila's tone and her ways of manipulating him and making him feel as though he was going crazy. Was she doing the same with all of them?

Sam stared at the notes. She had to consider that all she had to go on were the written texts; she had no way to know what was discussed during calls or in person. An idea came to her. She glanced at the time—it was nearly eight o'clock, not quite nine in Texas. She picked up her phone and found the number for a Richard and Donna Potter in Nuevo Laredo. Another new fact: Richard of the text messages must be a Junior. A woman answered warily—it was too late for telemarketers.

Sam quickly identified herself and asked if the Richard Potter who dated Lila Contreras was related to them. Donna Potter confirmed.

"Yes, such a sweet girl," she said, "so classy, her choices of clothes and everything. Richie is quite taken with her. And of course we're all *so* excited about the baby."

Uh-oh. She doesn't know. Sam felt her heart sink. She had hoped to ask about the relationship between Richard and Lila, whether he'd said anything about feeling manipulated. Now it was taking a different tack.

"Mrs. Potter, I don't know how to say this. I assumed you knew …" She took a deep breath and came out with it. "Lila is dead."

There was complete silence at the other end.

"I feel so badly about telling you over the phone. Really … I assumed the word had already reached you." She debated about saying there had never been a grandchild, but what was the point? They would know it was lost to them now.

She went into a little detail about the where and when. There was no gentle way to say that their grandbaby-mommy had been murdered, so she gave as little information as possible about that.

"I'm so, so sorry," Sam said.

Finally, Donna found her voice. "Richie doesn't know. I'm sure he would have told us."

"Probably not." Evidently, Lila had kept each of her lovers compartmentalized in ways that the extended families didn't know each other, or else Patsy or Danny's parents would have been in touch with the Potters.

"His dad and I chat with him on Facetime now and then. I'll have to tell him ..." Her voice broke, more for the fact of her son's heartbreak, it seemed, than for a love of Lila. "He wanted to be in his baby's life, and he planned to marry her next time he came home on leave."

Sam made some more soothing noises, glancing toward the living room where Beau's attention was elsewhere. She was tempted to get back to asking what Donna Potter had thought of Lila, but this wasn't the time.

Donna wasn't quite finished. "It's early morning over there right now. I suppose this is as good a time as any to try and reach my son. I'm not going to get any sleep until I've spoken with him." She ended the call abruptly.

Sam sat back in her chair, rubbing her temples. What a mess. Lila had ripped up more lives than just Danny's.

She got up, feeling her own creaky joints from sitting so long, and made her way to the kitchen for a cup of tea. While the kettle heated, she paced the room, considering everything she'd learned. She didn't feel any closer to figuring out who actually killed Lila.

She brewed an herbal tea for herself and made a cup of hot cocoa for Beau, carried them into the living room, and settled on the couch. Taking her mind completely off the case by staring at basketball players on the screen might free the tangle of her thoughts and allow her mind to rest enough to come up with fresh ideas.

It was nearly ten o'clock when her phone rang. She saw that it was the same number she'd mostly recently dialed.

"Mrs. Potter—how can I help you?"

"I've spoken with Richie—we've been talking for nearly an hour now. He took the news surprisingly well."

"Really? I mean, that's probably a good thing."

"I think so. I also learned quite a lot more about Lila." Her voice had lost the emotional tenor from earlier. "It seems Richard was trying to break things off with her, just before she informed him about the baby. He told me some things about the way she treated him."

Oh boy, Danny's story all over again.

"Well, anyway … He admitted he had given her a large sum of money."

Sam had seen the request, but didn't know he'd actually handed it over.

"So, as we talked … we're both wondering what happened to that money? Did Lila spend it so quickly? Or is it sitting in an account somewhere? At any rate, Richie would like to have it back."

"I can certainly understand that," Sam said, talking as she carried empty mugs to the kitchen. "but I'm afraid I have no idea. I'd suggest you get in touch with the San Antonio police and ask for an investigation."

"I suppose that's what we'll need to do. How complicated this has become."

"Yes, it seems Lila was fairly expert at leaving complications in her wake." Sam set the mugs in the kitchen sink. "Oh—could I ask you one other question? We're trying to track down others who had recent contact with Lila, in hopes of identifying her killer."

Donna seemed agreeable to that.

"Do you know anyone in your son's circle of friends, a male with the first initial S?"

"S—heavens, I don't know ... Let me think ... I believe Lila once mentioned someone named Sergio. But I don't recall Richie ever talking about him. I'll give it some thought and call you back if I think of someone."

Sam probably thanked her, but her mind was reeling. Sergio. Could it be? Surely not Danny's best friend.

Chapter 39

I can't believe I never connected S with Sergio," Sam said the next morning. She looked around the attic room at Kelly's. "It just seems so unthinkable that Danny's best friend would have taken up with Lila, and at the same time." *The guy doesn't even set mousetraps.*

Eliza, sensing Sam's upset, jumped up to the table and rubbed against her hand.

"Mom, those things happen in the real world."

"I know … I just …" She picked up a plum that was sitting on the big table, next to the book of runes, and squeezed it gently to see if it was ripe. "Serg impressed me as so honest and open. And so caring about Danny and wanting to help us."

"So, it's probably not him. Can't be. There are a zillion names that start with S—you have two of them, yourself."

Sam relaxed and smiled. "Well, at least I can absolutely swear that I'm not the one Lila was texting with."

Kelly fingered the leather cover of the old book. "Maybe we could just come up with a magical fix for this whole thing."

"A love potion—no, an anti-love potion—got us into this. What do you suggest to get us out of it?"

"Oh, I don't know … maybe we find a spell that gives you the all-seeing-eye. Whenever you look at someone you'll instantly know if they are guilty or innocent. It could make you the darling of every police department in the country."

Eliza meowed in agreement.

"And an outcast among all my friends."

"Hey, you never know—it could become a second career." Kelly was flipping the pages of the old book.

"Um, Kel, I just sold a business and am spending precisely as much time as I want to with the other. I don't *want* a second career."

"Okay, then, it's your loss."

"Yep. My loss." Sam closed the book on Kelly's finger, and Eliza laid her white paw on the cover. "For now, I need to talk to Danny again. Surely, if his friend was getting too close with his girlfriend, he would have had a clue." She called the detention center and asked if she could get an appointment. As it turned out this afternoon was one of the designated visitor days and she scheduled the two of them to go.

* * *

"For me, this is all the reason I need to stay on the straight and narrow," Kelly murmured as they followed a guard down the corridor to the visitation room.

They were escorted to a table and told to wait for inmate Flores.

"It's fairly new and it's clean and all that," she continued, "but wow—what a creepy feeling to know if you walk that hallway on the wrong side of the law, they'll slam the door and throw away the key."

Sam met her daughter's stare. "I hardly think they throw away the key, especially in a county detention center. Still, I'm happy to know I won't ever be visiting *you* here." She looked up. "Shh, here comes Danny."

As before, he arrived in handcuffs which were clipped to a ring in the table, on the other side of a plexiglass sheet just high enough for them to speak over. He seemed pleased to see both Sam and Kelly.

"We don't have much time, and I've got some difficult questions, Danny." Sam folded her hands, mimicking the serious tone the lawyer often took.

"First off, we've discovered that Lila was corresponding with two other men when she first met you, and that at least one of those affairs was going on while you were dating her. Have you heard the name Richard Potter, or Richie?"

He shook his head. She noticed he didn't seem especially shocked at the news.

"She told Richie Potter that she was pregnant, and she produced a test stick showing a positive for that."

"And she was pushing him to marry her, too?" he asked.

"No, it doesn't seem that way. But she did ask for money for the doctor and hospital expenses. Sound familiar?"

He slumped forward, pressing his forehead to his cuffed hands, until a guard warned him to sit straight. When he looked back at Sam and Kelly his eyes were weary.

"It does. She also showed me a pregnancy test and claimed I was the father."

"When was this?"

"When she got here, to Taos. She came to the casita one night and presented this as if it were a done deal—that I would marry her as soon as I knew."

"Gosh, Danny, what did you say?" Kelly asked.

"Well, she goofed up when she told me. She said she was six weeks along and I could either marry her or she would have an abortion. She knew how I felt about family, that killing my own child would be unthinkable, so this was her way of forcing the marriage."

"But you didn't agree, did you?"

"No. Quick math in my head and I knew she was lying. I'd been away from her more than two months at that point. It couldn't have been mine."

"And that's why you weren't surprised just now when I told you about Richard Potter."

"Exactly."

"Okay. Well, I'm glad to know that you weren't fooled by her claim. But what happened? Did you two fight about it?"

He shook his head. "Not about that."

Sam stayed quiet and let him think.

"It was about my grandmother's ring—I've told you that part. I refused to marry her and she threw out the idea that I'd given her the ring."

"Okay. Yeah, I remember." Sam picked at a cuticle for a second. "Danny, there's more. I mentioned she was with two other men ... Well, she refers to the second one just by the initial S."

No reaction.

"Someone tossed out the idea that it might have been Sergio."

"No way. Serg and me, we're best buds since grade school. If she came on to him, he'd have told me."

Kelly reached forward, then realized she couldn't touch Danny's hands through the plexiglass. "Sometimes sex does strange things. Secretive things, unforgivable things …"

"Danny, if it means getting you out of here, I'd recommend we at least tell the sheriff Serg is a possible other suspect. He can have the San Antonio police question him, just to be sure he's in the clear."

"No! I'm serious. I won't throw my friend under the bus." His expression was slightly wild, his eyes growing moist. "I won't …" He let the thought drift.

"Okay, then. I won't give out his name. The sheriff has the evidence that implicates this S, whoever that is. They'll track it down and figure it out. And we'll all just hope it's someone else." She knew she didn't sound very confident about this last part.

Danny changed the subject, asking about his family, whether Sam had talked with any of them recently. The separation was eating away at him, she could tell. She promised to call Patsy and see how his parents were coping.

"Just downplay all this with my grandmother," he begged as their time was nearly over. "I don't want her coming down here and seeing me. Not Tia Pauline either. They're both so religious." He turned his palms up and gave a tug at the handcuffs. Seeing him this way would be hard on them.

"Do you want me to give them a message?"

"Call them, if you get the chance. Just tell them I'm

doing fine, the food is great, and I'm getting lots of fresh air. Do it on the phone and don't let *abuela* see your face. She can spot a lie instantly." He gave an ironic chuckle.

The guard declared the end of visiting hours at that moment, and the ladies had to go.

"What will you tell his family?" Kelly asked, once they'd exited the building and were getting into Sam's car.

"Just what he wants me to—for Faustina's benefit. But I'm still going to call Patsy and get her take on Sergio and whether the local police should talk to him. Clearly, Danny will stand up for his best friend, even if it means losing his own freedom."

Chapter 40

She placed the call when they got back to Kelly's place. Scott and Ana were whipping up some kind of science experiment in the kitchen. The attic room was empty and quiet but for Eliza, who crawled onto the window seat and curled into a contented ball in the sunshine.

Patsy answered on the first ring.

"Do you have a couple minutes?" Sam asked.

"Sure. I'm cramming for a big test tomorrow and my brain is fuzzy. I can use the break."

Sam asked about the parents, how everyone was holding up, and passed along Danny's blatant lie about the conditions in jail, attempting to make it sound like the gospel truth.

"Patsy, a question has come up, a tricky one. Those two phones you sent—they're providing evidence that Lila was involved with two other men, one of whom she refers to as S. The idea came to mind that it might have been Sergio. Danny completely rej—"

"No way. Sorry, but I reject that idea too. Serg is as loyal to Danny as a cocker spaniel. Or maybe I should say a pit bull. He'd never go behind my brother's back."

"Okay. Okay." A pit bull, huh. The kind that would kill to protect someone?

Sam put that thought out of her head and brought up the subject of the money. Again, Patsy's reaction was swift.

"There's no way Serg could put his hands on twenty thousand dollars. Just no way. I doubt anyone in his family has ever seen that kind of money in one place, Sam. They're simple working-class people. And Lila would have known that. She wouldn't see him as a possible source of that kind of cash."

"That brings up another question. What would Lila need that much money for? You knew her pretty well. Did you get any feeling about her financial situation?"

Patsy was quiet for a few seconds. "You know, not really. She had expensive tastes—loved an elegant meal out, that kind of thing, but to need twenty grand—huh-uh. I never saw anything on that scale."

Sam didn't mention that the twenty thousand was only part of Lila's big plan. When Patsy began sounding restless to get back to her studies, Sam again sent well wishes to the family and then ended the call.

"So, what do you think?" she asked, turning to Kelly. "I don't get the feeling it's worth siccing the cops on Sergio."

Kelly shrugged. "Your call. You know Danny and Patsy aren't exactly impartial about this."

"I do. But she also made a valid point about the money. Where would Sergio get that much?"

"Um, Mom … Maybe it's not honest money. You think all crooks *look* like the ones in the movies? Drug dealers, money launderers …"

Sam sighed. "You're right. Appearances can be completely tricky. But Sergio? A guy's closest friends would know." *Probably.*

"Let's look at why Lila might think she needed all that money, enough to try and finagle it from three different guys." Kelly had opened the leather-bound book and was paging through it slowly.

"You think we'll find the answer in there?" Sam joked.

"You never know …"

"Okay, why does a twenty-five year old need a huge amount of cash all at once? To make a down payment on a house … to buy a new car …"

"To pay off her blackmailer … to get rid of the loan shark who financed her gambling habit …"

Sam drummed her fingers on the tabletop. "Well, you might have something there. If her need was legit, she would have gone to her parents, right? Her mom seems to be doing pretty well now, and her dad … well, he'd pretty much do anything for her."

"Except that, on a cop's salary, he most likely won't have a pile of spare savings or anything."

"And kids of divorced parents usually have the knack of playing one against the other pretty much down pat, especially when it comes to wrangling extra money from both."

"So—she didn't go to her parents, and we're back to thinking maybe she had an addiction or something. Gambling, drugs … those are expensive habits to keep up."

Sam wandered to the window seat and plopped down,

stroking Eliza's fur as she contemplated the possibilities. The cat stretched and rolled over to present her belly, purring loudly. Sam rubbed the underside of the cat's chin. "Tell me, Eliza, what's the answer to our riddle here?"

Eliza's body gave a quick twist and she sat up, staring at Sam's face with her knowing green eyes.

"She's telling you something, Mom. She does that to me all the time." Kelly turned to face them. "Usually when her food bowl is empty."

"Come on, cat. Let's see what you want," Sam said, standing. "I need to head out anyway. I think I should pay a visit to Sheriff Evan. Good thing we made up."

The two women started to leave the attic room, but the cat leaped smoothly from the window seat to the table, where she placed a paw on the open page of the book.

"Come on, you. I'm closing this door," Kelly beckoned.

Eliza stared and gave a quick *mrroww*, her paw on the page.

"Now," said Kelly.

Finally, the cat jumped to the floor and followed them downstairs. In the kitchen, her food bowl was full.

Chapter 41

Evan agreed to see Sam immediately, walking out to the lobby where she was chatting with Dixie the dispatcher, and leading her back to the private office that used to be Beau's.

"Must be strange for you, seeing me on this side of the desk," he said.

Sam shrugged. She'd become so accustomed to having Beau at home, it would actually feel strange to see him behind the desk again. She told Evan so.

"I'm guessing you're here about the Lila Contreras case?" Getting right to the point.

"I am. Delia Sanchez has asked me to look into a few things, mostly involving Danny's family and friends, just gathering information for his defense."

"You probably shouldn't be here talking to me about

that. Wouldn't Delia consider it a conflict of interest? You know that whatever I learn has to go to the prosecutor."

"Evan, I know. I just want to learn the truth. I feel sure Danny's innocent, but the reality is that I just need to know what happened."

"Fair enough. So ... go ahead."

She told him she knew Lila had been trying to extort money from three men, including actually stealing more than ten thousand from Danny's bank account. "So, my natural question is why—what did she want that money for? And since she was so sneaky about asking for it, was it needed for some illegal purpose—drugs, gambling, blackmail?"

He listened, leaning back in his chair with his hands resting in his lap. When she was finished, he reached for a thick file folder on the credenza behind him.

"I can pretty much tell you this from memory, but let's check to be sure." He paged through the sheets, which were bound at the top of the folder with a long metal brad. "Here's the autopsy report. It automatically includes a toxicology report where they've screened for the most common types of drugs. And, no. Lila had no drugs in her system."

"Maybe she was dealing, got into a bad spot where she owed someone?"

"It's possible, and that wouldn't show up in an autopsy." He was trying for levity but the joke fell flat.

"Obviously. But it's something worth investigating. She wanted all that money for something, and the person she was going to pay it to might have become very angry at the delay. Have you checked it out?"

"Sam, slow down a minute. We just received the two

cell phones, which you obviously must know about. Delia Sanchez brought them to me yesterday afternoon and we've barely had time to go through them. Once we establish this money trail—the demands or whatever they were— we'll have some more knowledgeable questions to ask. *If* it looks like the money is a viable lead, we'll have what we need to get subpoenas for Ms. Contreras's financial records, credit card charges, and all that. Most likely the prosecutor will want those anyway, to track her travel here to Taos, establishing when and how she arrived, to build his case."

Sam tried not to convey her edginess. She already knew about the phones and the money demands, but she couldn't very well blurt it all out. Evan was right—his department needed to follow things systematically and put it all together. And that would happen in its own time.

Meanwhile, all she could do was to thank him for his time and take her impatience home with her.

She arrived at the ranch to find Beau on his phone, walking back and forth in front of the barn. He put the phone away and waved her over.

"Want to be a real cowgirl for a few hours?" he asked with a grin.

"Ooh, a *real* cowgirl … What does that involve?"

"That was the driver of the hauler out of Arizona. The guy who's leasing our east pasture for grazing has shipped me the first twenty head. Getting them unloaded and settled where I want them isn't impossible for one man, but it's a lot easier with two."

"Sure—I'm in."

"Get your jeans and boots on. He'll be here in about twenty minutes."

By the time she'd changed clothes and joined him, he had both horses saddled and ready to go. Sam hadn't ridden in months, not even a casual evening jaunt around the property the way she and Beau used to do. Her thighs would be screaming about this tomorrow, she thought as she mounted the horse.

They trotted along a worn pathway that led to the east fence. Here, the truck could pull along the county road and the driver could back up to a gate they rarely used for any other purpose. Beau dismounted and unlocked the padlock and chain, pushing the gate fully open.

"You miss having Danny around for this stuff, don't you?" She watched as he tied the gate open.

"Yeah, sure. We work real well together." He walked over and stroked the nose of her horse. "What have you heard about his case?"

Sam told him about the cell phones and Lila's demands for money.

"My opinion? The money's at the heart of it. Just think—what are the usual motives for murder? Love, territory, money—which usually breed jealousy, greed, acquisition. Sure, there are the heat-of-the-moment flares of rage. But premeditated or not, most crimes like this begin with someone's being jealous over a love interest, or greedy for territory or money or something else they want to acquire."

Sam let that sink in.

"From what you've told me, it doesn't seem like this Lila girl was deeply in love—she was using these guys. And what was she using them for—money."

"I think it was also about control. Remember how she was manipulating Danny's emotional state, how she twisted things he said. And there's the fact that she showed up here because she wasn't able to control him from a distance the way she could when she saw him every day."

He nodded, one ear cocked toward the road where a plume of dust indicated that the truck was nearing.

"Okay, so control still relates to one of those things. In this case, I suspect she saw Danny as her territory. She couldn't bear to have him out of her sight because he was hers. It sounds like manipulating men was practically a sport with her."

"And because she wanted their money." Sam smiled at him from her perch on the saddle. "You are quite the psychologist, my love."

"Just an ex-sheriff who saw it all." He patted the horse's neck and turned to wave down the approaching truck.

It took a few minutes for the driver to maneuver the trailer into position, near the open gate. Before they lowered the back ramp, Beau called Sam over.

"Just sit here at the opening, making sure none of them try to sneak outside the fence. Most likely they'll stay together and go where I herd them. They're nervous and skittish after being in the trailer for hours, so we just need to keep an eye on them."

She nodded and reined her horse into place. Down came the ramp, and the driver gave a few shouts to get the cattle moving. Once they discovered the freedom of the pasture, they willingly left the confines of the dirty trailer. Within ten minutes, the job was largely done. The driver closed his trailer and drove away, and Beau closed and locked the gate.

"They'll stick together for the first couple of days," Beau said with a nod toward the huddled cattle, "until they get used to the place and the rest of our herd. We'll drive them toward the water tank and they'll figure out the rest."

Sam followed his lead. It didn't take much to convince the thirsty cows to gather around the small pond on the property.

"I'm going to watch them a few more minutes," Beau said. "You don't have to hang around if you don't want to."

But Sam was enjoying the soft breeze and the last of the warm afternoon sun. She remained astride the horse, sitting beside Beau and watching as the cattle settled down and began eating the grass near the water source. Once a few of them lay down to rest, Beau seemed content that they would be all right.

They rode slowly back to the barn and unsaddled the horses. Sam went inside to clean up, after Beau said he would stay and brush them and tend to a few other things.

The hot shower felt wonderful and she swallowed a couple of ibuprofen to ward off the upcoming muscle aches. Dressed and downstairs once more, she saw a call from Kelly on her phone screen.

"Hey, what's up?" she said when Kelly picked up.

"Doing some research online. I think I might have discovered what Lila wanted all that money for."

Chapter 42

Tell me more," Sam said.

"Something about our San Antonio trip was bugging me and I couldn't figure out what it was. Then I walked into Puppy Chic this afternoon and Riki had on an old rerun of *Keeping Up With the Kardashians*. She watches TV sometimes while she's brushing dogs. The background noise helps keep the dogs from going berserk every time the door chime rings."

"Kel. What?"

"Oh, okay, so I'm glancing at these ultra-glam girls with all the hair and makeup—and the clothes, oh my gosh. I'm seeing them and I'm thinking about Lila. And it hits me who her role models are, who she wanted to be."

"By dating a rancher from Texas?"

"Wait, I'm getting to that. Mom, I had my hands on

the clothes in her closet. Remember, she didn't own a lot of things, but what she had was quality. That girl liked shopping at the high-end department stores, Neiman-Marcus and such. The shoes, the bags … she had a small fortune in clothing in that small closet."

The light was beginning to gleam, but Kelly's idea didn't completely make sense. "I don't know, Kel. Maybe she admired those famous girls and their glamour, but she worked at The Gap and dated ordinary middle-class guys. Her own family … the dad's a cop, mom's a housewife."

"A housewife who upgraded to a richer lifestyle when she got the chance." Kelly paused a second. "But I'm getting off topic. I went and did a little research. You remember the girls we met that night at Thrashed? Emily, Taylor, Devon. Well, I had their contact info so I looked them up and followed them on Instagram. What a revealing world that was. Through the friends, I also started to follow Lila, who had a pretty big following, and it's all the same subject—clothes, makeup, designer labels. Most of Lila's followers seem younger, the teen girls who idol-worship celebrities."

"Interesting." Sam still wasn't quite sure where this was going and why Lila would choose the men she chose.

"To truly live the life of her dreams, Lila needed to move to a bigger city, meet classier—richer—guys. But she wasn't ready for that yet. She had a plan."

"To acquire the clothes and shoes she would need, to fit in once she got to …"

"She told her followers she had her eye on Dallas or Houston. She'd researched how many millionaires and billionaires live in each of those cities. Seriously. On her Instagram page she gave statistics."

"So, you're thinking …"

"I think Danny, and possibly this Richard guy, were practice."

"Her training ground for the big leagues."

"Exactly."

"And what about S, the guy with the other phone? Maybe another man similar to Danny and Richard, but maybe he was up a few notches. Maybe he lives in one of those big cities, and she was trying to snag him?"

"It's possible. I think it's entirely possible."

"Wow. Great research, Kel." Sam hung up, a dozen ideas floating through her head as she went into the kitchen.

In so many ways, what Kelly said made sense. Lila was a manipulator—they knew this. Everything from getting her father to fix her traffic tickets and hide at least one DUI charge under the rug, to the way she had treated Danny.

Sam pulled a container of green chile stew from the freezer, wondering if Lila actually would have gone through with a wedding to the young ranch hand, supposing he'd been agreeable. She thought not, not if Lila's real goal was a much bigger fish. Most likely, the girl just wanted him to agree so she could get money from him—much the same way she'd coerced both money and the promise of a future together from Richard Potter, simply by telling him she was having his baby. She must have known Richard was going to deploy overseas soon, so he wouldn't be there to find out she wasn't actually pregnant. It was almost the perfect test of her powers to get her way.

Or, Sam realized, maybe the demands weren't about the money at all. Maybe it was all about establishing her control over the men—if she could get them to relinquish money and make life-changing commitments, she held a lot more control than any of them realized. It would also explain why she was working the scam with more than one man. She needed a variety of scenarios to perfect her techniques before she tried them on a much more sophisticated class of victims.

Sam's supposition didn't quite explain why Lila had blatantly stolen the money from Danny's account—after all, for her control measures to prove themselves, he should hand over the money himself—but it gave Sam a lot to think about while the chile heated and she made a salad to go along with it.

Beau walked in, smelling of hay and earth and horses. While he showered, Sam placed a call to Sheriff Richards' office and was put straight through.

"I've had some more thoughts on Lila Contreras and her financial situation," she said. "Just wondering if you've learned anything new from her credit card and banking records?"

Evan sounded somewhat impatient. "Sam, I've got the warrant but the records themselves haven't come through yet. Things take time in the real world."

"When you get them, I'd like to suggest you look for charges at high-end clothing stores. The lady had very expensive tastes. My guess is that she was spending a lot more than she could have been earning."

"Fine. I'll check. Thanks, Sam, but I've got a call right now."

She thanked him but the line was dead practically before she had the words out. Okay. Way different than when Beau sat in that office, but she could chip away at Evan Richards until she got what she needed.

Chapter 43

When Sam *happened* to stop by the department the following day, Evan was out. She found Rico in the squad room with an array of papers on the desk in front of him. Rico was a buddy, a young deputy when Beau took over as sheriff, one whose law enforcement skills had increased over time. She wouldn't be surprised to see him as a viable candidate for sheriff, himself, one day.

He stood, stretched, and greeted her warmly. "Hey, Sam, what's up?"

She covered only the very basics. "I talked yesterday with Evan about some warrants for Lila Contreras's banking records. Just wondering if they came in." Her eyes trailed to the cluttered desk.

"Working on them right now," he said.

"Want some help?"

He shook his head regretfully. "Sam, you're not a deputy any more. I can't let you touch anything."

"If I promise not to touch, can you tell me what's in them?"

"Probably not, legally."

"Can we play Twenty Questions?"

"I kind of think we're already doing that …"

"So … did Lila charge things at expensive stores?"

"Sam, I have no clue which stores are expensive and which ones aren't. I haven't seen any charges at Walmart, if that's what you mean."

"How about Neiman-Marcus, Chanel, Coach, Manolo Blahnik …"

He held up a hand. "Sheesh, I don't know." He turned to the papers on the desk, rearranging a few so they sat near the edge, picking up some others. "Look, I need to make a quick restroom visit. I'll be right back and we can continue this."

He had picked up the bank statements but left the credit card bills. Taking him literally at his word about not touching, she kept her hands to herself. Her eyes, however, stayed busy. The front page of one Visa statement showed that Lila's balance was within mere pennies of her credit limit—good to know. The credit limit itself must have been backed by her parents, or else Lila had lied ferociously when applying for the cards. There was no way a retail shop employee could afford this.

The itemized portion of the statement showed two of the stores Sam had speculated about, along with a couple of cosmetic and perfume charges and some hair salon bills that nearly took her breath away. No wonder this girl was grabbing for money. She'd had no concept of spending within her limits.

What had Beau said? Most motives end up being about love or money.

But to get herself in this deep, without a plan already in place … it seemed Lila wasn't quite as sharp as she thought she was.

"Tell Beau to stop by some day." Rico's voice startled her and she jumped about a foot. "We still miss him around here. Tell him I'll take him out for a beer or something."

"Will do. Thanks, Rico. You're one of the good guys." She gave the young deputy a hug and left.

* * *

Sam left the sheriff's department, pondering what she'd just discovered. Her car went toward the Victorian, almost on automatic, and she arrived at Kelly's driveway without actually remembering all the roads and turns. Who needed a driverless car?

Scott called a loud "Come in" when Sam approached the kitchen door.

"What, all by yourself in the kitchen?" she asked. "And … baking?"

"Kel asked me to brush some oil over this loaf of Italian bread and get it into the oven. That's the sum total of my baking skills, I assure you. The girls are upstairs, our bedroom I think, and I'm afraid to go in there."

"Well, have fun with the bread. Don't forget to set a timer." She headed toward the foyer staircase. What had he meant—afraid?

Raucous laughter greeted her at the top of the stairs and she followed the sound to the master bedroom. Kelly and Scott had stripped off the dark, Victorian-era wallpaper, refinished the original hardwood floors, and redone the color scheme in soothing tones of taupe with purple accents. What caught Sam's eye was movement at the doorway to the adjoining bath, where Ana came tumbling through the doorway in a fit of giggles.

"Silly mommy," she shrieked, pointing toward the bathroom sinks when she spotted Sam.

"Hey, pretty girl. What's silly mommy up to?"

"You have to see her hair!" Ana spun in a circle and then dashed into the bathroom.

Sam followed.

The vanity top was strewn with hair gear—a dryer with diffuser on it, a flat iron, a half-dozen clips, and four bottles containing who-knew-what types of gels and other products. The carved box, Manichee, sat amid the chaos. Kelly stood in front of the mirror, surveying her mass of curls, which now resembled a reddish brown explosion gone horribly wrong.

"This did not go the way I envisioned," she said.

Sam suppressed a laugh—the sight was truly comical. "Two questions: What, exactly, *did* you envision? And, um, this isn't permanent, is it?"

Kelly gave a hard stare into the mirror, then a bewildered gaze at all the gear on the vanity. "You know what, you're right. I didn't quite start with a clear vision. And no, thank god, it's not permanent. I'd be better off to wash this out and start over."

"And this experiment came from ... where?" Sam picked up the box and lifted the lid. It was empty.

Kelly gave Ana a sideways glance.

"From me! Mommy wanted to look like Karsheean."

"She overheard us talking about ... you know, earlier.

And I said the name Kardashian, and she asked who that was, so I showed her some pictures. And she said my hair would be very pretty all long and wavy like that … and the rest is history."

"Yeah, natural curls like yours aren't exactly easy to tame into long and wavy, are they?"

"Not to mention, my hair isn't long, never has been past my shoulders, and probably never will be—not like those photos."

"Ah well, I say you give up on the experiment and let's go make some tea or something."

Kelly's eyes widened. "I am not going downstairs with—with this!"

"Even after nearly five years of marriage, you're conscious of your appearance around Scott. That's cute."

"I'll shower this off and be back to myself in ten minutes. You girls can go start the tea."

Ana grabbed Sam's hand and led the way. Scott had apparently gone back to his study, and they made their way, unseen, to the kitchen where the Italian bread was smelling heavenly. Sam filled the kettle and put it on a burner. By the time she had located a pretty china teapot and cups and a loose tea called Buckingham Palace Garden Party, Kelly reappeared with damp curls, sporting her normal casual style.

"Better," she said. "And it didn't even require a special potion—just water and shampoo."

"Better," Ana echoed.

Eliza meowed her approval.

They brewed the tea and settled at the small kitchen table, Ana swigging her watered-down cup in three swallows and heading off to find her daddy.

"So," Sam began, "we were talking about Lila's dream of becoming as glamorous as a TV star so she could snag a wealthy man. I got a peek at the evidence proving she was spending money as if she actually had some."

She related some of the details from the credit card statements.

"She's up to her credit limit everywhere, and it looked like she's paid the minimum for months now."

"How many different cards?"

"Six or seven, I think. Rico only left the room for five minutes. I had to read fast."

"Most likely Lila was applying for a new card every time she needed more spending power."

"Wow, hard to believe these companies would keep issuing new cards," Sam said. She carried two and paid the balances in full each month, but realized most of the world didn't operate that way. Especially younger consumers who were getting their first taste of their purchasing power.

As if reading her mind, Kelly said, "I know what it felt like. Remember, when I got back here from California I'd reached my own debt ceiling. Thank goodness I got some wise advice from you."

"I'm just glad you took it. You worked hard to get stable again. Doesn't look like Lila was anywhere near stable. Each of her charges was a thousand dollars or so."

Kelly made a *pfft* sound. "That's *nothing* in the world of designer clothes, Mom. A purse alone can run five to ten thousand, if she goes for the top brand and buys the real thing."

"Well, she certainly wasn't at that level yet."

"So, she was probably outfitting herself to fit in. When she got to Dallas, she wanted to look like the classy girl who could walk into a swank bar or somewhere without appearing like a complete rube. Then, when she met Mr. Right, he would outfit her in high fashion and she'd be the eye candy on his arm."

"Yeah, most likely that was the case." Sam picked up one of the tiny lemon cookies Kelly had set out on a plate. "But I cannot figure out how this relates to a motive for murder."

Kelly shrugged. "I dunno. No man was covering her bills—at least yet. Her parents didn't seem to have any clue about this, especially her father. Danny surely didn't know about her spending habits …"

"Let's *hope* Danny didn't know about her spending habits. The pressure to get married. Can you imagine if he actually had married her and then realized what a financial burden she would become?" The prosecutor would argue that was plenty of motive.

"She didn't want to marry him. Or Richard. Or probably not this S guy. I'm betting Lila Contreras was after a much, much bigger catch."

But who would that be?

Eliza meowed insistently, grabbing their attention. Kelly pushed her chair back and allowed the cat to jump up onto her lap. When she began kneading Kelly's chest with her paws, Sam noticed.

"What is she trying to tell you?"

"I have no idea, but she's been insistent ever since yesterday when we were in the attic. I even went back to the book and found the page she kept pointing to."

"And?"

"I read the entire page. It was some poetic-sounding bit about names. 'What is in a name, after all? A name shall appear, and that name shall be the chosen …' I don't know. You know me and poetry. I never quite get it."

"Hm. Almost sounds Shakespearean, but I don't recognize those particular words."

"Right. Shakespeare. My worst grade in all of high school literature was that segment."

As soon as Kelly quoted the passage she'd read, Eliza looked toward Sam.

"We were talking about Danny's situation. Maybe it's something about the names? We've pretty well talked to everyone whose name we got."

"Except the elusive S," Kelly said.

"*Mrroww.*" And then Eliza leaped off Kelly's lap.

Sam and Kelly exchanged a long look, eyes slightly wide.

"I guess we made the cat happy, but I still can't figure out why," Kelly said.

Sam drained her teacup and stood. "Hey, the tea was wonderful. I gotta get home."

Chapter 44

Sam's phone screen lit up when she started her car. She'd gone inside and left it on the console. "Okay, what's this?" she muttered. The number on the screen showed Delia Sanchez so she immediately tapped the button to call the lawyer back.

"What's up, Delia? Good news, I hope?"

"I'm not sure. I had a call from Danny about twenty minutes ago."

"He's all right?"

"I think so, although he seemed a little … something. Edgy."

"Did he say what it was about?" Surely prisoners didn't get to make calls just because they wanted someone to talk to.

"He had received a phone call, a friend from back home."

"Friends are allowed calls now?"

"No. I'm guessing that the young man used the pretense of calling from my office or something like that. Anyhow, Danny thought it unusual enough that he felt I should know."

"Okay, so who was it?"

"A guy named Chad. Danny says they were more like drinking buddies than close friends, and I guess that's why hearing from Chad was odd."

Sam vaguely remembered the young preppie looking guy sitting at the other end of the table at Thrashed. Kelly had spoken with him more than Sam did, but she didn't remember any special connection between Chad and Danny.

"So, Delia, are we supposed to take some kind of action? What do you suggest?"

"Well, Danny just said the phone call worried him. He said it sounded like the friend had been drinking, and he was going on about Lila, something about lots of fond memories and that kind of thing. But the call ended with this Chad turning on Danny, saying he hoped Danny would rot in prison."

"Really. Wow."

"Could be the drinking, could be ... I don't know ... anything."

"I can make some calls, see what I can find out. Maybe there was more to Chad's and Danny's friendship than I picked up on the first time?"

"Let me know what you find out." Delia seemed glad to have handed over the puzzle to someone else.

Sam put her phone on speaker as she started home. With a voice command to her contacts, she called Danny's sister.

"Hey, Patsy, I know you're crazy busy right now, but I just have a quick question. Danny has a friend named Chad. Do you have a number for him? I guess he called Danny today, and it's prompted some questions."

"Chad Smith? Um, yeah, hang on a sec."

Smith.

When Patsy came on the line again, Sam blurted out the first question that came into her head. "Was Chad ever involved with Lila?"

"Yeah. That was no big secret, except maybe from my brother. They started hanging around all chummy, about five minutes after Danny moved to New Mexico. Why?"

"Did no one think it strange that she also kept stringing Danny along?"

"Well, I guess, now that you mention it."

"Straight out—was Lila romantically involved with Chad Smith?"

The silence told her a lot. Then Patsy got her voice back. "Probably. She had a nickname for him—Smitty—that no one else used. She joked once that it was from some movie character, a guy who was strong and handsome and rich."

Smitty had to be S.

Sam barely remembered saying goodbye to Patsy; her head was reeling as the pieces clicked into place. He had bragged about having money and how he would inherit his father's business one day. She let the clues bounce around until she got home and parked the car. It was all starting to make sense now.

Her breathing was coming hard when she called the sheriff's department and asked for Evan.

"Please, Evan, don't question me right now." She

gave the highlights of her calls with Delia and Patsy. "San Antonio PD needs to bring in Chad Smith for questioning. I think he may have been here in Taos when Lila was killed. We need to find out. Whatever evidence you can get, please do. It's important."

Eliza had told them—*a name shall appear*. And this name fit. Sam felt the hair rise on her neck.

She couldn't say why she was feeling almost panicky over this. Maybe some insight from having handled Manichee earlier, maybe just the adrenaline blast from having figured out the connections with Lila, S, and Danny. But something in the case was breaking loose and she needed for Evan to understand its importance.

"Sure, Sam, I should be able to get to it this afternoon."

"Not just any time. Make the call now and please make them understand it's super important. Isn't there some kind of A-number-one priority or something?" She couldn't remember the terminology Beau used to use.

"Okay, then. Priority One it is."

"And call me back when you learn something. If you can arrange to be in on the interview, by video or something … I don't know … Can I be there too?"

"Sam, is there something more you're not telling me?"

That Lila was spending money like crazy? That she'd tried blackmailing three different men for large amounts by hinting they'd fathered her non-existent child? That one of them had become enraged enough to kill her? Evan knew all that. It just seemed he hadn't put it together with the same sense of urgency.

"No, not really. Just have the police question him about how well he knew Lila and, mainly, find out where he was when she was killed."

"Okay, sure."

She ended the call, not at all certain how quickly he would follow up. But she'd done what she could, for now. She walked into the house, pocketing her phone, but feeling a little letdown from Evan's reaction.

When a call from him came, not five minutes later, she stopped in her tracks in the kitchen.

"You could be on to something, Sam. Chad Smith has vanished."

Chapter 45

An LS500 was reported stolen from Addison Smith Lexus when the dealership opened for business that morning. In checking the security cameras, the previous evening it all appeared to be business as usual, nothing but the normal comings and goings of employees and customers. The dealership closed at eight p.m. A few browsers, probably those who didn't immediately want to be accosted by a salesperson, wandered onto the lot and meandered among the cars. But those were pretty much gone by ten.

At two in the morning, the cameras had gone on the fritz and didn't come back on until Gloria, the office manager, came to work at eight in the morning. She was one of those OCD types who bustled about while the coffee brewed, making certain every little thing in her world was precisely in order. She saw that the system needed rebooting, so she did that. Then she poured her coffee and went to her desk.

The service manager, Randy Biddles, had been on duty since seven. People liked to drop their cars off for maintenance on their way to work, so his was the earliest-opening section of the whole operation. He'd been one of the last to leave the previous evening, and he swore the car, which was valued at more than a hundred grand, was parked right next to his assigned slot. But he must have been mistaken. Either that or the buyer had convinced a manager to let him come in the early hours to take delivery—people did get antsy about picking up their new cars. And for Randy, the days tended to blend together, especially when you worked several twelve-hour shifts in a row because your worthless assistant manager was on a bender with his skanky girlfriend. It was impossible to get good help these days.

By the time Gloria and Randy ended up next to the coffee machine it was nearly ten o'clock. His chance comment about the white LS500 clicked in her precision-minded head, along with the inoperable security cameras, and they called in the sales manager.

No, the buyer of the pricey car hadn't come by to pick it up. His appointment was at noon today.

So, where did the car go? An all-out search was launched, because this buyer was a close friend of Addison Smith's and it wouldn't do not to have his car ready and waiting.

But the car wasn't on the lot. And a nervous call to Mr. Smith revealed that the family was concerned, too, because their son Chad was supposed to take his younger sister to her mandatory piano rehearsal for the big recital in two days' time. Chad wasn't home and his bed hadn't been slept in.

Two plus two sometimes really does equal four. Smith called the police and his insurance company first, then placed a call to the friend whose new car wasn't going to be ready for delivery quite yet.

By the time Sheriff Evan Richards from Taos, New Mexico, called the San Antonio PD, the missing car and the dealership owner's spoiled rich-kid son were far from tops on anyone's mind. But Evan finally reached an officer who knew the Smith family, and he passed along the details. The officer's name was Miguel Contreras.

* * *

"Why would he be on the way to Taos?" Evan asked Sam.

"Once I brought up the questions about big sums of money, and after Chad Smith's call to Danny in jail, he figured out that Chad was the one who killed Lila. He was ready to sit down today with his attorney and make a formal statement. Once Delia knew the whole story, she was planning to call you and lay it all out."

"So Chad Smith is rushing right into our hands?"

"I doubt he sees it that way. Chad probably figures if he can somehow get rid of Danny before he tells what he knows, he's home free." She shrugged and waved one arm, even though he couldn't see her over the phone. "Who knows what goes on in the mind of a rich young kid these days. They think they're bulletproof and above the law."

"He can't get into the jail."

Sam felt her patience wearing thin. "Right. So Danny's

Connie Shelton

safe. But you want to catch Lila's killer, don't you? It might be smart to set up a trap for Chad Smith."

"I'll get out a BOLO on the stolen car, and I need to talk to Danny ..." Evan seemed to be thinking out loud rather than talking to Sam.

But it was just the information she needed. She ran back out to her car and beat a quick path to the sheriff's office. Dixie waved hello but was busy on a call and didn't try to stop Sam from pushing through to the squad room. A briefing was in session, with Evan facing four deputies.

"... north of Santa Fe. We've got a little over an hour to get ourselves in place."

Chapter 46

Evan gave out assignments and the deputies dispersed. When he turned toward his office, he spotted Sam standing in the hallway.

"Sam, I can't—"

"I know. I'm not asking to ride along with the deputies, but could I go with you to the meeting with Danny and his attorney? I'm worried about him, Evan."

"You can't say anything to our suspect, Sam." He walked past her, his long legs striding toward the back door. Although he easily outpaced her, Sam scrambled to keep up.

Outside at his cruiser, he gave her a look of impatience but he didn't stop her from getting into the passenger seat. The ride to the courthouse and detention facility was a short seven minutes, during which he cautioned her again about saying anything to influence what Danny Flores might say. This was an interrogation by the sheriff, with the obligatory presence of the suspect's attorney.

"We just need to find out what this Chad Smith told Flores during their phone call."

Sam nodded and kept her mouth shut. She already knew some of it. Evan could ferret out the rest on his own.

They were just about to enter the building when Evan's radio squawked. The voice of Deputy Wilson came fuzzily through. The stolen Lexus had just passed the rest stop at the Overlook, headed toward Taos.

"Drop in behind and follow. If he doesn't head straight for the jail complex, pull him over on the stolen vehicle charge."

"Roger that."

"Come on," Evan said to Sam. "Let's get inside."

Delia Sanchez was waiting, and the three were shown to a private room rather than the main visitors' hall. A very nervous Danny was escorted in, wearing the usual handcuffs. Evan signaled the guard to remove them, and the four took seats at a metal table.

The sheriff took charge. "Danny—first, thank you. We're checking out the new lead you've provided in your case." He held up one hand. "It doesn't mean that lead will pan out or that we'll make an arrest. I'm just informing you. We're here right now because I need your formal statement attesting to the facts you stated to Ms. Sweet here. You may run each statement past your attorney first, if you wish."

"It's not much," Danny said hesitantly.

Sam sneaked a discreet peek at her watch while Danny talked. They had maybe twenty minutes before Chad could possibly be here. But Danny's story was short. He quietly confirmed everything he'd said earlier. Evan took it all down.

The sheriff was rechecking a few points when his radio came to life again. It was Rico's voice this time.

"Suspect has just pulled into the parking lot. I'm leaving my vehicle."

"On my way," Evan said, standing. "Ms. Sanchez, please verify that what I've written here agrees with your client's statement, have him sign and date it."

He was halfway out the door. Sam glanced at both Danny and the attorney, gave them a thumbs-up and followed on Evan's heels. He didn't seem to notice she was dogging his steps, but she wasn't going to wait quietly in the interrogation room. They reached the lobby and saw Rico standing at the open glass entry doors. Chad Smith stood one step down, speaking earnestly with the deputy.

"But I'm a very close friend, and I'm just in town for a few hours," he pleaded.

"Doesn't matter. Visitation is on certain days and only by appointment," Rico told him. His fingers were hooked casually in his belt loops, but the grip of his service pistol was mere inches away.

"Stay here," Evan said to Sam.

Chad continued, "Seriously? There's no way I could get a special appointment? I'm from out of state." His eyes were darting around, looking for some way past Rico.

Evan walked out the door, not looking toward Smith, just another cop going about his way. Until he reached the same step where Chad stood. "Hey, Chad," he said in a casual tone.

Instinctively, Chad turned to face the friendly greeting. Evan was already reaching for his handcuffs. "You'll need to come with me, sir."

"What! You can't—"

"You're wanted for questioning in the death of Lila Contreras."

"No way! Listen, I'm not even from around here. I'm from Texas."

The fatal statement. Rico didn't much like Texans. He stepped down and reached for the suspect's left arm.

Chad spun in a circle. With Rico on one side, Evan on the other, and two more cars full of deputies screeching to a stop at the bottom of the steps, he was surrounded. He slipped his right arm away from Evan and whipped out a knife.

Sam felt her eyes go wide as the switchblade flicked out, narrowly missing Evan's arm. She was out the door, ready to start slugging and kicking if need be.

"Back off!" Chad shouted. "You can't do this to me."

Evan made a show of backing away, giving Rico the perfect diversion to grab Chad's left wrist and twist it sharply behind his back. With one step sideways, he threw the suspect off balance and Chad went to his knees, hard, on the concrete. Evan stepped in and placed his foot on Chad's right wrist. His fingers opened and the knife fell to the ground. Sam dashed over and kicked it beyond the suspect's reach.

"Thanks—great job." Evan said it quietly, but Sam caught the words.

The rest of the deputies closed in and Chad was cuffed in a flash.

"Chad Smith, you are under arrest for grand theft auto, for assault on a law officer, and for the murder of Lila Contreras."

Smith's eyes went wild at the mention of Lila's name. His hair was flying out at crazy angles and spittle formed at the corners of his mouth.

"That bitch! I had every right! No way was she gonna ruin my life! She didn't know who she was dealing with." He twisted in the grip of Rico and Wilson. "*You* don't know who you're dealing with. My father's an important man. *There's no way you're getting away with this!*"

His stare landed on Sam. "You—you couldn't accept my warning, could you? You *had* to keep digging."

Sam went blank for a moment. Then it hit her—the man in the shadows along the Riverwalk. She and Kelly had decided the scary guy was one of Miguel's cop buddies. Evidently not.

Chad ranted on. "You'll pay for this! All of you will p—" He tripped over Rico's outstretched foot and his shouts echoed off the building as the officers hauled him inside.

Chapter 47

Chad Smith was right about one thing: his father wasn't sitting still for his entitled son being arrested. To give the man credit, he did try. But, ultimately, the only charge that got dropped was that of the stolen auto. Even that cost him. When word got out that one of his burly mechanics had been lured by Chad into threatening Sam and her daughter, the service department revenues dipped sharply. And the wealthy customer, who learned his newly purchased luxury car had been taken across state lines and driven by a killer, backed out of the purchase and took his business to another dealership. It seemed the bigger the fuss Addison Smith made on his son's behalf, the more notoriety it brought to the business, and the more customers he lost. Texans, in general, are a law-and-order bunch.

The elder Smith eventually backed down when it became clear it wasn't merely Danny Flores's word against his son's. Chad's own shouted "I had every right" confession had been overheard by many. But even that wasn't the final nail in the coffin.

The knife Chad had pulled on Evan was bagged and tested and, yes, Lila's DNA was on it. The tip of the knife matched with the horrible cuts on her forehead. Chad had not been able to resist taunting the dead woman with her own words—Sweet Dreams.

And there was other evidence from the crime scene— DNA on the victim's clothing and fingerprints on surfaces in the hotel room—proving Chad Smith had been there. All it took was a suspect to match them to. And although the young man would never admit to any part in the crime, there were gas station receipts showing he had been in Taos on the day Lila was murdered and a security camera in the hotel parking area showed his car briefly in the lot.

They had enough to put him away forever, and he had been stupid enough to provide nearly all the incriminating evidence. Evan told Sam and Beau all this over dinner at the Richards' home, a lovely roast and all the trimmings prepared by Riki, in the English tradition.

Sam was happy to accept Evan's muted apology for having jumped to conclusions about Danny. They were alone on the back porch of the couple's little house while Riki put the finishing touches on dessert.

"Danny's the one you should say that to," she gently reminded. "We'll all be at Easter dinner at Kelly's."

"I need to cultivate more of Beau's coolheaded manner."

"He does have a way with that. I've never seen him shrink down in the face of danger, but he always kept all the facts in mind." She patted his arm. "You'll get there."

Sam walked around the back garden for a few minutes, admiring Riki's daffodils and breathing the rich scent of the hyacinths in bloom. There were still a lot of unanswered questions in her mind, but she wasn't sure she would be up for what would probably be a weeks-long trial to learn those answers.

Chapter 48

Easter morning sunrise was always special, Sam reflected as she watched the light on the clouds from the back deck at the ranch. Whether this came from her small town upbringing and the religious connotations, or if it was just because spring is a magical time. Chilly air, pastel clouds, the first beams of sunlight warming the earth, where tiny sprigs of the new alfalfa crop were beginning to appear.

From the barn she could hear male voices as Beau and Danny tended the chores that would be there every day, no matter the season or the day of the week. She sat on one of the wooden Adirondack chairs, bundled in her fuzzy robe, cupping a mug of coffee, and soaking up the scenery until the fields were fully bright and it was time to go inside and get dressed.

Danny had been fairly quiet since his release, and she

knew it was best to give him space. He needed to process all that had happened, and had only been home a week. His parents had come and were staying at Faustina's. Sam and Beau had left them to their family time on Good Friday, and last night Pauline insisted on including the Cardwells at the Flores family dinner.

Heartwarming—seeing Danny and his parents. Heartbreaking—his father's obvious decline in health and the knowledge that it could have all gone so much worse. Sam felt her nose prickle and tears pooled in her eyes.

But the worst had not happened, not to this family. For the Contrerases, this must be the saddest holiday of their lives. Tears overflowed and tracked their path down Sam's cheeks. Happy endings didn't always come for everyone.

She wanted to talk with Danny, really talk. There would be a time for that.

Right now, her coffee was gone and she had a cake to decorate.

The fondant-covered cake waited on the kitchen counter while Sam put on clothes and her baker's jacket. She'd brought home enough tools to finish the job here rather than going down to Sweet's Sweets.

This one was a giant egg standing upright, with a jaggedly open top. Soon there would be a tiny chick peeking out. She piped decorative pink and yellow swirls over the blue shell, adding a sprinkle of colored sugar here and there. The Easter egg motif had been Ana's idea; the chick on top was Sam's own surprise. Piped green grass covered the base, and she added green-tinted coconut for texture and egg-shaped candies hiding in the grass. A few elaborate tulips and daffodils completed the garden ambiance.

Beau's boots stomped on the front porch and he walked in a minute later, with the smell of crisp morning air on his clothing.

"Cinnamon rolls will be out of the oven in five minutes," she told him. "Tell Danny. I made plenty."

The light breakfast was meant to hold them over until noon when everyone was invited to Kelly and Scott's home for a big dinner. Danny's family had begged off, saying Hector wasn't up to it. Danny would join them again at his grandmother's this evening.

Sam had prepared two large salads—ambrosia and coleslaw—and would make the deviled eggs at their house. Little Ana first had to scour the yard searching for them.

She expected Beau to go back outside and shout Danny's invitation to breakfast, but he pulled out his phone and sent a text instead. Woo—modern guy.

* * *

The Victorian looked resplendent, with the flowering plums in their full glory and the front beds filled with spring blossoms. Scott and a couple of helpers had spent the past week repainting the trim. Without the need for a parking area, as had been the case when the chocolate factory was here, Kelly had seeded the front dirt area with grass, and the lawn was just now starting to provide a carpet of green on the gentle slope leading to the house.

This place is meant to be lived in, Sam thought as they drove up. It's much better this way than as a business.

Danny and Beau carried the salad bowls inside, while Sam managed the cake. Before they were halfway to the door, another car pulled in. Evan and Riki got out.

Sam had been slightly nervous about the guest list—it would be the first time Evan and Danny were in a social situation since Danny's release. Would there be tension between the sheriff and the man he'd wrongly arrested? The hustle-bustle of the arrival, balancing the large bowls, greeting Scott at the door, and deciding where to set all the food helped cushion any awkward moments.

Out of the corner of her eye, Sam saw Evan approach Danny, hand extended, apparently doing his part to make amends. She felt the pressure ease.

"Where's Ana? I halfway expected to be jumped when she saw the cake."

"She had a social engagement," Kelly said, looking up from the open oven door. The scent of baked ham filled the kitchen. "Hannah invited her to go to church with them. I don't think she realized she would have to sit quietly for a long stretch. It'll be interesting to see how Myra handled two four-year-olds for the duration."

Sam chuckled, imagining. For the girls, the whole experience was most likely about wearing pretty dresses and whispering about how many Easter eggs they'd found this morning.

"Want me to set the table?" she asked. "Then I can come back in here and do the deviled eggs."

"All done," Kelly said, stretching a kink out of her back. "I wanted time to socialize with my guests, so I set the table last night and fixed the eggs right after Ana left with the Millers."

"Great plan. In that case, I'm going to peek out there and see how the guys are doing." See how Danny's coping.

She swapped places with Riki, who was on her way into the kitchen with her contribution to the dinner, glazed carrots. Sam found the men in clusters in the living room, where Scott had already taken care of their beverage requests. Scott was chatting in the foyer with new arrivals Zoë and Darryl, while Beau, Danny, Rico and Evan seemed to be holding a more serious conversation near the fireplace.

Sam gave Zoë's shoulder a quick squeeze then walked over to join the men. Apparently, the topic was centered around the loose ends from Danny's case and Chad Smith's arrest and indictment.

"Some great news," Evan was saying when Sam approached. "It looks like you'll get back the money that was taken from your account."

Danny's face lit up. "What … how?"

"I've been in touch with investigators from the bank. They tracked the money transfer to Lila's account, and once we established that it wasn't authorized, they assured me they would reverse the transfer. It should be back in your account in a day or two."

"Wow—I really appreciate that. I had anticipated a battle."

Evan shook his head. "Nope. You're good. Unfortunately, the others were not so lucky. We're still piecing it together—and this stays here in this group, you understand. It looks like both Richard Potter and Chad Smith gave Miss Contreras cash. She used some of it to pay down her credit card debt just enough to stay out of trouble, but there was plenty left, which she blew on another spending spree in Dallas last month. From talking with her girlfriends, it looks like she was known for those."

No one wanted to say it was lucky Lila died before she could also spend Danny's life savings; that would be cruel.

But Sam felt the vibe pass through the group.

"So, she had no actual plans to marry me? All that talk about planning a wedding, and the big fuss over my grandmother's ring?" Danny was clearly still trying to wrap his head around the extent of his girlfriend's deception.

"Nope," Rico said. "I tracked some of her spending. She had her eye on a big diamond she'd seen on a trip to Dallas. The jeweler remembered her clearly because she bragged that she was getting engaged to some oilman and wanted to get ideas for the ring he would buy her."

"Was there actually an oilman?" Sam wondered.

"We haven't found any evidence of one. So far, Lila's plans for hooking up with a rich guy only took her as far as Chad Smith."

Sam slipped her arm around Danny's waist and gave him a hug. "For the record, you are a much better catch—any day."

"And very lucky you avoided that trap," Beau added with a smile. "Can't imagine what life would be like with someone who lives so many lives and gets into that kind of debt without thinking."

A beam of light slid across the wall, reflected off the windshield of a car pulling up the driveway. Sam didn't recognize the vehicle, but she knew the perky girl who bounded from the back seat and dashed up the front steps.

On the front porch railing, Eliza reached out a paw toward Ana. They touched noses, and the little redhead giggled. The two gazes met, and Sam swore her granddaughter and the cat communicated, perhaps in their own secret language.

Chapter 49

The Sunday evening sunset lingered over the valley north of Taos, taking its time, much the way the sunrise that morning had done. Sam and Beau stood on the back deck at the ranch, watching Danny as he moved about inside the casita. The cattle in the north pasture were settling down, lowing occasionally.

"It was a nice day," Sam said, hooking her arm through his. "Ana had a great time, and I think all the adults did too."

"Did you hear Evan ask me if I wanted the sheriff job back?"

Her breath caught. "*No* ... What did you say?"

"I took it as a joke—he doesn't actually want to give it up." He smiled at her and then winked. "I said no. And I told him I don't even want to go back as a deputy. Ranching has its own challenges, but most of them come from the animals or the weather. I don't want to deal with people, their insane actions and motives. Not yet anyway."

She squeezed his arm. "It still feels like it's too soon for that."

The sun dipped behind the distant horizon and the air immediately felt colder.

"But don't you still miss it, in some ways?"

His eyes took on a faraway look and his answer seemed faintly wistful. "Not in the sense you're thinking. I miss the camaraderie of the guys, the times after the danger was over and we sat around having coffee and recapping our victory. I miss being involved in the feeling that I've made the world a tiny bit safer for people who just want to go about their days."

"You don't miss the action, the chase?"

Unbidden, the moment when Chad pulled the knife flashed through her mind, the gut-wrenching feeling that he was about to harm one of the deputies. When Beau shook his head in answer to her question, she understood. Completely.

Thank you for taking the time to read *Deadly Sweet Dreams*. If you enjoyed it, please consider telling your friends or posting a short review. Word of mouth is an author's best friend and is much appreciated.
Thank you,
Connie Shelton

There's more coming for Samantha and family!

In the meantime, if you've missed any...

Turn the page to get the the full list!

Watch for a new Charlie Parker in early 2021,

A teen girl becomes Charlie's newest client when she walks into RJP Investigations with tears in her eyes and a thick police-investigation folder in her hands. Cassie Blake's mother vanished from their home when Cassie was just a baby, leaving no clues and plenty of questions. The police chalked it up as either a young woman who got tired of being a mother, or a tragic murder victim whose body was never found. Either way, Charlie sees a lot of herself in this kid and can't resist taking on the cold case.

Get Sweethearts Can Be Murder at your favorite online retailer, available in 2021

And, in my other series, The Heist Ladies …

It's Amber's turn to call upon the Heist Ladies for help in this wrap-up to the series. The team's youngest member has taken a computer programming job and is on her way to a promising career. But a business trip to Europe with a fun side jaunt in Paris ends badly when Amber's luggage is searched by authorities and discovered to contain contraband. Even if she can convince them she's innocent, Amber knows she's been taken in by a con artist, and, well … that's the specialty of the Heist Ladies. Will the women be able to catch this oh-so-charming bad guy before he can pull the same sleazy con on someone else?

Get Show Me the Money at your favorite online retailer, available spring of 2021

* * *

**Sign up for Connie Shelton's free mystery newsletter at www.connieshelton.com
and receive advance information about new books, along with a chance at prizes, discounts and other mystery news!**

**Contact by email: connie@connieshelton.com
Follow Connie Shelton on Twitter, Pinterest and Facebook**

Books by Connie Shelton
THE CHARLIE PARKER MYSTERY SERIES
Deadly Gamble
Vacations Can Be Murder
Partnerships Can Be Murder
Small Towns Can Be Murder
Memories Can Be Murder
Honeymoons Can Be Murder
Reunions Can Be Murder
Competition Can Be Murder
Balloons Can Be Murder
Obsessions Can Be Murder
Gossip Can Be Murder
Stardom Can Be Murder
Phantoms Can Be Murder
Buried Secrets Can Be Murder
Legends Can Be Murder
Weddings Can Be Murder
Alibis Can Be Murder
Escapes Can Be Murder
Old Bones Can Be Murder
Holidays Can Be Murder - a Christmas novella

THE SAMANTHA SWEET SERIES

Sweet Masterpiece   *Sweet Payback*
Sweet's Sweets   *Sweet Somethings*
Sweet Holidays   *Sweets Forgotten*
Sweet Hearts   *Spooky Sweet*
Bitter Sweet   *Sticky Sweet*
Sweets Galore   *Sweet Magic*
Sweets Begorra   *Deadly Sweet Dreams*
Spellbound Sweets - a Halloween novella
The Woodcarver's Secret

THE HEIST LADIES SERIES
Diamonds Aren't Forever
The Trophy Wife Exchange
Movie Mogul Mama
Homeless in Heaven

CHILDREN'S BOOKS
Daisy and Maisie and the Great Lizard Hunt
Daisy and Maisie and the Lost Kitten

Made in the USA
Columbia, SC
11 October 2020